HOT TO

Also by Frank Palmer

Testimony
Unfit to plead
Bent grasses
Blood brother
Nightwatch
China hand
Double exposure
Dead man's handle
Dark forest
Red gutter

HOT TODDY

Frank Palmer

Constable · London

First published in Great Britain 1997 by Constable & Company Ltd,
3 The Lanchesters, 162 Fulham Palace Road, London W6 9ER
Copyright © 1997 by Frank Palmer
The right of Frank Palmer to be identified as the author of this work
has been asserted by him in accordance with the Copyright,
Designs and Patents Act 1988
ISBN 0 09 477200 2
Set in Palatino 10pt by CentraCet, Cambridge
Printed and bound in Great Britain by
Hartnolls Ltd, Bodmin

A CIP catalogue record for this book
is available from the British Library

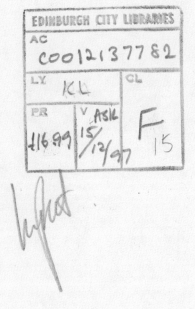

For Paul and Christine

Special thanks to Professor David Childs for his briefing on the former East Germany and its intelligence services, Major David Barnett for historical help and the staff at Nottingham Castle for a guided tour. Any mistakes are mine, not theirs.

The East Midlands Combined Constabulary, its cases and its characters are fictional.

The hospital nurses' former home next to the castle was transposed into a hotel for this story. In the way that fact sometimes follows fiction, a proposal has been put forward for a similar conversion in real life. If it takes place, any new management is welcome to the name and the décor; no consultancy fee required.

08.30 hours

'I was proceeding in a southerly direction . . .'

You know straight away when an old-time beat bobby is about to make a rare contribution to the overnight log. All start with 'I was proceeding . . .'

My grandfather, bless him, began every report on every incident he chanced upon that same way. Not that he submitted many. Veterans not bucking for promotion seldom do.

But, when they have to put pen to paper or, these days, two fingers to keyboard, their accounts become diamonds among the dross of domestics, pub brawls and break-ins.

Just seeing that intro is a tonic this morning, a remedy for a throat that feels like sandpaper which Lemsip has failed to soothe.

I'll just tip this chair back, lean this stuffed head against the rest, let a smile grow and read between the lines to seek the full flavour of the chaos described in phraseology that went out with high tech policing.

At the end of a ten-to-six shift yesterday, it seems, this old-time cop was cycling home in the rain through the poetically named Meadows, once riverside plains, now an unromantic mix of sixties estates and turn-of-the-century terraces.

'My attention was drawn to a traffic hold-up in Farringdon Street,' he understates.

Imagine the sodden scene. In a narrow side street which homeward-bound motorists use as a short cut to escape bottlenecks on bridges, he'd come across a pile-up of motorway proportions.

A dozen drivers had skidded to a halt in the downpour. The man at the wheel of the leading car was being berated by two motorists behind, who had shunted into each other. He was protesting that a policewoman had ordered his emergency stop.

The policewoman, it turned out, wasn't a WPC at all, but a lollipop lady, so fed up with rush-hour traffic using her quiet street as a rat run that she and a neighbour had taken the law into their own hands.

She plastered a crude home-made 'Police' notice over the circular 'School Crossing' on her pole, donned peaked cap and yellow cape, and took up position at the kerbside. The pole was in one hand, her black hair-drier in the other, pointing down the street. Her neighbour stood guard at the other end, with clipboard and pen, noting index numbers.

The first driver feared he was being gunned in a radar trap and braked so sharply that the following car hit him and so, too, the one behind that. A van, fourth in line, executed a wheelie, then backed up a cul-de-sac beyond a 'No Entry – Road Works' notice. Vehicles behind only just avoided splashing into the wreckage.

The motorists raged. The women wept that they were only trying to make their street safe for pensioners and children to cross to the corner shop after months of vainly pleading for humped traffic calmers which the veteran constable naturally described in the old-fashioned way as 'sleeping policemen'.

He made everyone sit tight until the storm passed, then got to work with his notebook. The women were booked for impersonating police officers. One driver was arrested for being over the top after a long business lunch. Another was cautioned for defective headlights and yet another for dodgy brakes.

The officer bemoaned the fact that he would have got the van driver for joyriding and reversing the wrong way up a one-way street where he abandoned what turned out to be a stolen vehicle, but, not surprisingly, he absconded in the mayhem.

Most important of all, the cop would have run up a couple of hours of overtime sorting it all out, and the same again writing his deadpan report.

Sometimes, I wish I was back in the front line, instead of sitting here, warm and dry, deleting files on reds-under-the-beds, Iron Curtain contacts who never were, and suspected sleepers whose only crime was an Irish accent, then feeding them all back again when the ceasefire blew up in Docklands.

Two years now I've been in Special Branch. One decent job in all that time and that only lasted for four days.

At least he'd have had a story to tell his wife when he got home last night. I'm boring mine witless. Vetting is hardly derring-do.

My eyes drop away from the screen to the in-tray, overflowing with the usual anarchist rants and revolutionary ravings. Trouble is, with the budget well bust before the end of the financial year and it being a bank holiday with massive overtime pay for the rank and file, there's no one on duty to read them.

No *Morning Star* today, the only daily paper we get delivered to the office. Odd it should be observing a holy day that even the postman isn't.

Always had a soft spot for it, ever since college days when I was lusting after a student with lovely legs, so left wing that they called her Shirl Guevara. To impress her, I scanned it most days in the library to brief myself for her 'meaning of life' debates, went to a couple of demos, never got close to running my hands all the way up those legs once she found out I came from a police family.

Sometimes I wonder if twenty years ago I featured under 'Known Associates' in the files we still keep on all nutters on the subversive scene.

I'll spend a few minutes recapturing my wasted youth, lift a day-old *Morning Star* from the in-tray, put my feet on to the desk, and begin to read letters defending China, calling for a united Ireland and complaining that a photo of a spider in its web which appeared last month had been printed upside down; a refreshing change from the other tabloids with never-ending show biz and royal rubbish.

It would be a shame to lose a paper that caters for other than middle-class middle-of-the-roaders like me. I think I'll run the risk of a re-entry among 'Known Associates' and send the fighting fund a fiver.

The desk phone rings. 'Step in a minute, will you, Phil?'

More routine chores, I fear; nothing that will make the overnight log or the wife laugh when I get home.

9

09.50 hours

I am proceeding slowly in a small queue towards a table with a sign 'Registration Desk' hanging over it, using the time to size up the place and its patrons.

The place is the Standard Hill Hotel, an elegant building, even in comparison to its next-door neighbour, a palace fit for (indeed originally built by) a duke in the grounds of the old castle.

Most of the patrons today are delegates at an international conference on tourism and leisure. There's a lot of the latter about.

Groups of them are sitting on deep sofas in the exceptionally large lobby. Some are chatting and laughing noisily. Some are reading papers, foreign publications among them. Some are drinking – and not just coffee. Others have their heads back, eyes shut, and look as though they never want to drink anything again.

Still more are window-shopping locally manufactured lace and, oddly in a beer-making county, a display of whisky in a row of boutiques at the far end of the foyer. Others are browsing at paintings on pastel-shaded walls, of kings and queens who stayed next door over the centuries.

Everyone seems to be hanging about, waiting for something to happen.

I wonder if John Beamish is hanging around, too, hope not; not till I've had the lunch that comes with the registration fee the taxpayer has footed in advance.

John Beamish is 'vaguely missing', according to the vague briefing I got from my chief less than an hour ago.

Normally, Assistant Chief Constable Carole Malloy told me, she wouldn't assign a superintendent to such a low-key inquiry, but Beamish happens to be an MI5 agent.

He'd booked into the Standard Hill yesterday, was seen by his

10

partner at lunchtime, but had missed a rendezvous with him in the evening. Nor had he made his usual contact call to his controller this morning.

'So, naturally, his chief is concerned and wants us to run the rule over it very lightly,' she went on, tapping the side of her nose, telling me to be discreet.

He and his sidekick, she explained, are following up a tip that an ex-East German espionage ace, wanted for blackmail and murder, might show up at this conference.

Every security and secret service in Europe has been looking for Jurgen Musters since he vanished from his embassy in London with an armful of embarrassingly confidential dossiers just ahead of the Berlin Wall coming down.

He'd been spotted only twice in the five years since; on both occasions at similar conferences. In his wake two bodies turned up. One was an academic in Dublin, the other a media consultant in Bruges; both women.

Each had virtually cleaned out her bank accounts before being found dead – the first in the River Liffey, the second in a hotel bath. For public consumption, the Dublin death was written up as suicide, Bruges as accidental.

The tip is that now spy handlers are redundant Musters is blackmailing his former sources to Western secrets. Malloy theorised his money-with-menaces demand this way: 'I paid you well in the good old cold war days, now you pay poor, out-of-work me or I'll tell all.'

The fear is that he is about to pull the same extortion on a British-based ex-spy.

The missing Beamish had been dispatched with a fellow officer to the conference separately and under cover to observe and report.

A thriller, eh?

Well, hardly.

The only thrill I'm feeling right now is that I've escaped the boredom of a stuffy office, logging new names from crackpot literature, working out the codes they give to operations that usually turn out to be sparsely attended demos.

Two years in Special Branch have given me an inside view of the fabled secret services, in which I play an increasingly unhappy and minor part.

OK, they're good on surveillance, but they have the manpower and latest equipment to do the job, and, true, they've had their much-publicised coups which look all the better for keeping their cock-ups quiet.

Some successes came, not from brilliant investigative work, but from highly paid moles behind the Iron Curtain, pointing out the leaks on our side.

And some such gift-wrapped pinches were handled so ineptly that there were no published confessions, no charges, no convictions, all achieved under the dubious guise of 'prosecutions not being in the public interest' – in reality, political decisions to avoid a public spotlight that would have exposed glaring shortcomings in our own intelligence gathering.

Much of their information that I've been weeding out of our files was unsubstantiated tittle-tattle; half of it made up, I suspect, by informers to justify their lavish expenses.

These days, with an on-off ceasefire in Ulster and hardly a diplomat worth trailing in London, they're muscling in on police work with offers of co-operation in drug smuggling and money laundering.

A far cry, the old boys from the branch moan in the canteen, from the days when they nicked a member of the Portland spy ring who hailed from this region and wouldn't let the local force even do the background inquiries. Or the radar specialist they caught passing on secrets from a local RAF station – and never bothered to tell them about.

So far, thankfully, I've managed to keep them at arm's length, although I've met a few on training courses where they talk mysteriously of their tradecraft, but haven't a clue how to collect and present evidence in courts.

I've written them off as overgrown, maladjusted schoolboys, playing games, often illegal games, that have long gone out of fashion. As detectives they strike me as duffers.

Lunch apart, I can't claim to be looking forward to this job.

The queue shuffles forward a couple of steps and I stifle a yawn. Espionage, I'm thinking, has got whiskers on it. Nobody wants spies, spy catchers or spy thrillers any more; boring.

Beamish, I'll wager, is just as bored as me and has gone off for a night on the town; a big lively city, actually, with lots of places to go, lots of mischief to get up to.

The chances are he's already back, here in this milling foyer, having explained away his absence with the sort of flannel I've sometimes used in my twenty years on the force.

I gaze idly around. Which one is he?

Well, unless he's in undercover drag – I smile to myself – certainly not the ginger-haired woman, sitting in a battery-operated wheelchair, as motionless as a robin on her nest, surveying the bustle rather intently, wearing a name tag on her rust-coloured jacket I can't read at this distance.

Could be the slight, sandy-haired man she appears to be observing, who is carrying a green Marks & Spencer bag, and is wearing an almost white raincoat that hides any badge, as he scurries towards the lifts beyond the long reception desk and the wide staircase.

Hope not. Don't want to find him too soon; not until I've had that free lunch. Then I'll spin it out a bit and knock off early on a day that's a holiday for the banks, but hardly anyone else in these secular times.

'Welcome,' says the plump, bespectacled woman clerk sitting behind the registration table when I reach the head of the queue. 'Name, please.'

'Phillip Todd,' I say, loud enough for anyone within earshot to hear. 'Eastmids Police. Replacing Chief Superintendent Dale.'

She looks rather alarmed. 'Can't he be here?'

'Sick,' I half lie. Carole Malloy summarily jocked off Dale to field me. She couldn't ask him to make the covert inquiries Beamish's boss had requested. He's about as covert as Dolly Parton. It's only half a lie because he will be sick over missing a day-long skive and a free lunch.

Her male colleague, fair-haired and lanky, begins to pen a white card in black ink, flowery copperplate, as she stuffs a pink wallet from separate piles of papers on the blue baize table, the usual talking shop bumf – timetable, list of delegates, hotel and sightseeing brochures, map of the city centre.

'You'll take his place?' She hands over the completed collection and looks up at me. 'As a speaker, I mean?'

Speaker? Malloy never briefed me on this. 'Pardon?'

Her head goes down to one of the piles. 'On the 11 a.m. panel.'

She reads: '"The most violent place in Britain. How far – in fact and fiction – does our host city live up to its reputation?"' Her head comes up. 'Eleven this morning.'

'Er . . .' This speaker is speechless. I open my newly acquired wallet and find the programme.

The panel, I read, is to be chaired by Lord Kenton, a kind of quango king, government appointees who have replaced elected representatives on various committees to make sure they reach the right decisions; the sort of democracy of which the *Morning Star* does not approve. Scheduled to be on the platform with him are Chief Superintendent Alan Dale, Head of Police Community Relations, and Mr James Jackson, former CID inspector, now a crime novelist.

Her expression is anxious. 'That's all right, isn't it?'

Lord Kenton, judging from his frequent appearances on TV, may be a fat cantankerous old fart, but Jacko is a long-time pal, close enough to have saved my life three years ago. With him at my side – and time to give my clued-up wife a quick call for background – I reckon I can just about busk it. 'Of course,' I say with more ease than I'm feeling.

The man slips what he's written into a clip-on lapel badge. 'Euro Travel Congress' is printed across the top. Within a plastic panel is: 'Chief Super Philip Todd.' Under that is: 'Head of Police Community Relations.' In two lines, he's promoted me, transferred me and spelt my first name wrong. I'm not going to complain.

Relief filling her face, the woman pats a pile of thick glossy magazines on the table. 'Help yourself to one of these, too. They're in with the fee.'

I slide off the top copy. *Talking Points*, says the white on maroon masthead. In much smaller print is: 'Spring edition. £3 quarterly.'

The cover carries two colourful photos with a jagged tear between them. The top left-hand shot is of a tower I don't recognise. The bottom right side has the duke's palace next door standing on top of the steep-faced castle rock. Printed across both photos in a double strap is: 'Full reports on the Bruges convention. Preview of the Nottingham congress.'

I turn from the table, quite slowly, attaching the badge to my jacket lapel with both hands, a difficult manoeuvre with folder

14

and magazine tucked under an arm, looking down, and walk away with an exaggerated limp, expecting a tap on the shoulder or a quiet word in the ear every step.

While I sat in her office, Malloy had phoned John Beamish's boss with my description – forty, five-ten, very blond hair, dark brown suit, walks with a pronounced limp.

I had given my name loud enough for Beamish's partner to hear if he'd positioned himself strategically, as a good operator should.

All I know is his name or, rather, the name he is using – Larry Wigmore – and the make and number of his pool car – an N-registered silver-grey Peugeot 1.9 GTI, nippy but nondescript, a good choice for a surveillance man.

I wasn't told what he looks like, so the first move must come from him. 'They're running the show,' Malloy had emphasised. 'It's their operation. You're liaison.' Cruelly, she'd added, 'Just the leg man.'

No one waylays me on a stroll down one of several long, wide, grey-tiled gangways which criss-cross the thick royal blue carpet of the foyer. Few delegates have stirred from their sofas.

Two women in figure-hugging light grey suits are busy behind the polished teak reception desk. One is on a yellow phone sorting out a queried bill. The other is having communication difficulties with a smiling Portuguese delegate in a baggy silvery suit who seems to be wanting to know about the availability of tickets for the European soccer championships in a couple of months' time. She, too, picks up a phone.

Behind them is a bank of pigeon-holes in four rows for keys and messages. Above it, a clock fitted inside what looks like a lifebelt with red and white stripes and 'Special Needs Hotel' written in black block capitals around it.

Beside the reception, at eye level, is a framed picture of cavaliers lifting their hats, swords and a flag towards a hairy man in armour. The caption is in a smaller matching frame and says: 'On this hill in 1642, King Charles I raised his standard to start the Civil War. The castle, then a Norman fortress, remained in Parliamentary hands in the four years that followed.'

A bit like a soccer skipper winning the toss and electing to kick uphill against the wind, I muse. The price for losing in those days was high and, no doubt, there'll be a picture somewhere of

Charlie Boy with his head on the block, but I'm not going to look for it.

Beneath the painting is a wheelchair, red-framed, folded out, ready for use, a tartan blanket on the canvas seat. Both legs ache today, the good one from this bloody chill, so, to take the weight off them, I'll sit and wait for service in the wheelchair.

For something to do, I slip the list of delegates out of my folder, skip through the As to: 'Beamish, John. Central Office of Information. Room 224.' Then the word 'Full'.

I have to go to the top of the column to work this out. 'Full' seems to mean he checked in yesterday for the three days' and two nights' duration of the conference which ends tomorrow.

To cross check it, I flick to the Ds. 'Dale, Alan. Police Community Relations.' No room number is given. Then comes 'Day'. Then I flip on to the last sheet. 'Wigmore, Larry. Heritage Foundation. Room 150. Full.'

So, I think grouchily, both of them are using government departments with a touristy flavour as cover. The fee for a day delegate, Malloy informed me, is forty-five pounds, so a double booking with rooms for the duration would run into several hundred. But then money was never any object to the gilded secret services while cash-strapped police forces were having to take real policemen off the beat.

A flick to the middle now, but it's no real disappointment to find that Musters, Jurgen, ex-ace spy handler in the Staatssicherheitsdienst, isn't listed.

A skip back and forth shows that a couple of hundred or more names are tabulated, mostly foreign.

Both receptionists are still on their phones, so I delve further into my wallet and come out with the hotel brochure.

It has a passport-style stamp over its photo on the front with 'Special Needs Hotel' inside a circle – politically correct language for a place that caters for the disabled, with this wheelchair, a flat foyer with wide gangways and the low-gradient ramps each side of the imposing front entrance on four white stone pillars to automatic sliding doors.

Only someone who'd spent weeks being pushed around in a bog-standard NHS wheelchair would have noticed, I suppose; someone who'd wondered if he'd ever make the stairs again, someone who got used to over-helpful folk addressing all questions to people like my lady and 'Jacko' Jackson who were doing the pushing. Not quite 'Does he take sugar?' – but close.

I turn inside and read that this lovely old building was once a nurses' home, a gift to the hospital which stood on this hill from grateful citizens in memory of servicemen and nurses killed in the Great War.

Bet there were some high jinks in this place in the old days, I muse pleasurably. Not sexual high jinks. I don't mean that. Only men who have never been nursed think like that. Fun, I mean, parties, like I used to enjoy in Special Ops before . . . oh, forget it.

The hospital, I read, moved into a vast new building across the ring road from the university. In those two places, I spent, first, three carefree years and, much more recently, three painful months.

After the move, the home was sold – another civic jewel flogged off, a bit like selling a precious present a much-loved relative has given you; obscene really.

Still, I suppose the nurses would appreciate the efforts being made for ex-patients like me.

I've sat here for several minutes, on conspicuous view, but no one has approached. Two MI5 amateurs missing now, I moan inwardly, and sigh outwardly.

Across the counter the nearest receptionist is giving directions to a branch of the bank that is handling ticket sales for the soccer tournament. Belatedly, she remembers today is a bank holiday and starts writing down something. Over the top edge of the brochure, I see baggy silver pants departing.

Before all the literature on my knees can be restowed, baggy pants are replaced by a pair of legs on a par with Steffi Graf's or that girl's who hosts the National Lottery on TV; good enough to model the black stockings they are encased in – long, slender, smooth, with tight calves, not at all muscular, and trim ankles. There's nothing knobbly about the knees, either, and the loose pleated black skirt is short enough to give a good view.

(I can't claim a medical interest in legs that's anything to do with nearly losing one of my own. I've ogled them since I was a pimply youth. Appreciating this, my wife, when a little bit pissed or randy or both, will lift up her skirt and do a can-can. Never fails.)

My eyes travel on up and are disappointed. A flattish chest in a tight white shirt, a pale, washed-out face and close-cropped blonde hair give her a look that's a bit too boyish.

In a neutral, rather nasal voice, she is complaining that her black suitcase is still missing and the receptionist reassures her that every effort is being made to locate it.

The clerk gives the departing back a perplexed look which doesn't vanish when she turns and finally looks down on me. 'Heavy night?'

'Just resting up,' I say, smiling, tapping my bad right leg. I get up and, after a couple of strides, lower myself with elbows on the counter, so she can read my badge and I can read hers. 'Try Room 224 for me, will you?' I don't add Becky, the name displayed on a firm bosom.

'You, too?' she says pertly.

Beamish's boss is also chasing him, I conjecture, while she fingers the numbers, listens for some time to rings that I can hear, then shakes her head so firmly that her long blonde hair wafts gently. 'No reply still.'

'How about Mr Wigmore in Room 150?' I ask.

She presses more numbers, doesn't listen long. 'Engaged.'

Well, if Wigmore is too busy to greet me, I may as well start solo.

10.10 hours

The Special Branch bunch of keys that can unpick almost any lock doesn't have to be taken out of its little black leather wallet to open Room 224.

The lime green door is ajar, a pile of damp towels on the deeper green corridor carpet that runs the astonishing distance of the second floor, almost the length of a football pitch, and continues inside the room.

I tap and walk a couple of paces in, stopping to listen alongside a small square table on which stands a lamp with a white pot base and a floral shade.

A completely scarfed head pops out of another door immediately to my left, startling me slightly until a woman in a long-sleeved lemon housecoat steps into full view.

Her brown eyes are startled, too, even after they've gone to my delegate's badge.

'Mr Beamish about?' I ask brightly.

A small woman, with a pinched face, pale without make-up, fortyish, she shakes her head dumbly.

One rubber-gloved hand holds a red bucket, with cleaning equipment and a small bottle of bath foam, empty apart from white bubbles. The other motions to the main room, double bed neatly made up, blue pyjamas folded on the pillow. On the floor by a wall papered with yellow flowers on green stems is a canvas suitcase, straps unbuckled.

'Mmmmm' is all I can manage as my eyes return to her, then over her shoulder into a sea green tiled bathroom that's sparkling clean and well lit. An ad lib is needed. 'Got some statistics he asked for.'

'I have seen nobody,' she finally says, somewhat haltingly. 'Sorry.'

She has a Continental accent I can't quite peg. French, I guess, from the way she lets her head and hands do most of her talking. 'I will go now and return later.' She half turns; an ungainly movement in brown flat shoes that are on the big side, backless, and don't hide ankles that are rather swollen.

'Was his bed slept in?' I ask.

She turns back. 'I beg your pardon?' she answers very formally.

'His bed. Was it slept in?'

She appears to be thinking, but makes no response.

'Have you changed the sheets?'

A timid headshake. 'I do those only.' She tilts her head towards the bathroom.

'Was the bath used?'

Now she flicks her head towards the towels.

I nod into the main room in the general direction of a dresser cum writing table with a rack of hotel stationery in front of a wall mirror. 'OK, if I leave him a note?'

She studies my badge again, gestures with one hand again. 'Please.'

I walk over a carpet that's less than spotless, flecks of grey ash here and there, and sit on a round stool at the dresser.

She shuts the bathroom door, but leaves the outer door slightly open. 'Close, please, when you have finished,' she calls from the corridor through the small gap. Having appeared in awe of me, she now comes across as a bit guttural and bossy; German, perhaps.

I put the folder I've been holding ever since registration on the table and lift a sheet of headed notepaper out of its rack.

I take a slim gold pen, a Cross Century, a Christmas present from my wife, from my inside pocket and reprise my ad lib: 'Got some info for you,' I write, then delve back into the folder and note from the programme that I am booked to speak in the Plantagenet Suite, add the suggestion that we meet there at 11 a.m., signing off, 'Regards. Phil Todd Eastmids Police.' I don't give my newly inflated rank or my branch, real or imagined.

I get up, pick up the case, put it on the bedspread, all greens and golds to match the wallpaper, and throw the lid open. It's empty apart from scuffed brown shoes, size seven.

A few steps return me to the bathroom. Shaving kit and toiletries have been neatly lined up on a glass shelf beneath an illuminated face mirror. Standing alone on the shelf between the bath taps is a two-inch bottle, the same size and colour as the one the cleaner removed, but not quite a twin. This is hair shampoo, honeysuckle flavoured, according to the label. The used foam has not yet been replaced.

Returning to the main room, I walk between the dresser and the bottom of the bed towards the window. On the way I stop to look at a stark, almost childlike painting of a strange face – white, long, narrow, hairless, downturned lips and dead eyes; white neck and upper chest, flaky grey skin on the rest of it, like a burns victim. 'Effigy of Edward III, probably based on his death mask.'

Had I been with an old mate from Special Ops, we'd have been joking by now, asking the portrait 'Seen anything, mate?' But, on my own, searching a place where I shouldn't really be, I feel a tingle of unease.

A wing chair stands under the window and I kneel on it to peer through vertical blinds that hang open. Nose through a five-inch gap, I can smell stale cigarette smoke on the heavy stiff cloth as I look out on a bright, breezy morning.

The view from here is not of the castle, but a splendid building all the same, Victorian, red bricks newly cleaned, with a roof-top clock with a black face and gold lettering showing 10.15. The block is linked in an L-shape to a tall round building, equally tasteful; all parts of the old hospital, I guess.

Between that and me is a car-park lined with grass banks. On the back row, where I left it, is my newish silver Volvo and two rows closer a silver-grey Peugeot, but not close enough to read the number plate.

I pull my knee off the chair and walk on to the far corner where a TV set sits on a locked refrigerated drinks cabinet. Now the branch bunch of keys is used.

One row inside the door is empty. The check-list indicates there should have been six of those airline-size bottles of various whiskies there.

He's supped some stuff, I think, looking around, but failing to find the glass out of which he'd supped.

The door is kneed shut and I retrace my steps, breaking new ground on the other side of the bed.

I slide open a wardrobe that covers the wall to the short

21

entrance hall. A chocolate brown suit, a fawn blazer with grey cords, a dirty brown raincoat, all off the peg to fit a jockey-sized man, and three off-white shirts are on hotel hangers. Add to that what he's wearing, wherever he is, and John Beamish is not a man who travels light or very smartly.

I slide back the door. From behind it comes a shrill cheep. I open it again. My ears follow the sound to the brown jacket which I frisk to find a bleeper, unhooking it from the inside pocket.

It's a Message Master, the sort I use, small and light in a square black plastic case. For some reason (probably because I know I ought not to be doing this after Malloy's briefing not to meddle) I cup it gingerly in both hands, as if holding a bird that might fly away.

A button at the side is pressed with thumb knuckle to bring up the message: 'Kenton returning your call. In Plantagenet Suite at 11.'

There should be quite a crowd of us, I think.

I keep pressing. Stored messages scroll across the small screen. 'Contact Merryweather – Urgent.' 'Meet me. Trip. 9 p.m. Larry.' 'Contact Merryweather ASAP.'

What sort of on-the-road operator skives off without taking his bleep? I'm asking myself. Even a rookie knows better.

The faintest of sounds comes from behind me, no more than a presence, really. A tell-tale knot begins to tighten at the heart.

'Don't move.' A man's voice, soft but very firm. 'Keep your hands where they are. Don't go for any pockets.' A heavy pause. 'Don't even think of moving.'

The knot is so tight now that blood is no longer reaching my brain. Can't think, let alone move, except that I don't want to wind up, pray I'll not wind up, looking like King Edward on the wall.

'Face me.' Cool; icy, in fact. 'Slowly.'

Just short of hyperventilating, I am looking across my shoulder into the barrel of a black .38.

It's being gripped in two hands, arms fully extended, textbook-trained. The rest of his stance isn't so well coached. Only one leg

22

is flexed. The other is locked at the knee like the movement of a golfer on the back swing.

His dress is City, not links – dark, pin-striped, three-piece suit and a colourfully striped tie, military or old school.

On a wide, hand-stitched lapel a name tag introduces 'Larry Wigmore – Heritage Foundation'.

My brain unties. The rest of me remains clammy. 'Looking for you.' Pause. 'I've been.' The sentence has come out back to front, but I did well to utter it at all.

'Who are you?' His face and voice remain stiff with tension.

Hands still, almost squeezing the life out of the Message Master, I swivel my chest to give him a sight of my badge. 'Got a warrant card in an inside pocket and, if that isn't good enough, you can contact ACC Malloy at HQ.'

Slowly, almost reluctantly, he lowers his pistol, lets go with one hand and points it at the green carpet. 'What the devil are you doing here?'

'Looking for your workmate.' The words are coming easier now.

'Covert.' His voice is still starchy, blue eyes fierce. 'Those were the instructions. What do you mean by breaking in?'

'Didn't break in. The cleaner let me in.'

He frowns deeply, looks aimlessly about the room, says nothing.

'To leave a note for him.' I look towards the dresser, then at the gun. 'And it will be covert if you put that away. The cleaner's coming back.'

With one final glare, showing me who's in charge, he unbuttons his double-breasted jacket with one hand and, sighing, stuffs the gun into a black leather holster at his left armpit. Head down, he mumbles something about cock-ups I don't quite catch.

Now that I'm out of immediate danger I judge it safe to grumble. 'Nobody told me this was an armed job.'

He looks up at me sharply, but makes no response.

I seize the initiative. 'You were supposed to meet me downstairs when I signed in twenty minutes ago.'

A defensive smile. 'Calls to make, I'm afraid.'

'Did reception tell you I was up here?'

A barely perceptible nod. Odd, because I told no one I was

coming up. I glance around the room. 'Checked in here before, have you?'

A headshake is followed by a shift of ground. 'Head office asked me to have a look-see. Find anything?'

My heart is beating near to normal again. 'No word from him yet then?'

Another headshake, giving nothing away. 'You?'

I tell him my ACC has organised the usual ring round of hospital casualties and morgues and would have bleeped me if there'd been anything to report. I hand over Beamish's radio pager. 'Who's Merryweather?'

With a surprised expression, he presses up the messages. 'Mmmmm.' He is wondering whether to answer. 'Our chief.'

Weakness washes right through me, delayed shock. 'Mind if we sit down?'

He turns away stiffly and walks with a limp worse than mine to the white, round stool in front of the writing table. Back towards me, his head goes down over my note. His dark brown hair is very thick and curly and hangs well below his collar.

I explain to his back that the note was just a cover story for the cleaner.

He swivels round on the stool. The tension in his face has dissolved into dimples. Smiling rather shyly, he nods me to the bed. 'Sit among the cytisus.'

The bedspread, now that I look more closely, has deep gold buttercup-shaped flowers on slender stems. Seen plenty of them growing wild in my boyhood when grandad used to take me hunting and shooting and, sometimes, out on his rural beat. He'd have called it broom, but then neither of us was ever any good at Latin names.

As the rather hard fabric and the green leaves fold about my bum, I place the pink folder at my side. 'Time for a tactics talk, perhaps?'

Well, he begins, he can't tell me absolutely everything, of course, but refrains from adding, 'Need to know and all that.'

He'd been working on and off with John Beamish for, oh, ten years. 'Since this – ' and he taps his left leg which sticks out rigidly.

I tap mine. 'Know the feeling.'

A sympathetic expression fills his face. 'What happened?'

24

'A railway line just out of town. Hunt for an armed killer. He got me. The train got him.'

He grits his even white teeth and a sigh sizzles out. 'A sod, isn't it?'

Not half, I think, nodding. Twice before I've looked down barrels, both of them shotguns. Last time, at least, I was armed, too, and talked him out of it. The time before, on the railway line, no chance. Now and then I still wake up in a sweat, gripping my leg which I thought had been blown away; reliving the panic and the pain.

Panic again today, of course, but this time, mercifully, no pain.

'Never mind.' His bottom teeth nip an upper lip that actually goes stiff. 'We have one decent pair between us.' We both laugh, both forced. 'Kept you on, did they?'

I nod.

'Curtains for me, of course, in the army.' Wigmore looks downcast. 'Not a great pension, either, so this job's a godsend.' A tiny shrug. 'Dogsbody, really, but I kept the civil grade for my rank.'

He's fortyish, my age, perhaps a bit younger and certainly slimmer. His little smiles and shrugs, his southern public school accent, his whole self-deprecating manner put me in mind of Hugh Grant. My guess is that he'd be a captain, a major at most, when he was invalided out. 'Intelligence?'

'Communications. All went wrong planting a bug down the Falls. A sniper.'

Suddenly he seems quite keen to talk about himself, but, I remind myself, he's not missing. 'What's he like – John Beamish?'

'Very experienced. Came up through the ranks. Fifty-two now, not in the best of health. Been in the game man and boy. Counter espionage, obviously.'

The MI5, I've learned on courses, like to see themselves as defenders of the Crown Jewels, while MI6 steal other countries'. 'Where does Jurgen Musters fit in?'

His thick eyebrows arch in surprise. 'Major Merryweather's briefed you?'

I nod. 'Via my boss.'

'John's Musters' case officer.'

'What background is there?'

Quite a lot, as it turns out, now that he knows who I am, and he begins to tell it in an irritating fashion as if he has a pound of plums in his mouth.

Musters served officially as a commercial attaché in the old German Democratic Republic's embassy in London in the eighties. He used his diplomatic post as a means to get about Britain, with flying trips to Dublin, too, claiming to be drumming up cultural exchanges. Really, he was recruiting spies.

'Mostly, you know, low-grade stuff. Academics. Journalists. The odd businessman or trade union leader. The odder politician.'

'What did he use for bait?'

'They'd – potential targets, I mean – they'd apply for a visa to get into the East for some story or research or sales drive or something. He'd interview them. The old slow-burn. Formal chat at the office. A short-stay visa. Just a taster to whet their appetite.'

He smiles knowingly. 'Then, with the next application, into a Soho restaurant. "We're not seeking to take your fine country over. What we're looking for is trade of mutual benefit, cultural intercourse, etc." That sort of guff.

'To the naïve journalist, he'd suggest articles, anti-American stuff, and, lo, the run of East Germany and lots of nice exclusives. For the academic, previously closed doors to research material would be opened.'

I feel I should throw in a question. 'What did he get in return?'

'Info about other politicians and academics whose writings or lectures were less than critical of the old red regime, so they could be targeted.'

'Compromised?'

He gives this some consideration. 'Not necessarily sexually, if you mean the old honeytrap, no.' More thought. 'But take a trade union leader. He'd tell his executive he was attending some symposium which turned out to be a luxury holiday with family or, better still, lover. He wouldn't want that coming out now, would he?'

I shake my head.

'Or the journalist who'd bravely campaigned against Cruise. He wouldn't want it known that his trips were being funded by a friendship society that was really a front for laundered Stasi money.'

A tiny shrug. 'The CIA did much of the same, only more. Us, too, all over the world.' He smirks. 'But there you are. That was the propaganda business.'

In the main, he sums up, Musters' contacts were what's called agents of influence, opinion formers; not your Portland spy ring.

With my 11 a.m. speech looming and a couple of calls to make before performing, I have to hurry him on. 'And when the Wall came down he took all these names with him, did he?'

'Some, certainly.'

For instance, he goes on, a research professor, a woman, attending an academic jamboree in Dublin who was found dead in the Liffey. She was on file as a contact of Musters, suspected of feeding him stuff on geological finds, never proved. She'd been cleaned out financially. There was a travel fair on at the Gresham at the time. Musters was spotted posing as a Lufthansa courier.

Beamish and Wigmore had been assigned, but never picked up his trail.

'Bruges?' I prompt.

Well, he gushes on, woman editor of some long-extinct pacifist mag, then working in PR. Musters was suspected of giving her more than Stasi handouts. Found electrocuted in her hotel room's bath, which, of course, Wigmore pronounces barth. Her bank accounts had been cleaned out, too.

Musters had been in town, organising cultural tours that never took place. 'Took down payments, too, cheeky bastard.' He smiles sickly. 'We were both there at the time, John and me, along with half NATO's security services. No one got a whiff of him.'

Increasingly pushed though I am for time, this background deserves a moment's muse.

OK, it would be damaging, certainly professionally, if it had come out that she'd been sleeping with the enemy, but she wouldn't have been charged, surely, not after five years of peaceful co-existence? So why pay hush money?

27

Well, hurt pride, I suppose. Imagine the world knowing that you'd been snitching on your university chums, writing puffs for a discreditable regime and getting rewards in cash or kind.

Why do it in the first place? I ponder. Apart from cash or kind, you mean?

When searching for a motive, I was taught on one course, apply the CIA test and hunt MICE.

Money – which means greed and talks for itself.

Ideology – Communism being the way forward, moral and just in the long term, despite short-term excess. Our way was decadent.

Compromise – that old KGB saying, 'Once you've got a spy, you've always got him.'

Ego – being a somebody, doing something that no one else knows about, the self-importance and the sense of adventure that come with leading a secret life.

Like me, I privately admit, before it dawned that all the routine makes this sexy-sounding job more boring in reality than being back on the rural beat.

I have been silent only for a second or two, but Wigmore is waiting for me to say something, so I look straight into his eyes. 'His old contacts must be sweating now.'

Wigmore looks away, unsure. 'Well, the idealist will tell himself that Communism was and remains right and will come again. It was corrupt leaders who fouled it up. They'll be OK. They'll never accept that they backed a loser.'

He looks back at me, smiling rather pleasurably. 'But – yes – for the rest, there'd be some lost sleep wondering if their treachery is about to be revealed in some old spy's memoirs. I'd certainly worry about being grassed' – which, naturally, comes out as grarsed.

Me, too, I think fretfully. I suffer early morning awakening when I think of a one-lunchtime stand with a red-haired solicitor. It was before marriage and parenthood and there'd been a bit of a breakdown in our relationship at the time, true, but I'd hate Em to know about it even now.

And I'd hate Malloy and other chiefs to know about some of my manipulating of informers in my CID days; smart ideas at the time, impossible to justify with the passing of it.

Inwardly a shudder runs through me. 'So who tipped you that Musters might be here?'

He looks shocked at a question I probably shouldn't have asked. 'Nobody.' His face features uncertainty. 'As far as I know.' He pauses, pondering. 'Given how and where Musters operates, it seems a reasonably educated guess.'

'So how are you two tackling it?'

They took out different credentials and travelled separately to Nottingham, he replies, Beamish by train, Wigmore by car.

They arrived within an hour of each other, but didn't communicate, apart from a lunchtime phone call when Beamish gave Wigmore fresh orders to scout other hotels.

The meet to exchange progress reports was for 7 p.m. last night in the Trip to Jerusalem, an ancient pub at the foot of the castle walls, a short walk from the hotel.

Beamish was keeping watch in the Standard Hill Hotel. Wigmore did a swing round other hotels in walking distance in case Musters booked a room away from the conference to stay out of sight.

Beamish didn't show at the Trip. Wigmore bleeped him with the rescheduled time of 9 p.m. When he didn't show again, Major Merryweather was informed.

Their chief, he surmises, studying the Message Master in his hand, paged Beamish with the ASAP call last night and, with concern mounting, the 'Urgent' message this morning when he'd failed to make his usual contact call.

I move things on. 'See anything of Musters on your tour of hotels last night?'

A sullen headshake. 'No. Nor on another swan round this breakfast time.'

'Weren't you in your room around ten?'

'No. Came straight here. Why?'

'I tried it on the house phone about then. Engaged.'

He looks distinctly puzzled. 'Perhaps someone else was also trying me.'

Perhaps, I concede, privately. 'What was your briefing?'

'Locate, report and keep tabs until a full surveillance op is in place.'

I pull out my notebook. 'Describe Musters, will you?'

He thinks before he answers. 'Outwardly, he's so nondescript, a face in the crowd. That's why he got the job, I suppose.'

He slows down to let me make notes. 'Fifty. Five-ten. Ten stone, no more. A lightweight. Sometimes wears specs, various frames. Sometimes his hair is grey, sometimes natural mousy. Teeth false, but he changes dentures. Brown eyes but they can change, too, with contact lenses. A real will o' the wisp, I can tell you. I did lots of the tracking of him in his London days.'

He waits for me to catch up and look up.

'Dressed like a tramp one day,' he goes on. 'Savile Row the next. Speaks excellent English. Four languages in all. The very devil to shadow.'

A tough task, I'm agreeing. 'Any distinguishing features?'

'Never got that close.'

I turn a page. 'John Beamish?'

'Why?' A deep frown.

'My chief wants it for hospital checks,' I fib.

An understanding nod. 'Fifty-two, five-eight, and nine stone, real skinny. Hair grey, eyes blue. Never changes. No need. MI5 are the Plods. MI6 the Pimpernels.' That self-deprecating smile again. 'Lost the left little finger.' A grimace, holding up his own, out of habit, I think scathingly, from drinking tea. 'Hedge cutter.'

'Ever been AWOL before?'

'Well . . .' Suddenly, he's tight-lipped.

I lower my head towards the bed. 'It doesn't look as though he slept here last night,' then shoot a glance to the bathroom. 'But he used that.'

Anxiety flickers across his face. 'What on earth is he up to, I wonder?'

I'm not sure what he's driving at. 'I need to know whether to put out the full alert on this.'

'Don't.' Anxiety is redoubled. He almost blurts it, then softer, 'Not without Merryweather's OK. OK?'

I nod.

His head drops. 'John's had a yellow card.' He squirms uncomfortably on his stool. 'He's married, but, well, separate lives for some time. No kids. Gets a bit lonely now and then, seldom at home. Not that he gabs or anything. Very correct in that way.'

I'm going to have to push him. 'But in others?'

'Well . . .' An unhappy shrug. 'Whisky and women. He's entitled to both, in my view. It gets to you in the end, doesn't it, this job?'

I nod, but privately disagree. No job is going to turn me into a pisshead and a womaniser.

'Not a fit man. Doctors have told him to cut the booze and the smoking. Managed the second, not the first.'

I yank my head at the drinks cabinet and tell him it's been cleaned out of whisky.

Wigmore closes his eyes. 'Oh, God.'

'How will he be dressed?'

'At the final briefing in town he was in his brown job.'

I nod at the wardrobe. 'That's in there.'

'Oh.' Surprised. 'Must have changed then.'

'Into what?'

He shrugs. 'Blazer? A light brown one?'

Another nod.

Another shrug. 'His old grey job then. Not seen it for yonks but it's all I can think of.'

I have one more urgent question. I glance at my watch: quarter to, and I have those two calls to make yet. 'Are any of Musters' suspected ex-Joes delegates at the conference, ex-contacts he might try to put the bite on?'

'Two,' he answers.

'Gordon Allen. Attends most of these dos.' Wigmore seems to sense my need to get away, and clips his sentences even shorter. 'Not only a travel writer, but a fellow-traveller in the old days, intellectual left and all that. Runs that.' He nods down at the glossy *Talking Points* magazine which is on top of the folder beside me on the bed.

'Established twelve years ago with cash Musters provided from some innocent-sounding cultural exchange society. Allen got a free run of Eastern Bloc countries for his features.'

'Did you tackle him about it?'

'We had him in for a quiet chat. Told us, in effect, to piss off. We didn't get too heavy. You can't with the media, can you? Made that mistake before.'

31

Irritatingly, he becomes discursive. 'Our MI6 cousins tapped up a promising undergrad, got turned down. When he became a celebrated TV presenter, he went public about the approach. Can't have that, can we?'

I stay silent, forcing him back on track.

'We just kept a weather eye on the liaison. It was all pretty low grade.'

'And who else?' I prompt.

'Lord Kenton.'

I can feel my mouth dropping open, can't prevent it.

'Tapped up when he went to the GDR embassy for a visa for some trade union do years ago.' Wigmore beams broadly. 'But surprise, surprise, he came to us.'

'And?' I ask, simply to close my mouth again.

'Musters inherited him and we strung him along. Slipped him chicken feed, misinformation. The odd spicy bit, out of date, now and then, to give the rest cred. John made up the packages. Kenton used to drop them off at pre-arranged dead letter boxes or Musters would switch attaché cases in crowded pubs; the old scams.'

'So who was Kenton's paymaster?'

'Both sides. And he still made the odd anti-American, anti-NATO speech to keep up his front with Stasi. A patriot, really. Good as gold to handle.'

I long for more, but have run out of time. I stand, leaving the impression of my backside in the bed of broom, and explain the appointment I have to keep to maintain my cover.

He tells me Merryweather's orders to him are to make discreet inquiries about Beamish in drinking and vice dens.

From local knowledge (professional from vice squad days, not personal from bachelor days), I give him the names of a handful of inner city shebeens and brothels masquerading as massage parlours.

To keep in contact we exchange pager numbers. I jot his down in my book, glancing back at the other notes I've made, something occurring.

'If Allen's info to Musters wasn't worth putting him in the Old Bailey dock for and Kenton's was dud and planted by our side, neither seem suitable targets for blackmail, do they?'

'No.' He shakes his head slowly. 'Unless, of course, there's a third man we know nothing about.'

Always is in spy stories, I think gloomily.

Time, I decide in the descending lift, for just one call, so long did I spend in Room 224. Time to choose between the two main women in my life. My wife gets the vote over my boss.

After giving Wigmore a smiling thumbs-up for good luck in his trawl around the city's low life, I head for a triangle of hooded phones beneath the wide staircase in the foyer, rapidly emptying as delegates drift off – to hear me, it occurs with rising alarm.

'Hello.' A man's voice after I'd passed my home and my credit card numbers. Blast.

I like my father-in-law, am always pleased to see him for a holiday weekend of sports spectating, while mother-in-law fusses over Laura, seven months old now and in need of entertainment every waking minute.

But it's his daughter I want, and quickly. A font of information, she was – 'is' she'd insist – a journalist; weekly paper, radio, TV. She was on better pay than me when she quit to await mother-hood. She talks often of going back; something I'm trying to talk her out of.

Yes, I confirm, I've got the tickets for Forest versus his beloved Tottenham Hotspurs tomorrow, had to queue for half an hour to get them. And, yes, 'Jacko' Jackson will be coming with us, as usual.

To cut things short, I tell him Jacko is waiting for me to join him on the platform at some seminar, but I need to cross check something urgently with Em.

She's out in the garden, cutting the first of the daffodils, he reports, then tells his wife to call her and I'm forced into chitchat until she comes in.

Remembering that overheard conversation at reception, I ask him if he fancies tickets, too, for the European soccer if any are still available.

Surprisingly, he wants to know why.

Because, I remind him, Klinsmann, every Spurs fan's favourite after one super season at White Hart Lane, will be taking part.

He points out his idol isn't appearing for his native Germany in group games being staged in Nottingham, so, no thanks very much, he's not interested in the likes of Portugal, Croatia and Turkey who've been drawn to play here. Anyway, he's off to Wembley to see England.

No Em yet, so he compliments me on the changes we're making to our house, a between-the-wars detached. Such is my lack of style and taste, I have little say in the alterations. Now Em is about to tackle the walled garden and I face a summer of heavy labouring.

All the time I am racking my brains for the name of a programme she presented in her radio days some years ago. What was it? Something Watch? Something File? Can't be. She complains about every other current affairs show being called one or the other. It was something clichéd with a media ring, nonetheless.

Got it. *Stop Press*. And, to make sure I don't forget it, I rest the pink folder on a narrow ledge beside the phone and note it down in capitals while I hum and ah and laugh, where appropriate.

Finally he hands me on to Em. 'What's up?' Eight years in the East Midlands have diminished the class of a southern accent.

I inquire after Laura, who's 'Champion' – another word she wouldn't have used eight years ago.

She doesn't inquire about my cold which I made something of a fuss about over breakfast.

I tell her what Malloy has me lumbered with, the question I have to address and what little time I have. She chuckles.

'Remember that *Stop Press* thing you did on inner city crime?' I ask. 'Run it past me, will you, in about ninety seconds?'

The old pro in her takes over and she rattles off a couple of hundred words, me making scribbled notes on the folder.

'Simple,' she sums up. 'Do you mean to say we taxpayers are footing the bill for a cushy day like you're having?'

I make time to point out that at this moment in her life, as an out-of-work recipient of child benefit, she's an even bigger drain on the state.

She laughs again and tells me not to be late for dinner at eight. 'Baked halibut,' she adds.

Lovely, aren't they, these lapsed Catholic girls? She hasn't been in a church since I've known her, not even for our wedding, a register office do, with just a dozen around us.

The shops, the pubs, all commerce with the exception of banks, may no longer observe this holy day, but, just like the God-fearing grandma who raised me, she always marks Good Friday with fish.

I should tell her I love her, but all I say is 'Chill some Chablis' and 'Thanks' and hang up.

11.00 hours

I succeed in arriving, almost out of breath, at the opened double doors to the Plantagenet Suite precisely as a clock in an ormolu laurel above them ticks up the hour.

Lord Kenton waits outside, shuffling, just short of pacing. His large frame is expensively suited in smooth light grey with no name tag on his hand-stitched lapel – either because he doesn't want to snag it with a clip or because everyone knows him anyway.

He's unmistakable – sixtyish, sixteen stone, dark hooded eyes with pouches underneath, full head of black hair. His creased leathery face is not displaying the bonhomie you see on TV programmes like *Question Time*. He looks about as happy as a bloodhound that has lost his sense of smell.

He doesn't offer a Hallo, let alone a handshake. 'And where's our fellow panellist?' he whines in an accent that's close to Birmingham.

I mumble a Don't know amongst opening pleasantries. He mutters impatiently about schedules to keep. Abruptly, he turns, hands behind his prominent backside, to survey the room which emits the low, loud babble of lots of conversations.

Looking for inspiration to pad out my thin piece, I gaze at a puzzling painting on the wall next to one of the hooked-back lime green doors.

Two shafts of pale light, one round, one oval, break up a background so dark that it's hard at first glance to make out a line of helmeted men rounding a rocky corner that links the two.

The framed caption reads: 'The young King Edward III and allies enter Nottingham Castle by a secret tunnel in 1330 on their way to usurp his mother Queen Isabella and her paramour Roger Mortimer, later hung, drawn and quartered.'

Not much inspiration there, except, perhaps, don't screw around with royals.

I hear a puffing behind me and turn to see an approaching Jacko taking off his raincoat to reveal a slate grey suit as creased as his face.

Kenton about-turns to listen to apologetic waffling about a traffic jam caused by overnight floods from blocked drains near Trent Bridge.

Again without a welcome, Kenton cuts Jacko short. 'We're late. Best get in.' He turns his back on us to lead the way, striding, light-footed in polished black shoes, into a brightly lit, over-warm room wider than its length with around ten curved lines of chairs, twenty or so chairs to a line, all but a few filled. All the occupants crane their necks towards us, some pulling on headphones.

Stage fright grips me and, to avoid their eyes, I look left to the passing wall alongside which we're walking. It's covered with the same gold buttercup-like flowers on entwining silvery green stems as in Beamish's room, only much larger. Bigger broom, but I can't recall the Latin name Wigmore gave it.

Across my shoulder Jacko tilts his head up, like a dog with an airborne scent, to study my lapel badge through his bifocals. He drops his head sharply in a single, frowning nod towards it. Knowing my real rank and department, he is querying it.

A reply is avoided because the ginger-haired woman in the wheelchair I saw in the foyer when I arrived is partially blocking the aisle and I have to drop back into single file.

The platform is raised about a foot from the bottle green carpet. The table on it is covered with matching baize. Kenton sits in the centre one of three steel-framed, canvas chairs, overfilling it.

I sit to his right, nearest the aisle down which we walked, gaze over the audience, an unnerving mistake, and promptly look down again.

Jacko is smoothing his thinning brown hair with one hand and a thick wad of notes on the table with the other. All I have is three or four lines I made on the cover of my folder while Em talked on the phone.

'Sorry for the delay,' Kenton begins when the audience settles silent. He motions towards Jacko. 'He travelled through floodwater to reach us, apparently. Not to worry. The Trent's not overflowing. Just a blocked drain.'

'Apparently' was spoken with a smirk, as if he didn't accept the excuse, and, after a short pause, there's a brief, disbelieving ripple of laughter.

Encouraged by the reception, Kenton beams broadly. 'Glad to see so many of you here after our wonderful whisky tasting last night.'

Several members of the audience don't look at all glad, heavily hungover, in fact, and the delayed laughter this time is a touch self-conscious.

'Now . . .' In a deep, clear voice that has lost its origins he gives us short introductions, pointing out that I'm a late substitute in the advertised list of guest speakers. 'They are here to help us nail this canard about crime on our streets so that you can all be reassured that visitors you send us will return happy and safe.'

He reads out loud from the programme the question – 'The most violent place in Britain – how far in fact and fiction does our host city live up to its reputation?' – which he's already answered, but then a place out to boost its tourist trade isn't going to admit to much crime. 'Over to you, chief superintendent.'

Immediately I lean forward in my chair, say 'No' firmly into four small microphones and a small silver-cased tape recorder on the table and immediately sit back, trying to look relaxed.

It's a ploy I've used in response to long rambling questions in defence cross-examination, stunningly effective in court. It's an absolute failure here.

So deep is the sudden silence that the red light on the voice-activated tape which shows it is recording flickers out.

What Kenton should say (and very jovially) is something like 'Can you expand on that for the jury?' Instead, he gets the red light on again by blustering, 'You're going to have to sing louder than that for your supper, superintendent – or, at least, your free lunch.'

The audience laughs (against, not with me). One word, and I've lost them already.

I lean forward again, shoulders hunched, and try to expand on the quick briefing Em, having covered the question in her *Stop Press* days, had passed on.

Looking down at the jottings, which have swum into indecipherable scrawl, I stammer out among ers and mmmms the remembered fact that outdated Home Office statistics had put the city at the top of the table for offences against the person, but how a more localised breakdown showed the main cause had been one huge flats complex with a disproportionately high incidence of crime and vice.

Most of the recorded offences were thugs committing violence against each other, I point out. The crime wave receded when the flats had been pulled down, but the myth remained because of all the media attention it had originally attracted.

All solid stuff, but delivered so stodgily, with not a trace of Em's fluency and no humorous asides, that the woman in the wheelchair appears to be fighting off a yawn.

No red light again as I sit back to silence, having spoken for no more than three or four minutes that seemed to drag out like an hour.

'Mmmmm,' says Kenton, totally unimpressed, turning from me to Jacko. 'And what's your view?'

'I agree with the chief super,' he starts, making me feel a bit better. And he goes on to blame over-zealous clerks in Records. 'If one mugger wants to mug another mugger, I don't see that should worry the tourists.'

He tells of a top Fleet Street writer who'd lodged for a weekend in the crime-ridden flats, intent on cribbing the title of locally born Alan Sillitoe's book about life in the city's back streets, *Saturday Night and Sunday Morning*, for a feature on all the violence. Unfortunately for him, not a noteworthy crime was reported during his stay. 'No news isn't good news for newspapers, so the story never made it,' he adds.

The popular press is always a target, soft, but legitimate, at almost any convention, so it wins an easy laugh.

Then he moves on to media myths in general, arguing that the city's long-time reputation of having the prettiest girls in Britain was created in the *Stars and Stripes*, the American forces newspaper, by wartime GIs seeking to flatter them into bed; risqué stuff and some female listeners giggle.

I am not about to interrupt him, but I know he's made that up. I've read somewhere that women's work created by firms that founded the lace and textile trades here gave them financial independence which others of their sex didn't enjoy elsewhere and this won them the national reputation of always looking so good.

In his post-police career as a crime writer Jacko has grown used to flamming up radio interviews and library talks. He's performing so well that I suspect he's getting a handsome fee for turning out.

The gratitude I felt at the outset when he backed me up has vanished now. The longer he speaks the worse he is making me look by comparison.

I realise too late that I have made a complete chump of myself. Secretly, I am railing against Malloy for landing me in it at such short notice. Top secretly, I am having to admit that I am no public speaker.

Now Jacko turns to Robin Hood. 'The greatest myth of all,' he calls him. Most of the audience are clearly enjoying it, but a group from the local tourist office in the front row begin to smile somewhat thinly at the idea of their biggest money-spinner about to be debunked.

I am coming out of my cringe, sit forward again, taking notice.

The over-sized presence of Lord Kenton obscures a full view of Jacko. Expensive aftershave has been liberally applied to his rutted cheeks, mixing with traces of cigar smoke from his suit. A gold chain stretches across his paunch between the two pockets of a waistcoat.

He smiles without mirth, menacing almost, and strums the baize impatiently with multi-ringed fingers as Jacko craftily works in the occasional plug for his latest book.

To find out more about him, I slip the conference brochure out of my folder, thumb through to the pen portraits of guest speakers and read: 'Born Walsall 1930 into a family of ten . . .'

Having pegged him as younger, I am surprised by his pension-able age, but not by his birthplace.

'Joined Post Office as telegram boy during the last year of the war. Elected full-time official of his union ten years later. Became

Labour MP in 1970s for coalfields constituency, after two unsuccessful attempts in rural divisions . . .'

His rise through the Labour movement and, judged from his hand-stitched suit and the size of his paunch, his love of gold and good living would have made him a target for a spymaster like Musters.

'Under-Secretary, Ministry of Fuel and Power in last Labour government, charged with the task of nuclear waste disposal . . .'

I wonder what part MI5 played in placing him in that sensitive position, conning Stasi into thinking they had a prize mole close to the top, all the time feeding his East Berlin masters with duff stuff.

'On change of government, elected founder president of Union of Satellite Communications Staff. Created peer in 1990 for services to the environment, appointed chairman of Conservation Coalition two years later.'

So, when the voters kicked him and his party out, he hadn't returned to the push-bike technology of the Post Office, but had organised the scientists and technicians in the expanding new world of satellite and mobile communications into a new, élite union.

His peerage, I suspect, has less to do with protecting the environment or union rights than with his services to the secret service. His thank-you for fooling the old Eastern Bloc had been a well-paid posting to a quango, plus attendance allowances every time he turns up at the Lords, and all that on top of his state and union pensions.

Nice work? Not sure. I've dealt with a lot of informers in my time. Spies, agents, double agents sound sexier, but that's what they really are – informants. It's a devious, dreadful job.

Jacko is advancing the theory now that Robin Hood never existed, pointing to the lack of contemporary records of his alleged life in King John's time. The first mention of him was in a fourteenth-century ballad, and that, he argues, is a bit like basing Argentina's history in two hundred years' time on the musical *Evita*.

All the audience, except the local tourist executives, guffaw.

Over their heads is an interrupted view of the press bench where three journalists sit, backs to a plain lime green wall, beneath one of several 'No Smoking' signs. Place-names in stencilled black capitals on white cardboard identify who they represent – BBC, *Evening Post* and *Talking Points*. Behind the third is a gaunt-looking man with a brown chin-strap beard that makes the rest of his face look very pale. He is wearing a crumpled blue suit; white shirt, no tie.

With all eyes on Jacko, it's safe to fish out the complimentary copy of Gordon Allen's magazine which I'd tucked in the wallet.

I flip quickly through lots of adverts from cities, hotels, universities with conference facilities, several pages from Bruges including an oddly posed photo of Kenton in dinner jacket, four more pages on Nottingham with stories and pictures about the soccer stadium, theatres, the castle, the rabbit warren of caves beneath the city, and a double-page write-up on whisky.

There's no pen portrait of him, just a photo by-line on a feature in the Nottingham section with the eye-catching headline: 'Royal Scandal'.

These days, editors know that if they want to boost a flagging circulation all they have to do is stick the magic words 'Royal' and 'Scandal' together, but this piece is a real con.

It is centuries old, all about the history of the castle next door, how its defences never allowed attackers to take it by storm and were only breached by the stealth of Edward III, avenging himself for Mortimer's connivance in the murder of his father, who died with a red hot poker up his back passage.

Ouch. I stir uncomfortably in my seat, glad I've not married into the royal family, then or now.

My eyes return to Allen who is fiddling with a black camera, not even making the occasional note.

Further along the wall from the press bench is another table enclosed on both sides by sound-proof panelling that gives the appearance of a temporary box for radio commentators.

In it sit three women. All have headphones. One has close-cropped blonde hair, but a lacy tablecloth drapes down the front blocking any view of legs, so I can't be sure it's the woman with the missing black suitcase. All are talking soundlessly into mikes, instantly interpreting for delegates who don't follow English.

'If he did exist,' Jacko is saying, 'he was the biggest mugger of them all.' He sits back.

The audience breaks into warm applause. My eyes go back to them. Theirs are on Jacko, not me.

He has talked for so long that Kenton has time to permit only half a dozen questions.

In response to one, from a Swiss woman, Jacko opines to gales of laughter that William Tell was a far better shot than Robin Hood, citing his last words, 'Where the arrow falls, there let me be buried,' pointing out that it missed the whole of Nottinghamshire and landed in Yorkshire, pulling a pained face to give the impression that being buried up there was a fate worse than death.

Only one question is directed to me, about what precautions can be taken to reduce the risk of street attack, and I reply with standard crime prevention stuff: go out with a companion, take only the cash and credit cards you need, don't wear jewellery, stick to well-lit streets, avoid underpasses – a bit difficult with the duelled Maid Marian Way cutting across ancient streets like Castlegate and separating the castle, the Playhouse and several hotels from the old market square, but I'll not mention that.

Kenton delivers most of his vote of thanks towards Jacko, but finally turns his head to include me. 'And you, too, chief superintendent, for standing in at such short notice.'

The inspiration I failed to discover as a public speaker finally hits me. I pitch forward on my elbows and lie, 'My pleasure.' No pause to lean back this time. 'Perhaps someone can help me.' I pat my folder. 'I have to hand over these stats to Mr John Beamish, of the Central Office of Information, whom I don't know by sight. He's not in his room, so if he's about here or anyone knows where he is, perhaps they'll let me know.'

'Certainly,' gruffs Kenton. Then, sounding like a vicar wrapping up his sermon at Evensong, he announces he has a special notice.

The noon session, he booms, will be about the city's newest tourist attraction: a Victorian courthouse that's been turned into a museum of justice.

I think I'll give that a miss. It was in that court that I learned the mistimed trick of Yes/No answers. Now it's a museum piece. Forty, and I'm already part of history. I feel old enough as it is.

By special arrangement, Kenton goes on, the lecture scheduled for midday on the city's caves has been put back to eight thirty in the evening and will take place *in situ* – in the castle grounds

43

with a tour of Mortimer's Hole, returning via the Western Passage.

Count me out of that, too. After what I've just read, I'm not going down anyone's hole or up anyone's passage, thanks all the same. By then, I'll be home eating baked halibut.

'That', Kenton goes on, beaming, 'gives us an extra happy hour beforehand to resample the delights provided by our Scottish friends in the Stuart Bar.'

I get it now. The plug for whisky in *Talking Points* is in return for some sort of sponsorship.

Well, apologies for absence from that, too. I can't even stand the smell of scotch, not since I drank half a bottle of it as a teenager at a sixth-form party, vomited my stomach inside out and staggered home, as my grandma often recounted, 'daft side out'. I was ill for two days; never touched a drop since.

'Coffee is now being served in the Tudor Room,' Kenton concludes, rising. So does almost everyone else, me included, feeling depressed.

As he steps round the table, Jacko is immediately waylaid by a woman radio journalist with a tape recorder in a black leather case like a handbag.

Kenton sits again, feeling his waistcoat for a pocket diary, to answer some query by the tall, fair male clerk from registration on his availability for a future engagement.

The ginger-haired woman in the wheelchair appears to be heading down the right-hand aisle straight for me. Her advance is almost soundless, just a slight noise from the four small tyres.

She gets close enough for me to read her badge – 'Rosalinda Falke, Football Association of Germany' – and to see that the black-bodied wheelchair is as deluxe as a golf buggy with fingertip controls.

There's something about it – or her – that makes me stare, but there is no time for a double take as I'm tapped on the shoulder.

I look across it at the slight, sandy-haired man I saw hurrying through the foyer when I arrived. No M&S bag now, no raincoat either to hide his ID: 'Peter Maurer, Deutsche Telekom, Frankfurt'.

'Your colleague Mr Beamish . . .' His accent is sing-along, not at all hard. 'He was certainly here at around seven last evening.'

'Whereabouts?'

'In the Stuart Bar with Mr Allen.' He inclines his head towards the press bench where only the bearded man remains, rearranging his folders.

'Thank you,' I say gratefully.

'I hope you find him.' He nods, smiles and about-turns. I look towards the woman in the wheelchair, but her heavily made-up eyes are on Maurer. She noisily backs her wheelchair, which gives off a shrill sound like a goods vehicle in reverse, and follows him up the aisle.

I amble to the press table. 'I gather you may know the whereabouts of Mr John Beamish?'

'No. Why?' A Liverpudlian accent, not the normal whine, a sharp edge to it.

'Col. Smallish chap. I gather you were with him in the bar around seven last . . .'

'No.' He looks into my face for a second, long enough to realise he doesn't like what he's seeing, then down, resuming his packing up.

'Mr Maurer, of Frankfurt, tells me he saw you two together.'

'Then he's mistaken.' he tells the table.

'Sure?'

'Absolutely.' Now he does face up to me with a defiant expression, chin up, the gritty northerner.

'Oh.' Like some of the kings from the castle next door, I've learned over the years when to storm the barricades and when to fall back on stealth. 'Sorry,' I say, retreating.

The babble of conversations, some in fast foreign languages, fills the Tudor Room where coffee is being served by waitresses moving around with trays of black or white and bowls of sugar.

I take black, don't add sugar, and gaze around. I'd like a longer chat and a closer look at Peter Maurer, of Frankfurt, not only to cross check the disputed info he's just given me about Beamish drinking last night with Allen, of *Talking Points*.

I just don't like the size of him. He's so lightweight that he could fit the description of Musters in my notebook. It's just the seed of a feeling, that's all; that indefinable stirring that every detective knows and should never ignore.

What I'll do is use my hankie to bag the cup he drinks from

and hope MI5's got and kept Musters' fingerprints from the eighties in his GDR diplomatic days when they had him under surveillance.

Better still, I decide on second thoughts, I'll bleep Wigmore to get back here to eyeball him; much quicker.

I wander around the light, airy room, plenty of space to seat two hundred, despite two long counters, one steel and permanent, one a row of covered trestle tables, on opposite walls, both being stacked with food.

A few delegates look up from tables to give me smiles of recognition, sugared with a touch of sympathy, I suspect, but no one stops me wandering across a thick fawn carpet with red and white pattern.

Unsurprisingly, my début as a conference performer has won me no fans who want to crowd around and hang on to my words. I'm left alone to recce.

Even without distractions I can't pick out Maurer in the crowd, though Jacko's easy to spot, grandstanding for an adoring knot of middle-aged women.

Allen doesn't appear to have followed me in, so plan A – get him together with Maurer and sort out who Beamish was drinking with and when – goes on hold.

I'm about to slip the folder from under my arm and rummage through to find Maurer's room number, give him a call on the house phone or knock on his door, when the woman in the wheelchair swishes in.

Now let's not get carried away with feelings and hunches, I caution myself. OK, Wigmore tipped me that Musters is a quick change artiste. That doesn't make him a disabled drag act, of course, but there's something about her that nags.

Time for that delayed double take now, as she peers up at a framed portrait, one of several on the deep red and off-white walls, women amongst them for a change, this one looking very queenly in a long, wide, burgundy-coloured gown.

What is it about her? Not her trouser-clad legs. Her face maybe, so waxy pale with overdone eye-shadow that she looks like an actress fresh out of make-up.

Actress? Stage? It won't come.

Is it her name – Rosalinda Falke? Why does that ring some

distant bell? I don't know a Rosalinda and the only Falk or Falke I can recall plays Columbo on TV.

A stupid thing for a detective to think and I smile at myself, and in that relaxed second it comes.

What's a representative of the German Football Association doing boning up on tourist attractions in a city that her national team and stars like Klinsmann, and, therefore, their supporters, aren't going to visit? If Em's dad can't be bothered – and he's got a free bed – why should they? It doesn't make sense.

Good question. So what are you going to do about it? I ask myself. A gentle chat and probe perhaps?

Jacko picks that moment to join me, not what I need when I'm deep in thought.

He points at my badge. 'What's with promotion and the dead legs' department?' He's always regarded any police job other than CID as being among the dead legs, Community and Public Relations worst of all. Speaking personally, I do wish sometimes that he wouldn't use such phrases.

I shrug casually. 'A mistake at the registration desk.'

'Still with the spooks then?'

I reply with the briefest of nods. His old-fashioned look, suspicious. 'You're not here under . . .'

'No. No,' I butt in desperately, too desperately.

'Yes, you are.' A gleam rises behind his bifocals and he strokes the back of his dark brown, thinning hair, a sort of self-congratulatory pat on the head.

I've given the game away and groan to myself.

Jacko uses me for raw material for future yarns. I've filled him in on two jobs I've done in the last two years – a corruption inquiry and an investigation into a fraud which used animal lib terrorism for a cover. He plans to ghost them when his current character runs out of steam.

He was with me when I got wounded on the railway line, his last job before retirement, aged fifty-one, almost three years ago. He tackled the gunman, stopping him getting in a second barrel, so I owe him a thank-you, I suppose.

Don't read me wrong, because he's amongst my closest pals. I'd trust him with my life. I have trusted him with my life. But I've always thought he could and should have done better in the police service. He spent his last ten years as an inspector, content with one big inquiry a year, counting the days until retirement so he could write his bloody books.

He had no other ambition, no career plan. Well, it wouldn't do for me. I'm already two ranks higher than he ever attained and I don't intend to stop at this.

I want chief super, then ACC, then chief constable. I want to be a policy maker, not a thief taker, and the first thing I'd do would be to disband this branch, give the job to MI5 and get those HQ desk jockeys back on the streets.

The great cottage industry of specialist units and interminable meetings would be slashed by half.

Ethnic minority, working-class kids, graduates. I'd recruit as many as money would allow. All would mingle for a few months in inner cities, collecting intelligence and signing up informants for the future.

And one other thing. Highly paid, idle sods like Dale, my personal hate figure at HQ, whose place I've taken here, would never again be permitted to attend a junket like this.

'Same deal?' Jacko asks, very quietly and seriously.

The deal is that I put the tale on tapes for him and, when he gets round to them, he will change all the names and locations, keep shtum about his source and make no inquiries of his own in the meantime. It can be time-consuming, but, then again, it's time he's given me rescuing me from that railway line gunman.

'Not sure there's anything in it.' My reply is honest, because I still half expect Beamish to stagger through the door in a worse state than me after my youthful binge on whisky.

'If it works,' he says solemnly.

I shrug and change the subject, patting my pen pocket. 'Got the tickets for the match tomorrow.'

He fixes the time and pub where the three of us will meet, then switches topics himself. 'What did you make of Kenton?'

Tactfully, I say nothing.

'Ignorant sod.' Jacko has no such tact. 'It was perfectly true about that hold-up. Just north of Trent Bridge. A couple of side streets from the Meadows blocked off. Water everywhere. All right for him, booked into the honeymoon suite here, no doubt, no need to travel, and a chauffeur-driven limo when he must. Seen his biog in the programme?'

I nod.

'Reckon he's more a conservative than a conservationist these days, don't you? Fancy a socialist ex-MP, this union pioneer . . .' It's building up into quite a left-of-centre rant. '. . . prattling on about the past when he should be campaigning for future jobs, real jobs, not seasonal, low-paid work as tour guides and counter assistants in souvenir Robinhoodland shops, fat bastard.'

I am not going to tell him that the fat bastard has made a delayed appearance and is coming up behind him. Lord Kenton, a small cigar clamped between his teeth, gives him a hearty slap on the back. 'Very entertaining,' he enthuses through a cloud of blue smoke. 'Fancy an encore at our Robin Hood Festival in the summer? Same fee?'

'Certainly.' Jacko looks back at me without a trace of shame. 'Thank you.'

I wish like hell he'd go now, annoy somebody else. I need Kenton on my own, to ask him when and from where John Beamish made that call to him which he returned on his bleep around 10 a.m.

My own bleep sounds in my inside pocket. I pull back the left-hand front of my jacket and half bury my head inside to read the message, avoiding having to bring out the pager in front of them. Jacko is bound to look over my shoulder at it.

'See me urgently in the Trip at noon,' it reads.

My head re-emerges. 'Got to nip up to Central nick for ten minutes,' I announce.

'Oh, you'll miss the next lecture,' commiserates Kenton. 'Should interest you. Courts and all that.'

'Pity,' I say as sadly as I can manage.

'You won't miss lunch, will you?' asks Jacko, much more pertinently.

'I'll be back,' I say confidently.

It's not a promise I'm too sure of keeping. The message isn't, as expected, from Larry Wigmore, with a lead from his trawl of the city's low life for his senior partner.

It's from ACC Malloy.

And it adds: 'Subject located.'

12.00 hours

I am proceeding at a brisk pace (for me, anyway) towards the Trip to Jerusalem, only a short walk, downhill all the way.

Just round the corner from Standard Hill, cold in the shade, is the twin-towered gatehouse to the castle grounds which partially obscures the view of the ducal palace on its rock.

A few steps along, in a tranquil little garden, stands a statue of Robin Hood, a squat, bronze figure, not much bigger than man-sized, taking aim with his bow. Sightseers queue to have their photos taken beside him.

The steeper the street descends, the higher the eastern wall becomes. Half-way up, where Norman wall meets later stonework, bushes and trees grow robustly in natural colonies and ivy and wild flowers thrive among crevices in the sand-coloured rock.

Along the foot of the wall, behind well-tended beds of shrubs, arched entrances to caves that once led to cellars or cells have been bricked off.

The bright midday sun is high, a welcome sight after a long hard winter, eye-squinting to look up at. The blue sky overhead gives way to patchy grey to the south, last night's rain clouds slow to break up on a cool wind from the east.

Beyond a bend the Trip, a student days' haunt of mine, comes into view – two-storeyed, steep slate roof, white plaster clad, a sort of extension, an afterthought tacked on to the wall, rising sixty or seventy feet above it.

The front entrance is through a small courtyard hedged with trimmed privet. '1189 AD', says a black-painted notice above it.

Inside is a small bar with an opening the size of an average kitchen window. Several real ales are advertised on an impressive array of beer pumps.

Before them stands Carole Malloy, short ginger hair un-covered, as usual, but, unusually, wearing a thick fawn, belted coat over the knitted green dress I saw her in this morning.

She seems to be holding herself awkwardly, as though the brown leather bag on her shoulder is weighing her down. She looks pale and perished, muffled up with a striped knitted scarf hiding her chin; much older today than her mid-forties.

She pulls down the scarf. 'What will you have?'

My real ale days are over; just haven't got the capacity any more. I doubt that this dry throat would appreciate a dry white. Actually I fancy another hot Lemsip, but settle for a Perrier water, still, no ice.

She orders a double Bells, rare for her at any time, unheard of at lunchtime, mumbling, 'I think I'm coming down with the flu.'

You don't need to be a detective to tell that and I feel a stab of envy. My chill isn't the red-nosed, bleary-eyed atishoo variety where bosses compliment you on your bravery in coming in to work and then promptly order you home to bed in case you infect them with your germs.

It's the insidious sort that no one knows you've got – an ache behind the eyes, the roof of your mouth cemented to your nasal passages, and that tired feeling; so, so tired.

The bearded barman is tall and the black beams in the ceiling low and he has to stoop to fetch a jug of water; hardly worth the effort, because she adds only a drop.

She pays, picks up her glass and turns to lead me into a small, unoccupied room that's been hewn out of rock. Inside is dim, with a slight fusty smell, but comfortably warm.

We sit at a round table fixed to a beer barrel, she on a dark red leather bench with a back that runs half up the wall, me with my back to the almost empty bar, too early yet for the lunchtime crowd. I put the folder I've carried under one arm on the table.

'Well?' I begin, anxious to get on with it. 'Where is he?'

She sips her scotch and grimaces. 'On his way to the morgue.'

'Beamish?' I ask naïvely, so shocked I take a long drink, wishing it was stronger. 'When? Where?'

'Found head first down in a drain in the Meadows.' She nods in a southerly direction towards the river.

Don't be naïve enough to ask if it's murder, I caution myself.

51

You don't accidentally fall down a manhole, except in slapstick comedy, and no suicide on record has killed himself by diving head first into a sewer. 'How?'

'No obvious marks of violence.' She's got a date with a Home Office pathologist at the University Hospital in an hour, she adds, and will find out the cause of death then.

'Stand well back when he opens his stomach,' I advise, rather insensitively. I tell her about the row of miniature bottles of scotch missing from his bedroom cabinet.

She pulls a face. 'Whitehall are airlifting up their own doctor to do the post-mortem examination.'

High-powered, I think, and whistle softly.

'It gets worse,' she goes on grimly. 'He was wearing a woman's nightdress, white, size 12, M&S.'

A transvestite MI5 agent, murdered while I was looking for him. Why I should ask this next question now, I'm not sure. It just springs into my mind, self-preservation, I suppose. 'Find any gun?'

She looks away, sharply, reprovingly, holding something back.

I rate Malloy highly. She's more than experienced and efficient. She's shrewd and sharp, highly intelligent and streetwise and they don't always go together in the police service. She's her own man, as it were, usually open and honest, but she can be devious. She likes to conduct her briefings from A to Z and only entertains questions at the end.

She looks back. 'No,' she finally says, still holding back. Then: 'Ready?'

For the briefing, she means. My reply is a dumb nod.

'Right then,' she resumes nasally. 'The water company got calls around 10 a.m. this morning, reporting floods in Farringdon Street.'

Farringdon Street, I think, recalling that old-time cop's note-bookful of pinches last night. This time I hold my tongue. Malloy reads the overnight log more assiduously than anyone at HQ.

'The blockage wasn't there, but in a drain in a cul-de-sac that runs north uphill from it. Water was coming out of a manhole and flowing through the street following the landfall to the river.

'Their engineers were working on crumbling brickwork in the

down section all yesterday. They couldn't resume until they'd pumped out the hole after the rains. They went down and there he was, bare feet sticking out horizontally.'

I chance an interruption, to let her know I've been getting on with the job. 'Left little finger missing?'

She looks suitably impressed.

I tell her I already knew about that disfigurement, patting a pocket which holds my notebook, adding, 'From his mate Wigmore's description.'

'Made contact with him, have you?'

Yes, I answer, but I don't reveal the terrifying circumstances of our introduction. Instead, I tell her I've just bleeped him from the public phones in the hotel to meet me here.

Now she looks distinctly unimpressed, doesn't explain why, but speeds up. 'It's a dual drain, storm water and sewage, so you can imagine the state of him.'

I prefer not to.

'The on-the-spot prelim shows he'd been dead at least twelve hours – before we were even asked to look for him.'

I nod, selfishly relieved.

'Read the overnight log?'

I nod again. 'Any connection?'

'Oh yes. That abandoned van. It was stolen from outside the Playhouse between five and six p.m. yesterday.'

The Playhouse is a stylish theatre Em often takes me to, another short walk from the Standard Hill Hotel.

'Any thoughts thus far?' she asks invitingly.

Plenty, and I number them off, thumb to little finger first. 'One, he was killed at or near the hotel.'

Thumb to ring finger. 'The van was pinched to transport the body. The killer or killers were probably going to launch him into the Trent.'

I don't have to tell Malloy that rivers are favoured by professional killers. The flow distances the corpse from the scene of the disposal and, if it stays submerged long and travels far enough, you may never find the waterside spot from which it was thrown, ruling out most of your forensic evidence.

Thumb to middle finger. 'He or they panicked when they ran into that neighbourhood watch radar trap. One bobby on his bike was already there. How many more would show up, examining headlights, brakes and index plates? All it would take was a quick computer check. And they're in a hot vehicle with a body inside. What would you do?'

She leaves the stage to me.

'Back up the cul-de-sac,' I continue. 'There is the reason for the road closure, roadworks barriers around a manhole under repair. Maybe the cover was still off.'

Malloy shakes her head. 'Just come from there. Seen everybody. They insist it wasn't.'

A memory occurs to me now of a trip down a much bigger sewer which the gang of commercial extortionists had used as an underground route to the pay-off. 'It's a two-man job to lift those lids. They're heavy, cast iron.'

'So I gather.' She's clearly been well briefed at the scene.

I speculate. 'They lifted the lid and tossed Beamish down before our beat man had time to turn his attention to them. He was so occupied clearing up the traffic chaos they just walked away.

'It could have taken hours for Beamish to reach the sewerage farm,' I continue. 'There, his body would have been buffeted about in deep tanks until screw pumps dragged it into the processing screen. It could have taken weeks before we found what the rats had left.'

'We're lucky,' Malloy agrees.

More than you can say for John Beamish, I muse morosely.

Malloy conjectures that getting a body out of a busy hotel could have been a major problem.

A couple of wheelchairs are pottering about, I report. 'One's the hotel's. Could have been borrowed, I suppose. It's easily checked. The other, a de luxe job, is always occupied by a woman delegate.' I pause. 'There's something not quite right about her.'

I tell Malloy of the soccer question Em's dad raised in my mind. 'Her name bugs me, too.'

'What is it?'

'Rosalinda Falke.' Yet again, as I am saying it, I finally latch on to why it bothers me; in good form today, despite all my handicaps.

I first came to this city, a country boy from the next county, to study music at the university, a gorgeous campus in parkland

54

on the western outskirts. I never mastered the subject well enough to earn a living out of it, so I followed my grandad into the police service.

One of my few public performances was in the pit orchestra as second clarinet when a college operatic society staged Johann Strauss' *Die Fledermaus*. It went down with the audience no better than my more recent stab at public speaking and received a panning in a students' arts magazine.

'The lead soprano is called Rosalinda. There's also a male character called Dr Falke.'

'So?' asked Malloy, puzzled.

'I wonder if she's borrowed the names. Check her out with the German FA, will you?'

With an unaccustomed lack of enthusiasm, Malloy fishes her notebook out of the shoulder bag resting beside her.

I retrieve the delegates list from the folder on the table, spell the names, add 'Football Association of Germany', and give her room number: 012.

'So . . .' I get back on track. '. . . there are two wheelchairs about, at least. One could have been used to push a very dead Beamish out of the hotel, well wrapped up against the rain, without attracting too much notice.'

Malloy completes this train of thought. 'And outside the stolen van is waiting.'

A new thought is emerging. 'There's a woman's suitcase missing which might explain where the Marks & Spencer nightgown came from.'

'What? Where from?' Malloy demands, her normal zest returning.

'Dunno. Not yet. A translator's, I think. Not sure.'

She gives me her very cross look.

I return it. 'I've only been there two bloody hours and one of them was wasted giving a bloody speech.'

'Sorry about that. Jocking Dale off was the only way I could think of to get you in.'

She seems to have relaxed a little now, so I dwell a while, telling her of my embarrassment and Jacko Jackson's dazzling display. She is very fond of him, often joins him and his wife for dinner, normally tells affectionate tales about him.

Today she shows no interest in him at all, more important

things on her crowded mind. Her expression is becoming impatient. 'Take a look at your list.'

I do as I'm told. Three interpreters, all women, are given in a separate section. She notes them all, then asks, 'Anything else I need to know?'

'Two loose ends.' First, I explain the 10 a.m. return call from Kenton on Beamish's bleep which I haven't had a chance to check with him yet.

'If', says Malloy thoughtfully, 'Beamish's message for Kenton was left in the last twelve hours, it was made by the killer or accomplice to make us think he's still alive. He's been dead that long, at the very least, longer if we're right and he was dumped amid last night's traffic chaos.'

I ponder. 'Against our 6 p.m. theory is the fact that the last reported sighting of Beamish alive was in a hotel bar at 7 p.m. last evening.'

She looks deeply disappointed. 'But it's in dispute,' I add hurriedly.

She asks what I mean.

The delegates list is flipped through again as I recount that the report came from Peter Maurer, of Frankfurt, from Room 010.

'Next door to your Fraulein Falke,' she points out, more or less to herself, head down over her notebook.

'Mmmmm,' I mmmmm, having missed that. My eyes go back to the top of the list. 'Anyway, he claims to have seen Beamish drinking in a hotel bar with Gordon Allen, of *Talking Points*, from Room 251, at seven. Allen denies it.'

Pending further checks, I go on, I'm not accepting either's word. Allen, after all, was a Stasi talent spotter in the eighties, an agent of influence who'd got away with it. He can't be trusted.

Neither can Maurer. His physique is uncannily close to Wigmore's description of Musters. So are the two names.

Malloy will know that conmen and informers who use aliases often assume names similar to their own. If they trip up, forget who they're supposed to be for a second (and it's easily done, as every undercover cop knows), they can talk themselves out of a tight corner, create enough time and doubt to make their getaway.

While she is noting two more names and room numbers, my mind wanders on. It's the same with code names, even in the police service. Look at that huge inquiry a provincial force conducted into allegations of corruption at Scotland Yard. Operation Countryman, they called it. Why? Because the investigators were hicks from the sticks.

And what did they call that nationwide crackdown on burglars last Christmas? Go on, have a guess. Operation Cracker. Simple, eh?

It's the same with the military. Even the dimmest of the thieves of Baghdad might have hazarded a goodish guess at what Desert Storm heralded. You can sometimes crack a code or an alias just by thinking about it.

She has finished writing. 'If we're right about the time Beamish went head first down the sewer, i.e. just after six during that traffic jam, then Maurer is wrong about that 7 p.m. sighting in the bar.'

I nod.

'What have you done about him?' she demands.

Into the forefront of my mind pops a mental view of Maurer walking into the hotel foyer with a Marks & Spencer bag. I study it for a second. But that was at ten this morning, I remind myself, hours after Beamish was dressed in his white gown. Anyway, every overseas visitor makes a beeline for M&S.

Don't even mention it, I decide; means nothing. Instead: 'Paged Wigmore to meet me here to see if he can eyeball him as Musters. He's trailed him often enough. He should be able to recognise him.'

'Why here?'

'Because it is – was – Beamish's chosen rendezvous spot, away from the hotel. They were operating separately.'

She thinks for a moment or two. Here it comes, I fear. She's going to jock me off, like she robbed Dale of his day out and free lunch.

It's murder now, a job for the Major Crimes Squad, not for Special Branch. She might retain me in an advisory role, but that's about all. I've done the legwork. CID will get any credit that's going. It's so bloody unfair. I need to shine, to get away from this desk job, win a promotion.

Well, if she sends me back to HQ, I'll go home instead, pleading a heavy cold. I snort, loudly and thickly, take out my handkerchief and bury my nose in it for a good blow, preparing the ground for an early getaway.

She looks down and speaks huskily. 'Don't tell Wigmore about Beamish.'

'What?' I can feel myself pulling a disgusted face. 'Why?'

'Don't.'

'But he's his sidekick. I can't keep him in the dark about that.'

'Orders. I'm not running it.'

'Who is?' I'm going to impress her again with my grip on the case. 'Major Merryweather?'

A tiny nod. 'The Home Office are taking a close interest. Handled well and a good result and . . .' She leaves it there, to tantalise me with hopes of quick promotion. 'No one must know about Beamish yet.' Then, for emphasis, 'No one.' She pauses. 'That apart, play it the way you see it.'

'Aren't you launching a murder inquiry?'

'Not yet. Only us two in the entire force know what's happening.'

I sniff, wondering what I am letting myself in for, needing to know. 'What about the gun?'

'Told you,' she almost snaps. 'We haven't found it yet.'

'But Beamish was armed?'

'How do you know that?' she asks, virtually confirming it.

'Because Wigmore is, so it stands to reason.' I pause. 'What about me?'

She shakes her head.

'Why not?'

'The Home Office don't want a shoot-out in a hotel packed with overseas visitors.'

Bad for the tourist trade, I quite agree, but, I repeat to myself: What about me?

She seeks to reassure me. 'There's back-up on immediate hand if you need it.'

'I haven't even got a portable phone to call for it,' I point out, a shade sullenly.

'Mobiles are out on this job. Land lines only.' She's spelling out a lesson the current royal family is yet to learn about intercepted calls. 'Don't phone HQ either. I'll bleep you with a special number when I've established a base.'

I fall silent, drinking up, thinking: Christ, this is mega top secret. They're pitching me against two killers with at least one gun, and not even a mobile phone to summon back-up.

'You trust me, don't you?' she asks with a concerned look.

I know what's troubling her. She was in charge of the railway line manhunt when I got wounded and didn't issue guns because we all thought the killer had got rid of his weapon. I don't blame her and never have, and, even if I did, I wouldn't tell her. 'Of course.'

Suddenly I don't want this job, but need a reason, other than cowardice, for the anxieties that must be filling my face. 'Doesn't the Home Secretary know that we have a couple of hundred or more delegates here who will disappear to the four corners of the earth when the conference breaks up tomorrow lunchtime?'

She finishes her drink. At last she smiles, and very wickedly. 'You'd better solve it today then.'

12.30 hours

Larry Wigmore arrives so soon after Malloy's departure that they must have passed each other in the courtyard; a close squeak.

He joins me at the bar where I am standing alone. We exchange Hi's. 'Another Perrier,' I tell the barman, then look at Wigmore. 'And?'

'Same for me. Thanks.'

The barman crouches with knees slightly bent to pour them. He looks between the beer pumps at Wigmore and asks him, 'Did you find your friend?'

'Sorry?' A flustered expression fills Wigmore's face.

'Last night,' the barman prompts. 'Your friend. The one you were waiting for when you came in looking like a drowned rat.'

'Oh. Er.' Wigmore shakes his head. 'No.' He smiles at me and glances around. 'Interesting place, eh? Must be named in honour of the Crusaders.'

My mind is not going that far back – only to last night. What time was his scheduled meet with Beamish here? Seven, by which time it had stopped raining, according to the overnight log. Yet Wigmore looked like a drowned rat. Well, he would, if he'd walked all the way from the Meadows after dumping a body and a stolen van; makes sense.

I'm not going to let him change the subject. Neither do I want to appear suspicious, just casual. 'Didn't take your car, then?'

He sighs. 'Always get lost in a strange city.'

Fair enough, I decide. I'd have walked round other hotels looking for Musters rather than drive in a one-way system in the tail end of rush hour in a city centre I didn't know. Makes better sense. Don't become paranoid about him just because Merryweather and Malloy are playing internal politics and cutting him out.

The barman places glasses on a draining tray. 'Another scotch for the lady, sir?'

My turn to be startled. I mustn't let Wigmore know about Malloy's briefing. 'Gone.' I know I owe him an explanation. 'A girl from the office with a bit of useful background.' I pay two pounds and twopence.

We pick up our glasses and I lead the way back to the table where I've left the pink folder.

From behind me, Wigmore says, 'Sorry I'm a bit late.' He'd been checking a couple of addresses of massage parlours I'd given him. Like last night, he'd left his car at the hotel and had to walk to Trent Bridge to find a cab when I bleeped him.

I sit. 'Any joy?'

He sits. 'Not a sniff, and I've only a couple more places to visit.' He takes a drink. 'But you have some useful info, though?' There's anticipation on his face. I can't think of anything to say. 'From the office?' he persists.

'Well . . .' I'm going to play safe in case he was here early and watching the entrance, checking up on me, like I'm about to check up on him. I don't yet know how good he is.

'The woman from the office . . .' I flick my head backwards at the barman. '. . . it was my ACC, actually, on her way to a conference at Central. Nothing to do with this. She dropped by for an update, didn't want to phone or come to the hotel.'

Wigmore nods approvingly.

'Pity you missed her.' A thoughtful sip. 'She's dead worried about your mate.'

He sighs mournfully. 'So, increasingly, am I.' He looks it, tired and drawn. He lists the vice and booze spots he's visited, the ruses used and the blanks drawn. He is doing a conscientious job, by the sounds of it.

'We're to up the pace a bit,' I tell him, taking the plunge. 'Still covert, but turn a few screws.'

'Good,' he declares.

'How well do you know Musters?'

'Only by sight.'

I am not going to tell him I think I've pegged him as Peter Maurer, of Frankfurt, based solely on physique. It's just a hunch. I'll wait until Malloy has checked with Deutsche Telekom. He may not be him. Be too specific on a surveillance and you get tunnel vision, see what you're told to see. 'Reckon you can ID him again?'

A pause, hesitant. 'Think so. Bear in mind it's five years, more, since we were tailing him, and we didn't catch up with him in Bruges in December, unfortunately.' His expression becomes more positive. 'Yes, I think I can. Why?'

'Will you stake out the foyer of the hotel, cast an eye over all the delegates?'

A doubtful face. 'John's orders were to work all the other hotels.'

'So you haven't checked the Standard Hill then?'

'Well, I was there overnight, but only to sleep. I spent most of last night in here waiting for him to show. I've not registered yet for the conference, attended any of the lectures or anything. John's supposed to be working them.'

'Not right now, he's not,' I point out bluntly. 'There's no trace of him in there today. And we need someone to watch for Musters.'

He sips silently. I finish my drink. 'Another?' he asks. I need more time to work on him and say Please, but No thanks to his follow-up question, 'Something to eat?'

We get up together, he to go to the bar, me to follow signs which lead through another bar to toilets in another slabbed courtyard out the back.

Afterwards, as I retrace my steps, Wigmore cuts diagonally across my path. He is wearing an animated expression. 'Something I want to see.' He leads the way into a passage. I follow.

'Just wanted another look at the south wall,' he says over his shoulder.

We emerge among a triangle of very old, tall, red-brick buildings, housing a museum, in a railed garden. Towering above them is the southern wall of the castle, well over a hundred feet high, topped with a mini-jungle of naturalised vegetation – trees that are more than saplings, thick bushes, evergreens. The only thing planted by man is a white flag-pole in front of the palace, most of which I still can't see from this angle.

He points towards it. 'Thought I spotted a rare cytisus up there.'

With nothing in flower, I can't even make out the common variety of broom.

'What a coup, eh, if it's a direct descendant from the Plantagenet period?'

'For who?' I ask, not a clue what he's talking about.

'A botanist.'

'Why?'

'They all wore a sprig of broom on their helmets.'

'You a historian or a botanist?' I ask, trying not to look bored.

Neither, he answers. His university degree was in electronics but his family runs a nursery in Sussex. A sad smile suggests he'd rather be arranging flowers than here on this job. He decides on another inspection from the top, if he can find the time.

Walking back inside, the subject of Plantagenet broom sparks off a hymn of praise from him for the Standard Hill Hotel. Clever, he enthuses, the way they've used real history, instead of tacky trappings like the Friar Tuck tuckery and the Little John john.

His first-floor room was in the red of the House of Lancaster with rosa something floribunda on his bed-cover and a portrait of one of the Henrys on a wall. 'Very stylish.'

I'm about as hot on history as botany. For some reason, I always remember royal disfigurements, hunchbacks, for example, to which I'll now add Edward's arse, but I'm useless on dates.

I get back to business as soon as we resume our seats. A large bread roll filled with hot pork and stuffing has been delivered to our table.

Refilled glass in hand, I lean forward confidentially. 'What's worrying my chief and what she came here to tell me is this. Musters could be in there . . .' I flick my head forward in the direction of the hotel. '. . . blackmailing or murdering an ex-Joe while we're looking for Beamish who, for all we know, may be on a razzle.'

He eats, daintily, almost in a feminine way.

'The priorities have changed,' I go on. 'She'll put fresh legs . . .' He smiles faintly. '. . . on Beamish. I'm to concentrate on Musters. I don't know him. You do.'

He's still eating slowly, not biting on anything I've said, so I go on, 'How well?'

Politely he empties his mouth before replying. 'Not to speak to or anything, naturally. Like I told you, John was the brains, handled his sources.'

'How was it worked?'

'He'd get copies of anything passing over across Kenton's desk. Now and then he'd include something from those papers in the packages for Musters. To the East Germans, it would look juicy, but was really past its sell-by date.'

He smiles conspiratorially. 'He'd parcel and seal them up. I was the errand boy. I'd deliver to Kenton at his flat or office. Then I'd trail him to the drop – a Tube lav, a park bench, whatever. I'd hang on and try to snap Musters collecting; not difficult. Kenton told us exactly where he'd be and when.'

'So you saw quite a bit of Musters?'

'Yes, mostly through a camera lens.'

'And so would Kenton?'

'Much more than me. He'll know him well. Face to face. Personally. Embassy parties. Collecting Musters' cash.' He ponders. 'Can't you ask him?'

'Already have, in effect.' I go on to tell him, exaggerating a little, of my torture by panel in the Plantagenet Suite, and he laughs merrily. 'I appealed to the whole audience to let me know if they'd seen Beamish of the CoI around because I'd statistics for him in here.'

The pink file on the table is patted. 'Kenton was sitting by my side when I made that appeal. He never volunteered a word about seeing or knowing Beamish.'

'Did anybody?' he asks urgently.

'A delegate did say that he'd been drinking with Allen of *Talking Points* at seven last night . . .'

A disgruntled sigh. 'He was supposed to be here then.'

I complete it. '. . . but Allen denies it.'

His face is even more disgruntled. 'He denies everything. Told you this morning. We had loads of photographic evidence of his meetings with Musters in the mid-eighties. We had his bank account, even the cheque, showing thirty thou from this international media outfit, Stasi-funded, to help set up his magazine. We got nothing out of him. Not a word. And John's a terrier, a terrific interrogator. Had him in for two days.'

'So you know him, too?'

'After two days of no-nonsense northern bluntness, will I ever forget him?'

'What's his background?'

'Just over fifty. Sort of Red Mersey, one generation removed.'

He is back in his clipped mode. 'Dad a docker. First-class degree in communications, despite lots of sixties political activity, picketing against this, demonstrating for that. Started in journalism as a campus corr for the *Worker*.'

I tilt my head, frowning.

'What the *Morning Star* used to be called. Changed its name thirty years ago. Too plebeian for the intellectual left, I suppose. Too tame for Allen eventually.

'Recruited, we think, when he sought a visa to go East on some feature for a far-out revolutionary magazine. Saw a gap in publishing when the conference circuit started to expand in the eighties and filled it with his magazine which Musters funded.'

'Is it making money?'

'Struggles. So dull. You've seen it, of course?'

He saw I was carrying it in Beamish's room, but if he hasn't registered for his conference bumf yet, how has he seen the current issue? Let's find out. I nod, then, 'You, too?'

The answer comes immediately. 'We get it delivered every quarter, just to keep an eye on him.'

Like we take the *Morning Star*, I concede, satisfied. 'Flicked through it.' I slip it out of the folder and turn the pages slowly, finding the Bruges photo of Kenton.

Even with a longer look, it remains an odd pose, eyes shut, hands together, in front of his groin, as if standing in prayer. The headline reads: 'Lord Kenton warns on honeypots.'

The story reports his speech at the final night dinner in which he cautioned sales representatives travelling overseas on export drives against unwise liaisons. 'Governments in the East may not need state secrets any more, but rival companies do want your commercial secrets. Pillow talk is dangerous.'

While I read, Wigmore explains that the magazine is heavily dependent on Kenton's goodwill, authorising expensive display adverts and bulk ordering copies for free distribution to delegates at the next get-together.

My eyes go down the page to a panel edged in black. 'Death of PR,' says a smaller headline, very routine. It's the third word in the text that makes me start:

Delegates were shocked by the sudden death of Denise Albert, 35, who was engaged as a PR consultant by the Bruges

65

organisers. She was found in her hotel room on the last night of the conference. She was a charming and efficient addition to our team. Condolences to her family in Brussels.

What shocked me is the word 'shocked'. She was electrocuted, after all, but the media are not supposed to know that. OK, the report doesn't say so and the use of the word 'shocked' could be coincidence. But it could hint at Allen's inside knowledge.

I point to the piece, but don't comment on the word.

Wigmore glances at it. 'Yes.' He nods solemnly. 'She was the Musters mole I was telling you about – the one he cleaned out financially, then bumped off in the bath while we were all having dinner downstairs.'

The dumb cluck, who knows she was electrocuted because he told me, has missed the potential significance of the word 'shocked' entirely.

I return to an old theme. 'Will you stake out the foyer while I check up on Kenton and Allen?'

He stays silent.

'I can't count on Kenton,' I continue. 'If he's not going to help me find one of our side, he's hardly likely to finger the opposition for me, is he?'

He gives me a long look. 'Any specific target in mind?'

What comes immediately to mind is this: (a) it's a stunning question and (b) he's not so dumb after all. Well, I reply as easily as I can, there's a telecom man called Maurer, a German of about the same build. 'Just cast an eye over him.' I widen the net. 'Or anyone.'

'What happens if it is him?'

Another fair question. MI5 agents have no powers of arrest. That's why Special Branch always accompany them on the final showdown. 'Stick your gun in his back and lock him in the hotel strong room till I get there.'

'Sounds more fun than working massage parlours,' he agrees with a shy grin.

Walking back, both of us rather slowly uphill, Wigmore chunters about the starkness of the college buildings across the road distracting from the quaintness of a medieval shop that sells lace. I'm not going to tell him the college was there before the shop was moved, lock, stock and timber frames, from the Lace Market to make way for a shopping centre.

I can't work him. He comes across as a harmless, chinless wonder, a forty-year-old fogey, full of olde worlde charm, yet give him half a chance to wave his gun and he'll do it with gusto.

Is he playing some game with me, stringing me along, testing me out? Well, he can forget it.

I'm not some flawed character out of le Carré, damaged by his upbringing and his shadowy job. I'm not playing intellectual chess.

This is a murder from yesterday; not a spy saga a decade old. I'm a traditionally trained detective and I'm going to crack it in the old-fashioned way.

I'm going to find out where my suspects were from six to seven, eliminating them one by one, until there's only one left.

Even as I draw up the battle plan, it occurs to me with a chill that has nothing to do with this cold spreading right through me that the man at my side is without an alibi.

I worry, not that I'm keeping secrets from him, but that I've already told him too much.

13.00 hours

I am proceeding to nibble a buffet lunch, back in the Tudor Room, looked down upon by Henry VIII, hands on the hips of a gold skirt under a fur-lined black cape, black beret at a jaunty angle.

Normally I'd have had a plate of smoked salmon, but there's fish tonight. Still thinking of Beamish and where he'd ended up, I didn't have an appetite for what's billed on a chalk blackboard by the door as 'Regional Speciality – spicy Lincolnshire sausages with mashed potatoes, thick brown sauce and mushy peas.'

Instead, I've gone for a plate of cold meats on to which a waitress behind the long counter spooned some green salad. All morning I've looked forward to this free nosh. Now I've gone off it.

I move to the nearest empty table, put the folder on it.

For a silly second, I look around for Beamish among the crowd, some sitting, some standing in small chattering groups on a carpet dotted with a repeated pattern of red and white Tudor roses.

I'm getting the hang of the themes now, beginning to see what Wigmore meant and, yes, the décor is clever.

On quick inspection between mouthfuls, still standing for a good view, I can't see Peter Maurer anywhere.

Jacko is very noticeable, tucking into salmon beneath the imperious gaze of Queen Elizabeth I, with a gold crinoline that makes her look as broad in the beam as her father. He is making the Swiss miss laugh so I won't join him.

In a far corner, Lord Kenton is jovially holding court at a round table to a cosmopolitan circle. Without benefit of instant translation, they have the fixed smiles of people who aren't fully understanding what he's saying, a bit like English viewers trying to follow Rab C. Nesbitt on BBC2.

Much closer is the short-cropped blonde with the glorious legs – and the missing suitcase – talking German in a relaxed, almost intimate, way with a man of about my size and age.

She is near enough to smell her expensive perfume, to hear mention of the town of Bonn and to see the badge on the chest of a sharply cut black jacket that matches her pleated skirt: Irene Kinsley, Interpreting Services.

Out of earshot, Rosalinda Falke, in her wheelchair, plate on her knee, is chatting to a burly man I haven't seen before.

Allen stands alone; odd for a journalist who should be mixing and listening, like Em does at parties. Plate in hand, he is studying a portrait among a collection of half a dozen regal-looking women, Henry's wives, I guess, one of whom, if memory serves, had a deformity. Odd that, too, for a red republican.

Who to tackle first? Allen is targeted as he turns away, grimacing, not liking what he's just seen.

The decision is immediately changed when Kenton gets up, excusing himself by demonstrating, left hand to ear, that he has a phone call to make, and heads towards the door.

I fall into step, abandoning my meal, half-eaten, and retrieving the wallet from the table. 'A quick word, please, sir.'

He is not stopping or answering.

'Privately, if poss. It will only take a minute.' He marches on, so I'm going to halt him in his tracks. 'It's about John Beamish.'

He slows, but doesn't stop by the blackboard and continues out of the room into the almost deserted foyer.

'You know him, I gather.'

Now he stops, turning, glowering. 'Met him, yes.'

'Seen him today?'

A firm headshake.

'Yesterday?'

No response now, staring at me.

'What time?'

No response still.

'Where?'

Nothing, just simmering silence.

'Look, I do need to know. Nothing to do with crime stats for the CoI.' I hug the wallet tighter to my chest. 'I have to trace him urgently.' I am going to float in a name. 'Major Merryweather's orders.'

He is looking down at the carpet.

'I know who he is, his real job, same as you do. I know he's not CoI.' I tap my badge. 'This isn't my department, either.'

His head comes up, eyes examining my name tag.

I put on a pleading expression. 'I have to trace him quickly.' Not wanting him to know I've searched Beamish's room, a lie is called for. 'According to his partner, you bleeped him at ten this morning in response to an earlier call from him.'

'What the devil . . .?' His fury is so bottled up that his craggy face is a shiny blood pressure bronze and he can't complete the sentence.

I decide to feed his ego. 'It's of national importance.'

He holds himself in check, leaning forward threateningly. 'You have no right to approach me in a public place; most irregular.'

Eye contact is maintained. 'We both know his line of business. He's bound to have given you a contact number, for emergencies. We have one now. Might I suggest that you use it, to check me out, get the all-clear to talk to me.'

Abruptly, without another word, he turns away, across the foyer, fiddling for and finding his small diary in a waistcoat pocket as he strides purposefully in the direction of the public phones beneath the stairs.

I don't follow, but neither do I return to my meal, just stand in no man's land for some time.

Jacko strolls out, the last person I want to see right now. 'Old bloke stayed in a place like this in London once. Knock comes on the door at midnight . . .'

Oh, God, another of his awful jokes.

'. . . Standing there is this incredibly beautiful girl in a see-through négligé. "Do you want super-sex?" she says and the old bloke replies, "'I'll take the soup, please."'

He ambles on towards the toilets, laughing far louder than me.

Kenton reappears from under the stairs and beckons me. I follow him towards the automatic doors. Beside them is Wigmore, sitting in a low armchair behind a lunchtime *Post*, fully out, back page leading with the team news for tomorrow's big match. I stoop without stopping and drop the folder on his table as I pass. He doesn't look up.

Walking down the wheelchair ramp, rows of cars to our left,

Kenton says nothing. As we pass through the hotel's black iron gates into the short, steep hill, he finally breaks his silence. 'You're vouched for.'

He begins to lead me through the streets – and his story.

Left first, up a slight rise, away from the castle. A party of orientals are taking photos of a square, compact house with a plaque recording that Lord Byron, the poet, once lived there.

He caught the nine o'clock out of St Pancras yesterday, Kenton begins, intent on getting to the Standard Hill well ahead of the lunchtime registration rush.

Unexpectedly, Beamish joined him in first class for breakfast. They had not seen much of each other for the last five years or so. In the decade before that they had been in regular touch. 'You'll know why.'

I nod, no need for more.

Kenton doesn't see it that way. Now he's got official approval he clearly wants to talk, share his secrets.

Having fought Communism as a National Serviceman in Korea, he'd gone through a spell of pacifism. Through that and contacts he'd made in his early union days, he'd met hosts of fellow-travellers.

It was in the sixties at a peace rally that he was first tapped up 'to help the cause'. A democrat, not a revolutionary, he didn't want to know.

The approaches became so worryingly persistent that he finally sought the advice of a trusted colleague, a senior figure in his union.

An invitation to spend a weekend at a hotel in the Cotswolds quickly followed and there he met two members of the security services for the first time.

All through the late sixties he allowed himself to be sucked deeper and deeper into an underground organisation called Comintern which plotted to have activists in key positions – like phone exchanges and power stations – to throw the switches when the great uprising came.

He saw his two handlers regularly, feeding them the names. 'Even my wife . . .' He corrects himself. '. . . wives didn't know.'

On his election to the Commons, things changed. He reported

71

all, of course, to the Cabinet Office, but Harold Wilson had no fondness for the secret and security services, thought they were conspiring against him, and kept them at arm's length. So did Kenton.

Musters came on the scene after he'd lost his seat and was setting up his new high tech union in the eighties. He'd applied for and been granted a visa for a union fact-finding trip to East Berlin and was invited to an embassy party afterwards. 'And how did you find our country?' Musters asked. 'Let's have lunch soon and you can tell me all about it.'

From experience Kenton knew what was coming. He re-established contact with MI5 only to discover that his two old handlers had retired. Beamish was assigned to him.

'I did what he told me to do – accept all Musters' bribes, keep all the meetings he arranged, hand over stuff Beamish had vetted.'

'Like what?' I ask.

'Documents on new developments. They were light years behind us on communications.'

'Was any of the stuff – well . . .' I tone down 'hot' to 'useful to them?'

'The good stuff was weeded out, as I understood it, but yes, now and then, he told me he'd slipped in something interesting – things we'd looked into, couldn't make work, and had abandoned, or which had been overtaken by developments.' He gives me a sideways look, almost a smirk. 'You have to give them something to keep them on the hook.'

Using the CIA's MICE test, I suspect the money Kenton was making counted for little. His ideology ran counter to theirs. Compromise, on the face of it, was out. Ego was everything. He'd loved it all, the achievement, the adventure.

In the nineties, of course, he concludes rather sadly, he'd had little to do, apart from secreting away a couple of accounts amongst his conservation and conference financial empire which the service could use in emergencies.

Anything to hang on, stay in the game, I'm thinking. Useful background all of this, of course, fascinating, but I've already decided this is a murder inquiry, not an espionage investigation, so I get back to yesterday by asking what Beamish told him over breakfast on the train.

Kenton gives a direct quote in reply. '"Prepare yourself for a shock. We suspect your old controller will be turning up incognito at your conference."'

Only then did Beamish reveal to Kenton that Musters had gone missing with files on his ex-sources and that, in the last year, two had been subjected to his blackmail.

If Beamish didn't tell him both had died after renewing their cold war acquaintance, then neither shall I.

He did tell him, 'We suspect you could be his next target. Can we count on your co-operation again?'

Kenton shrugs. 'Well, naturally, I told him "Yes".'

'Naturally,' I concur. I compliment him on the way he'd played ball with the security service in helping to feed the East Germans misinformation, hoping I've made his conduct seem both brave and patriotic.

'Everything I did,' he's at pains to reiterate, 'every scrap of paper passed on to Musters in my active days, was vetted by Beamish himself.'

'Naturally,' I repeat.

He's walking erect, quite proud of himself. 'Of course, I've nothing to fear. But, equally, Musters would not have known of our ruse, so I could see that I was liable for an extortion attempt.'

'So what was Beamish's plan?' I ask, passing a recognisable multi-storey car-park after lefts and rights up and down hills, so absorbed in his story that I'd lost track of my whereabouts.

'"Don't approach Musters," Beamish said. "Let him approach you. Act shocked, frightened. Find out what his money demands are, vacillate."'

'And then?'

'Bleep Beamish . . .' He pats the waistcoat pocket to tell me he had a note of his number. 'Fix to see him and tell all.'

He looks across his broad shoulder at me. 'We hadn't prepared anything beyond that, except that Beamish arranged the necessary money. He'll get me to collect it, no doubt, and meet up with Musters for the handover and he'll pounce.' He breaks off, frowning. 'Where is he?'

I'm not going to say anything until he has answered two questions burning within me, the first of which is: 'What do you mean – Beamish arranged the necessary money?'

He looks about him. 'This is strictly QT.'

'I'm vouched for,' I reply dully.

'Like I told you, I control an account for the security service – money that doesn't appear in public accounts.'

Slush funds, they're called, non-traceable.

'It's in the name of Heritage Foundation; no such thing, of course.'

It's also what Larry Wigmore is pretending to represent, so I should have guessed.

'Beamish came to my room yesterday afternoon and asked me to authorise a withdrawal of twenty-five thou.'

'What for?'

'Well, I just sign the occasional release upon request. I don't ask questions. There'd been a bite, I suppose.'

The second burning question now. 'Is Musters here?'

A brief nod.

'Has he spoken to you, tapped you?'

'Not me. No. But he must have approached someone.'

'Did you sign your authorisation?'

'Of course.'

'So where's the money?'

'Beamish will be handling all of that. Where is he?'

I shake my head, still not answering with the truth. 'We don't know. That's the emergency.'

'Aren't you worried?'

Worried? An agent dead, a gun missing and now twenty-five grand washing about somewhere. Only out of my mind.

We are approaching the Playhouse now, a modern building with black-and-white panelling. Its current production is advertised as 'a domestic drama'. It can't be a patch on the drama I'm caught up in.

I see no point in lying, say 'Yes,' but don't expand. Instead, I recap. 'Thus far then, as far as you are aware, though there's cash available to bait a trap, it hasn't reached the stage of you collecting it and setting up a meet?'

'Musters hasn't even approached me,' Kenton repeats. 'I haven't spoken to him. We've ignored each other. Those were the instructions.'

To our left is a terrace of bay-windowed Victorian houses, all offices now, the local coroner's among them. To our right is a two-hour parking zone, empty of cars and taped off. Inside the tape three scenes-of-crime officers are on their hands and knees.

The van used to transport Beamish's body must have been taken from here. It should be of some comfort to know that I'm not entirely alone on this job, but I don't feel any.

I have to cover old ground, to make sure I've got it right. 'But you have seen Musters here?'

'Oh yes. He sat in the audience at a couple of lectures yesterday afternoon, large as life, Beamish two rows behind him.'

'Have you seen either since?'

A vigorous nod. 'Both. Beamish was around early evening yesterday at the scotch sampling.'

'Did you speak to him?'

'No. Those were the instructions.'

'But you have tried to contact him since?'

'This morning. Sent him a message on his pager.'

I decide to double check. 'Saying?'

'"Returning your call." That's all.'

Well, that partially checks out. 'Why?'

'Why?' A querulous expression, not a man who suffers fools gladly. 'Because he was trying to contact me.'

'How?'

'A note pinned to the message board behind the registration desk this morning.' He digs into his pen pocket to find it, hands it over.

Skirting a tree-lined circular green, he dawdles to let me read: 'Contact Beamish CoI. Room 224,' under the hotel letterhead.

While I'm studying it, he explains it was taken by a conference clerk called Simon about 10 a.m. this morning while he was in a short meeting rearranging the caves lecture.

10 a.m. I remember what Malloy said. Someone must have been posing as Beamish. He could have been dead sixteen hours by then.

'I used a house phone,' Kenton goes on, 'but there was no reply from his room. I thought it might be important, new instructions or something, but I couldn't hang around to try again, had to have coffee with some council execs and then, of course, I was in the chair for your little session. I told him in the message where I'd be at eleven. He never showed up.'

75

That fully checks out. 'And have you made contact with him at any time this morning?'

'Haven't spoken to him since the train.'

'But you have seen him since then?'

'Not this morning, no. Last evening, five thirtyish, yes, but like I've said, we didn't speak. In any case, he was heavily engaged in conversation in the foyer.'

'Do you know who with?'

'That photo journalist.'

'Gordon Allen?'

He nods.

We are heading uphill again, a different way back to the hotel, the spire of the Catholic cathedral and the tower of a Methodist mission behind us. I take a few strides in silence, thinking this through, wonder how far I dare go. 'I was told Beamish was with Allen in the bar last night at seven.'

'Could be, I suppose, but I doubt it.'

He's given me a gift-wrapped opportunity to check his alibi. 'Were you in the foyer or the bar all the time from five thirty to seven?'

'Lord no.' A brief laugh. 'I had a quick one, then went upstairs for a snooze and a bath. Got down again about seven for a drink before dinner.'

He hasn't got an alibi, either, I realise with a touch of despair.

'It was a bit crowded, true, but I didn't see either Beamish or Allen. In any case, Allen doesn't drink much.' He pauses. 'What do you make of him?'

I tell him we chatted only briefly.

'A strange sort of chap, I find.'

I want more of this, but decide against direct questions. 'Not a bad mag he produces.'

'Think so?'

I don't say what I think.

'Seen that dreadful picture of me in the latest?'

I nod.

'Looks for all the world as if I'm playing with myself. Lots of chums have taken the mick. I was saying grace, for heaven's sake, before dinner. That's why my hands were there, but he doesn't explain that.'

76

He grumbles on. 'I'm going to have a sharp word with him. Don't want him using that picture again.'

'Er . . .' A gentle probe now. 'I saw on the same page that you had a fatality at your last conference.'

'Very sad.' He nods solemnly. 'A fall in the bath. Accident.'

Mmmmm, I think. So he claims not to know the real cause of death. 'Did you know her?'

A headshake, not too positive. 'She was only on a week's local contract to handle public relations.'

He's not really answered the question, I note.

We are nearly back at the hotel, among a collection of special-ised medical units left behind when the hospital moved.

'And Musters – have you seen him again?'

A baffled expression. 'At our session.'

I can feel myself gulp, fearing the worst. 'Where was he?'

'Good lord. Don't you know?'

I shake my head, knowing the worst.

'He was pretending to be that German telecom rep, the sandy-haired chap who came up afterwards and was talking to you.'

13.40 hours

Wigmore is studying the *Post*, reading so slowly that he hasn't reached the back page in the twenty minutes I've been out.

I flop down beside him on the comfortable sofa, drained by an exhaustion that has nothing to do with walkabouts on a bad leg or a bad cold.

The lobby is milling with well-lunched delegates, waiting for the next lecture. Mercifully, Jacko is not among them; gone home, I hope.

I slide the folder on the table towards me and look inside to check the subject on the programme – an illustrated talk on local boys made good, from Lord Byron to General Booth.

Wigmore nods at a page of small ads. 'Kenton's just caught the lift up.'

It was at Kenton's suggestion that I returned a couple of minutes after him. Why I'm agreeing to all this cloak-and-dagger I'm not sure. If I were running the show, I'd have the hotel sealed and crawling with detectives and scientists by now, searching all rooms and questioning all delegates and staff – and to hell with bank holiday overtime rates.

'Any joy?' asks Wigmore, peeping from one side of the paper.

I lean forward, elbows on knees. 'Maurer is definitely Musters.' He takes the news calmly enough. 'Any sign of him?' I ask.

'No.' He folds up the paper. 'The key to Room 010 is in its pigeon-hole. He must be out still.'

I don't know whether he is trying to impress me with his expertise as a watcher. If so, he's failed. Wigmore told me at the Trip he's spent so little time in the hotel that he hasn't registered for the conference and, therefore, the bumf. The name, fine. I gave it to him, but not his room number.

I look down at the opened folder in front of us. He must have had a peek – and why not? I would. Forget this inside job bullshit, I tell myself.

As one wave of suspicion ebbs another crashes in. If he didn't register, how did he get hold of his lapel badge? They were doled out with the bumf. I can't ask him point-blank. He'll start to read what's building in my mind soon.

'Hasn't seen John today, he claims,' I report. 'He phoned his radio pager in response to a message left about 10 a.m. at the registration desk. No contact or sighting since.'

'10 a.m.?' Wigmore repeats musingly. 'So, if he didn't sleep here last night . . .' Anxiety fills his face as the sentence dribbles away.

'It was a phoned message,' I explain. 'He could have made it from anywhere.' Anybody could have made it from anywhere, I add privately.

On the registration table there's no male clerk on duty to question about the message. Come to think of it, there's another question for that desk clerk now – about the distribution of badges.

I'll sit here a while and wait for him to return from lunch. I have a feeling this little interlude of peace is the lull before the storm that's bound to break when it leaks out that I was face to face with Musters, chatting to him, thanking him for his help even, and let him go.

He'd conned me, pointed me in Allen's direction to distract me. He knew I'd know Allen was an old Stasi source and I'd take the bait. Distract me from what? I can't work it out.

Wigmore breaks into my thoughts. 'I've an awful feeling about this.'

So have I. He's about to question Beamish's fate, to put me on the spot. 'Why?'

'Well, given that he's been gone overnight and Musters is missing and he's killed twice at conferences like this . . .' A heavy shrug, unwilling to spell out his fears.

I'm going to pass the buck. 'Have you told your office of your worries?'

A brisk nod. 'They're very laid back about it. Say John's been AWOL before.' A puzzled headshake. 'But always with good reason. You know, something better turned up to chase.'

'In Bruges, for instance?'

79

He thinks. 'Well, having taken evening dress all that way for the last night dinner, he didn't bother to show up. Said he had drinks with a contact instead.'

To change the subject, I tell him of Kenton's annoyance over his photo in *Talking Points*.

He smiles. 'He was annoyed at the time, too. Quite rude in public to one or two latecomers interrupting grace. He's a stickler for time-keeping.'

'He says the woman in the bath died from an accidental fall.'

'That was the official line.'

'How about Dublin?'

'What about it?' His guard is up again.

'Did Beamish behave himself there?'

'As far as I can recall. I had to talk myself into the trip. Merryweather wasn't keen on sending ex-military intelligence to the south. We both worked bloody hard.'

And unsuccessfully, I think sourly.

Wigmore is giving me an unfriendly look. 'I don't know what gossip Kenton's been passing on, but I do know that John's a good operator. He doesn't do this often, you know.'

He's covering for him again. I'm not going to push for more on Beamish's background and behaviour. He wasn't bumped off in a booze-and-sex session. He was killed because he'd discovered someone's secret here.

'Er . . .' Wigmore wants to say more but is uncertain how to express it. 'Look . . .' Pause. 'If he turns up . . .'

If, I note. Does he suspect he's dead or does he know?

'. . . is there any way, you know, of minimising the fall-out?'

'How do you mean?'

'He's a helluva good stick, you know, despite his . . .' He shrugs to avoid saying 'faults'.

'What you driving at?'

'Well . . .' Wigmore fidgets on the deep cushion, very uneasily. '. . . he thought he'd have to go after the Wall came down.'

That figures, I think, remembering reading somewhere that hundreds of old MI5 hands were made redundant, a dividend of peace.

'They kept him on because he's the tops when he's on form.'

So good, I think, that he was sitting two rows behind Musters yesterday and didn't alert anyone, let alone his partner. What was he playing at? Trying to grab some personal glory to hang on to his job, paying for it with his life, poor sod?

'He's already had one caution and the next might be his last,' he goes on.

'What are you suggesting?'

'Well, when he turns up . . .'

When, I note. Is he looking on the bright side or has he corrected an earlier mistake?

'. . . provided he's not in any real trouble, can we tell London he, sort of, well, was taken ill on inquiries, a state of collapse, or something, and had to book himself into a hotel, down, say, at Trent Bridge, to sleep it off? To explain his missing night, I mean.'

Nothing I tell Malloy and she tells Merryweather is going to alter Beamish's future, so there's no harm in going along with him to stop him suspecting Beamish is already dead – if he doesn't already know, that is. 'Perhaps.'

He gives me a puppy-dog look, close to adoration. 'Now you're back and you know who you are looking for, perhaps I ought to polish off those two outstanding addresses where north meets south.'

I give him my quizzical look.

'Down by the Trent. That's the geographical border, isn't it, twixt north and south? That's what we were taught at school. What are you?'

Oh, Christ, I think, he babbles more than Jacko. Still, I'll humour him. Derbyshire-born, I tell him, now living in South-well, a lovely old minster town, on the west bank of the Trent, so difficult to say.

'If I'm chatting to a no-nonsense professional northerner, like, say Allen, I claim to be from the south, just to get up his nose,' I continue. 'If I'm with a southern softie . . .' I'll mention no names, let him guess. '. . . then I act the gritty northerner.'

Whether he guessed or not, he laughs, unoffended. 'I can see there's a distinct advantage in being a Midlander.' His smile fades. 'What do you think, then?'

I can't make up my mind if I want him at my side where I can keep an eye on him or out of harm's way. I play for time, telling him to hang on until I've made a quick call at two.

He reopens his paper. Soon, from behind it, he says very softly, 'Your gritty northerner is handing his key in.'

I stretch and yawn and look, as idly as I know how, at reception.

Gordon Allen is looking at me.

'What do you think?' asks Wigmore quietly but urgently.

I don't know what to think about anything any more.

'Shall we follow?' he persists.

I can see the point. Odd that he's walking out on the next session. Magazine editors like a little sex and titillation from history, like centuries-old royal scandals, safer than contemporary figures who could sue. There's not much sex in the founder of the Sally Army, but Byron should be worth a listen, right up his magazine's street.

'He might be going somewhere interesting,' conjectures Wigmore. His face breaks into a beam. 'To meet John privately, maybe?'

Not unless he's going to the morgue, I think gloomily.

'Or to see Musters, perhaps?' Wigmore adds eagerly.

I pat my leg, inwardly cursing it, and nod at his. 'He'll recognise us and all he'll have to do is break into a trot to lose us both.'

Allen is going through the automatic front doors, pulling a dirty white raincoat over his blue suit.

Wigmore tosses the paper on to the table. 'Not if we . . .' He rises quickly. 'Come on.' He's taking command now, the ex-officer coming out. 'John'd expect me to follow. Come on.'

I get up, collecting my folder, and follow as he walks awkwardly across the foyer, left heel grinding into the carpet.

At reception, he puts a hand on the wheelchair, parked in its usual spot beneath the painting. 'Mind if I borrow this?' He pats his thigh. 'An old wound rather playing up.'

'Well, sir . . .' Becky, the receptionist, is the one caught on the hop.

He lowers himself, taking the tartan blanket from the back rail, tucking it round his legs. 'Back in half an hour.'

'Room?' asks Becky.

'One five zero,' says Wigmore with a touch of the military.

His shoulders hunch. Both hands grip the outer rims. He pulls away, slowly at first, faster over a tiled gangway as his hands work rapidly.

The door slides open for him, me some way behind. 'Let's split up. First one to spot him bleeps the other, right?' he calls over his shoulder, like an excited schoolboy going out to play.

He works his left hand to execute a sharp right, smoothly and expertly. He clearly spent much longer in convalescence in a wheelchair than I did.

Outside, Allen is nowhere to be seen. Wigmore is heading down the ramp, hands operating anti-clockwise over the top half of the propelling rim now; so fast that he could wheel for England in the Para Olympics. He takes another right when I'm only half-way through the car-park and vanishes from sight in the direction of the castle.

For five minutes I've been mooching about aimlessly, mainly retracing the route Kenton led me, but avoiding the street to the Playhouse and coroner's court, not wanting the forensic trio to look up from their fingertip search, recognise me and stop me to chat.

A worrying thought springs into my mind. There's going to have to be a public inquest at that court. We've got a body, for christsake, in the morgue: a death that's anything but natural.

You can't write off a corpse in a sewer as an accident like they did the body in the bath in Bruges. How the hell's that going to be explained away?

Can't be. It's going to have to be made public in one court or the other; all of it, whether we catch the killer or not.

Killers, a voice from deep within prompts. Right. Killers. Lifting a manhole cover is a two-man job.

OK, Musters is the prime suspect, but who's with him? Who? Come on. Who? Go back. Work out the possibilities.

This, I caution myself, is subject to there being no third man, as yet undiscovered. OK?

OK, then. Forget the 7 p.m. sighting Musters gave you. He's a blackmailer, killer and liar. Stick to the theory you agreed with Malloy. Beamish was dumped in the drain at around six last night.

Well, Wigmore has no apparent alibi for six. Opportunity then. Motive? He was the courier. Could he have been slipping something naughty into the packages Beamish made up for Kenton to deliver to Musters? And Musters blackmailed him? And Beamish rumbled it?

Go on. Kenton. No alibi, either. And he's released twenty-five grand. Where is it? OK, he doesn't look as though he needs money, but neither did those Lloyd's underwriters who went broke. Opportunity and possible motive then.

And Allen? Let's see where he leads us first, shall we? If we catch up with him, that is.

The bleep goes off in my pocket.

The unsigned message says: 'Got him. Meet at castle.'

14.05 hours

I am proceeding to thumb through my folder yet again, trying to look inconspicuous and studiously occupied.

Sitting in the wheelchair, grinning slyly, pleased with himself, Wigmore was waiting for me on the flagstone approach to the castle gatehouse where knots of sightseers huddled around their guides.

He'd greeted me with, 'Spotted him on that dual carriageway' and he nodded east towards Maid Marian Way. 'Met up with one of those yellow Secure World armoured trucks. Signed for a package. Put it in a green bag he had in his raincoat He's gone into the grounds.' Then he yanked his head behind him.

'Did he spot you?' I'd asked.

'Don't think so.'

I pushed him in the chair up a slight rise under an arched stone entrance and through an opening in black railings next to a turnstile; no admission charge today.

Inside the grounds Wigmore took over the wheels himself, heading left down a tree-lined asphalt path between rolling lawns.

I took a left, too, down a lower path between the waist-high top of the castle wall and beds of multi-coloured primroses and crocuses and wallflowers and tulips, not yet in bud.

Allen wasn't hard to spot. He was sitting on a stained slatted bench, head down, fiddling with his camera at his chest. A bright green plastic bag was beside him.

I stopped by the wall, leant back with one elbow on it, for a view through bare plane trees of the east front of the ducal palace towering above Allen.

Wigmore reappeared behind a glass-enclosed bandstand, where I once played in a college concert band, woodwinds ruining sounds great composers wrote for strings; another ghastly performance.

I've decided not to dwell on failure today, but to think of success; only success.

For ten minutes now Allen has sat still, staring, like a lover stood up on a heavy date. Not once has he turned round to observe the colonnades and balustrades on the east front of the palace behind him, much less take photos of it.

I am now sitting on the steps of a marble sundial, folder opened on my knee, repeatedly glancing down at it and up towards Allen. Wigmore has wheeled himself into a gap in a circle of park benches to keep Allen in full view.

The way all three of us seem to be pretending not to be looking at each other unnerves me. Try as I might, I just can't find that lucky feeling today.

Now Allen is examining his watch. He gets up. Surprisingly, he is making a deliberate detour over the grass in my direction. The black camera is bouncing on a strap, Marks & Spencer bag swinging in his right hand.

As he passes, out the corner of his mouth, he says, 'Abort, right?'

Enough. I've had enough. 'Wrong,' I say, standing up. 'You're under arrest.'

He's shocked into stopping in mid-stride, mouth open, trying to find some words. 'What for?' he finally manages.

Good question that, so I pause. 'For starters, let's try breaches of the Official Secrets Act in the eighties.' Good answer, too.

'But . . . Impossible . . .' He's gone deathly white.

Wigmore wheels himself up, swiftly, almost silently, as if borne on the chilly wind from the east.

'But . . . but I've been, was promised immunity,' Allen stammers. 'All arranged.'

'Bullshit,' snaps Wigmore, catching the confrontational mood. He steps out of the chair, flicking off the rug and, in the same movement, without looking, throwing it across the seat, as expertly as a matador with his cape.

He takes the green bag with one hand, not peering inside, and the camera, a 35 mm Nikon, in the other, pulling it so close to his face that Allen has to crane his neck forward.

'A promise. It was a promise,' whines Allen, all trace of northern grittiness gone.

Satisfied with his inspection, Wigmore lets go of the camera which bounces against Allen's stomach.

Wigmore's free hand runs over Allen's white raincoat. 'Open it,' he orders. Allen undoes two buttons. Wigmore starts to frisk his suit. Searching for what? I ask myself. Does he think he's armed? Or does he know a gun is missing?

He stops suddenly. 'What's this?'

'My tape.' Allen fumbles into a pocket, takes it out, hands it to Wigmore. 'It was a promise,' he repeats. 'In writing.'

Wigmore examines the silver-cased recorder. 'All along you refused to co-operate with us.'

'Not then.' Allen is almost spluttering. 'Here. Yesterday I've done exactly what he asked. He promised. "It's a deal," he said. We shook hands on it. Where is he?' He looks around as if expecting to find whoever he's talking about.

I lead the way to the nearest bench, sit down and pat the place next to me. 'You'd better tell us all about this deal.'

Allen sits next to me, groggily. Wigmore climbs back into his chair, puts the green bag and recorder on his lap and wheels himself into a position directly in front of us. He hands the tape back to Allen, who grunts ungratefully as he pockets it.

I wonder whether to intercept it, record what's about to be said as evidence, but that would mean cautioning him and inviting a solicitor to join us. I decide against, wanting some facts, and now.

Wigmore's hand goes into the shopping bag. A thick bundle of twenties comes out of a padded bag inside. He waves it at Allen. 'Explain this, if you'll be so kind.'

'You know.' Allen rubs the flat of a hand down his mouth, so his reply is muffled. 'You must know. Surely. It's for Musters.'

Now his hand is working his bearded chin so vigorously I can hear the friction from the bristles against it.

'Explain,' Wigmore says.

'He – Musters, I mean – came to my room yesterday, just after I'd checked in. Didn't even give me time to unpack.'

'Tell us exactly what he said,' I say slowly.

'I've been through all of this with . . .'

Wigmore cuts in, speaking quietly, but very firmly. 'Go through it again, please, old man.'

'Remember me?' Allen reports Musters as saying.

'Of course,' he claims to have replied.

He looks at me mournfully and gets no further with the verbatim. 'Last person in the world I wanted to see. God, it was a lifetime ago. Thought it was all over.'

'Thought what was all over?' asks Wigmore.

Allen gives him a soulful look. 'You were right. You and Mr Beamish. I did those things – some of them anyway – you accused me of.' Pause. 'In the eighties, I mean.'

'Like what?'

'You know.'

'He doesn't.' Wigmore flicks his head at me. 'Tell him.'

Allen shrugs heavily. 'Talent spotting.' He rushes on, embarrassed. 'I didn't give him secrets myself. I haven't any. I did do the odd paper for him.'

'On what?'

'Political assessments and the like, analysing which way trade unions might jump on any given issue; the sort of stuff he could have read in any political magazine.'

He looks at Wigmore pleadingly. 'We've been through all this before.'

Wigmore jabs a finger at me. 'He hasn't.'

Allen's eyes drop, avoiding both of us. 'But, well, yes, I did keep an eye open on my travels for people, sympathisers, who might, well . . .'

Wigmore completes the sentence for him, a sickened look on his face. '. . . be useful to the enemy.'

A mournful nod. 'I admitted as much, all of it, all this to Mr Beamish.' He breathes in deeply. 'OK if I smoke?'

'Just keep your hands where they are,' scolds Wigmore, then, without a pause, 'When?'

'Yesterday, made a clean breast of the whole . . .'

Wigmore breaks in. 'Why the sudden change of heart?'

'"Forget it," Beamish said. "It's what you do now that counts."'

'Why?' Wigmore asks ambiguously.

Allen mumbles, bearded chin close to his chest. 'A load off my mind, I can tell you.'

'When did you talk to him?' asks Wigmore. He may be a fair frisker and a good watcher, but he's not a great interrogator, getting us too far ahead in the story.

'First,' I cut in, 'tell us what Musters wanted.'

'That.' He nods at the green bag on Wigmore's knee. 'Twenty-five thousand.'

He pulls a tortured face. 'He was on the run, he said, out of work and broke and needed money. He'd got me a grant to start up. Now he wanted it back. Otherwise – and he made no bones about it – he'd talk.'

'Who to?'

'Didn't spell it out. Just a few words in the right ears, he said.' A tired look, done for. 'Any leak like that would mortally damage the magazine, its credibility, its independence.'

The patriotic Kenton would certainly end his patronage; end of incoming revenue, too, from government advertising and councils plugging their towns. They don't sponsor disloyalty.

'I haven't got that kind of ready cash. The grant he organised only funded launch costs. These days I operate on a tight overdraft.'

'So what did you do?'

'Played for time, told him I'd have to speak to my bank. He told me he'd be waiting around reception about five.

'I thought about running away, going to the police, jumping in the river, everything. Then I saw Mr Beamish picking up his key, got his room number, took my life in my hands and called him.'

'What time was this?'

'Soon after two.'

'What did he say?'

'To stay where I was. He came straight to my room. I told him what I've told you.'

'What did he tell you to do?'

'Nothing there and then. He locked me in and went off.'

To contact Kenton, I guess, and get his hands on the money.

'When he came back he told me to tell Musters the cash couldn't be raised immediately, but I'd meet him at 2 p.m. here today, both of us carrying M&S bags which we'd switch.'

'How was the money raised?'

'He did it. Beamish. Told me where to collect it and when. You know . . .' He looks at Wigmore. '. . . that security van that was waiting for me. Like clockwork. Mr Beamish arranged it all. Hasn't he told you? Aren't you in on it?'

I hide behind the old 'communications breakdown'.

He looks ashen. 'I thought he'd arranged for you two to protect me. Didn't he? He must have, surely? Weren't you waiting in the foyer?'

So much for our surreptitious surveillance, I brood.

He looks back at Wigmore. 'Bloody pleased I was to see you when I collected.'

Wigmore colours slightly.

'Where is he?' Allen raises his voice a note. 'He told me to wait ten minutes. No more. Then abort. His precise word. Is that what he told you? Where is he?' He looks frantically around him. 'He signed; signed an immunity.' He goes for a pocket in the suit under his unbuttoned raincoat.

'Don't move,' barks Wigmore, so loudly that I flinch.

'I . . .' Allen is so shocked he can't say more.

Wigmore reaches forward, feels with one hand under the coat and pulls out a headed sheet which he hands to me, eyes never leaving Allen.

The paper feels thick between finger and thumb. The top centre is embossed with what looks like a seal and stands proud under my thumb. Inside a circle is 'Crown Offices'. Beneath is a post office box number and a London postal code.

On it, handwritten, is: 'This is to certify that Gordon Allen and any company of which he is a director is indemnified against any financial loss that may occur out of transactions authorised by me during the period April 4–6.' It was signed 'J. Beamish' and dated 'April 4'.

I hand it to Wigmore, who studies it intently, then slips it into a pocket. 'What if, for whatever reason, the money couldn't be switched?'

Allen answers immediately, well briefed. 'Go back to the hotel and await further contact from Musters. Sometimes, Mr Beamish explained, operators like him do a dry run to check that their victim is carrying out their orders. Do you think that's what's happened?'

Well, if it has and Musters has been following us, I've totally blown it now.

The same thought is occurring to Allen. 'Is it safe to go back? I mean, if he's seen us together . . .'

It seems to be dawning on him what he's let himself in for. 'You will protect me, won't you? But I've done exactly what Mr Beamish said. You'll vouch for that, won't you? So the deal's still on, isn't it?'

'Remind me of the details,' I say dully.

'No mention of me in any blackmail case arising out of this and amnesty for anything that happened in the past. Right? That's fair enough, isn't it, for helping now?'

I don't answer. 'Why didn't you help me when I spoke to you this morning?'

'For God's sake.' His anger subsides as fast as it flared. 'I didn't know you were working with him.'

I tap my name tag. 'But you know I am police.'

'He told me not to say anything to another living soul. Besides, you'd been talking to Musters.'

'What?' Wigmore's face almost drops out of his wheelchair.

I have to let mine follow suit, not wanting him (or indeed anyone) to cotton on to the fact that I already know I've chatted to a spy and suspected triple killer and let him go.

'That German telecom man. He's Musters. That hair is just a disguise.'

I look suitably shocked. 'He said he'd seen you with Beamish at 7 p.m. last night.'

'I know that. You've already mentioned it. But you don't believe him, surely? Not him. He's lying.'

'So when did you last see Mr Beamish?'

'Five.' He stops to think. 'Or thereabouts, last night. A bit after, perhaps.'

'Where?'

'In the foyer,' he replies, confirming to within half an hour what Lord Kenton told me on our stroll through the streets.

'Just to hand me that.' Allen gestures to the letter in Wigmore's pocket.

Beamish, Allen explains, told him he'd got authority for the release of twenty-five thousand pounds. Realising banks would be closed for the weekend, he'd instructed Secure World, a private security firm with a nationwide fleet of armoured trucks, to act as courier for the cash and given them details on where it was to be delivered.

So, I'm thinking, Beamish got money out of a secret slush fund on Kenton's signature to bait the trap for Musters. But somehow Musters rumbled the plan before he could brief Wigmore and killed him.

That doesn't make sense, I rebuke myself. He had all afternoon, from two to five or half-past, to bleep Wigmore and brief him. Why did he cut him out? Why is Merryweather cutting Wigmore out?

And now, I think, panic rising within, I've blundered into a security service trap that's been funded with laundered MI5 money. On top of that, there's no denying that the killer of one of their senior agents escaped from under my nose and I didn't have a smell of him.

Wigmore begins another question. 'What happened . . .'

I interrupt. 'Five o'clock or soon after was the last time you saw Beamish?'

He nods gravely.

'What was he like?'

'How do you mean?'

'Well . . .' Was he drunk is what I mean, but I can't say that. 'Was he stressed out?'

No response.

'I mean, it was a tense time for everyone.'

'Well, he seemed on top of everything. He complained he had a cold coming on.'

'Had he taken anything for it?'

'Not that he mentioned.'

'Did he, when you parted, mention anything about going into the bar, perhaps, for a warming scotch, inviting you, maybe to join him?'

'I don't drink, not much.' He thinks. 'Anyway, he said he was off to his room for a hot bath to try to sweat it out, to be on good form for today.'

Wigmore gives me his puppy-dog look. He's not to know whether it's by accident or design but I've begun to lay the foundations for the excuse he wants to give to Merryweather for Beamish's long absence. 'What happened . . .' He's so impressed that he's forgotten his question and he falls back on 'next?'

'Musters came to my room just before six o'clock,' Allen answers. 'I told him the money was available and confirmed this rendezvous.'

Six, I groan inwardly. The vital time. And his only alibi witness is a blackmailing killer I can't find.

If the Home Office are taking an interest in this case and all of this gets back, I fret, then forget the promotion that Malloy hinted at. I'll be lucky to keep my rank, even the job.

'What's going to happen to me?' Allen, understandably, has a more pressing problem. 'Am I in danger?'

If Musters has witnessed this tête-à-tête, if this is a dry run, yes, I'm forced to accept. Now I look frantically around me, looking for a sandy-haired man, lurking in the bushes, holding an M&S bag for the switch, but see nothing apart from strolling tourists.

On the other hand, I think, trying to find some calm, some crumbs of comfort out of all this chaos, all of this could be bullshit. Allen could be Beamish's killer.

I toy with the idea of taking Allen in. Suspicion of espionage is a good enough holding charge. I've made no bargains with him, no amnesty deals.

But if he is telling the truth, he's more useful out and about, rather than in a cell where even Musters wouldn't try to renew contact.

I've made up my mind. 'Mr Wigmore will watch over you and the money. He's not as handicapped as he sometimes looks.'

As if to confirm it, Wigmore gets out of the wheelchair again and pushes it with the bag of money on the seat as we walk slowly back to the Standard Hill.

Allen does most of the talking, repeatedly and profusely apologising for not telling the truth to Beamish and Wigmore years earlier, expressing his shame, blaming his political naïvety.

Musters, I order myself, you must find Musters. He has all the answers. But will he, after all his years of spy training, talk? Will he tell me who is lying? Allen here? Or Kenton? Or, until I resolve these ever-darkening doubts, Wigmore? Or is there a third man?

'Tell me.' I break a long silence going through the iron gates of the hotel. 'The talent you spotted for Musters in the old days. Has any of it turned up at this conference?'

'Only one,' he answers immediately.

Not the third man, as it turns out. Not a man at all.

And no lady either, if what Allen is saying about her sex life is true; the sort of lady, in fact, who features in Jacko's joke about super-sex, catering for special needs the hotel didn't have in mind.

14.45 hours

The pager in my pen pocket cheeps as we walk up the wheelchair ramp outside the Standard Hill Hotel. I pull it out and look down on 'Phone Malloy. ASAP.' followed by a seven figure number I don't recognise.

Wigmore returns the chair to reception with fulsome thanks. Allen remains at his shoulder, as close as he can without getting inside his pin-striped jacket, nervously looking about the almost empty foyer.

Needing to talk to Wigmore privately and right now, I throw an arm over his shoulder, but address Allen. 'Excuse us for a mo.'

I shepherd him towards the staircase. Allen follows us with eyes as pathetic as a child about to be left in a pushchair outside a shop. Wigmore rounds on him. 'Piss orff,' he says imperiously, his poshest voice. Allen slinks away, but not too far away.

'That document . . .' I nod at Wigmore's chest. 'Is it genuine?'

'Think so. And John's signature.'

I ask how the system works and learn that MI5 has access to several secret accounts, all topped with public money that's lost in Whitehall.

Eyeing his badge, I decide not to tell him I know the account used in this transaction was Heritage Foundation, the organisation he's pretending to represent. I don't want him to rumble just how much I've been holding back.

'A senior officer in the field, like John, can draw on them in an emergency to buy essential information,' he continues.

'Happen often?'

'Not as much as it used to when the Wall was up. Last month, for instance, a grand to someone to keep him inside an Arab fundamentalist cell.'

'Do you use Secure World as cash couriers?'

'In emergencies, yes.'

'But twenty-five grand – isn't that excessive?'

'Unheard of, in my experience. But still, if it's part of a plan to catch someone as big as Musters, and we'll get it back . . .' His expression dissolves into a mixture of sadness and betrayal. 'Why hasn't John told me any of this? I'm supposed to be working with him, after all. What's he playing at, do you think?'

Two thoughts spring to mind – one, we in the police put up public money, more than that on occasions, to fund a ransom that will lead to a hostage, but there'd certainly be no use for a middleman like Kenton whose part in the deal is beginning to scratch at my brain and bring up a sore; two, Beamish didn't trust Wigmore and, with no real evidence, I think I know why.

'I'll get on to Merryweather. I'm going to have to sort this.' There's a flush of anger on his cheeks and a flash of it in his tone. He's beginning to see through the plot, I fear.

'I mean,' he goes on, quickly composing himself, 'after I've tucked up the cash in a deposit box and seen Allen safely back into the conference hall.'

All I can do is nod. Wigmore returns to Allen whose face fills with relief at their reunion.

I move on to the bank of phones, spot a male clerk on the registration desk and take a detour in his direction. 'Simon?' I ask. He nods.

Lord Kenton, I inform him, name-dropping, has authorised this query, fishing in my pen pocket and producing the message he'd taken. 'What time was this call?'

He doesn't have to stop to think. 'Just after ten. Soon after I wrote that.' He lowers his eyes towards my badge.

About the time reception was trying Wigmore's room for me and getting engaged, I recall. 'Do you know Mr Beamish?'

'No. Is he German?'

'Why?'

'Well, the caller spoke good English, but in a vaguely Teutonic tongue.'

Could Wigmore put on a German accent? Why not? He's ex-army and Germany is about the only regular foreign posting they've had for years.

I say Thanks, half turn and turn back. 'These badges.' I finger mine. 'Are they always issued on registration?'

'To day delegates, yes.'

'What about residential delegates?'

'We always leave them in their pigeon-holes at reception.'

Ah well, I think, turning fully and walking away, in soccer terms, that's one-one with extra time about to be played.

'The preliminary,' says Malloy, not a nasal word wasted after I'd tapped out the numbers from the pager display. 'Death by drowning. Not in sewage, though. He was dead when he went down the drain. His lungs were remarkably clean. Fragrant, in fact.'

I ask what she means.

'The scent of honeysuckle.'

She means he was drowned here, in a foam-filled bath in Room 224, and the cleaner has taken away the evidence. I groan to myself.

'So,' she continues in a voice thickened by her cold, 'we could be right about the scene of the crime and how and when the body wound up there.'

'Are Forensics joining me?'

'Stick to the Trip briefing.'

Work alone and let no one know Beamish's dead, she's still telling me. OK, it's doubtful that the lab boys will find much after the spring cleaning that domestic gave the bathroom, but I've not told Malloy that. Yet, here she is, passing up the chance of finding evidence from the scene.

Confused, I ask for the approximate time of death, but Malloy says that the pathologist couldn't be more specific than between 4 p.m. and 8 p.m. yesterday until tests on organs are completed. 'He hadn't eaten since breakfast . . .'

So Kenton told me the truth about their meal on the train trip north.

'. . . but you're wrong about the booze. It will be some time before we confirm the blood-alcohol content, but he hadn't had a skinful.'

So who helped him clean out his cabinet of scotch? I ask myself. Must be Musters. Surely, a spy catcher wouldn't invite a spy handler to his room for an afternoon drinking session?

Unless, of course, Musters realised he'd been pegged, got into

97

Room 224 while Beamish was running around seeing Allen and Kenton, a safe place to hole up, settled his nerves with a few tots while he waited, hid when Beamish got back, struck while he was in his foam-filled bath.

I tell Malloy I'd positively IDed Musters as Maurer but couldn't find him. I expect a bit of gentle abuse, her style (you know, 'If you did less talking etc.'), or an outright bollocking ('Bloody well get on with it then').

Instead, she says, 'Well done.'

A bollocking would have been better, eased my guilt feeling, a throwback to schooldays, I suppose. If you'd misbehaved (played truant or had a crafty fag, for instance) detention or lines seemed to square things up. OK, you'd moan to your mates about the injustice of it but, in your conscience, you knew you had paid a price and settled your account.

'We're having the devil's own job checking those bona fides,' she goes on. 'Good Friday. Lots of people off.'

She'll stop chasing telecom companies in Frankfurt, thanks, and concentrate on Rosalinda Falke with the German FA. She'll flash me with anything firm.

'What do I do with Musters . . .' I was going to say 'if' but change to a confident 'when I do find him?'

'Have you anything local on him yet?'

I tell her about the attempted blackmailing of Allen and Kenton's role in raising the money.

'That'll do. Take him to Bingham lock-up. I'm off there myself as soon as I'm finished with the doctor.'

Bingham? I query mentally. A small town station, not continuously manned, half-way between here and HQ, not Central, just a walk away, with all its high tech.

I don't ask why. I suspect I know. A team will be waiting there, the grillers from MI5.

I'll do the work and run the risks and they'll exclude me from the interview and all the insider dealing. And the deals will be done behind closed doors in a station that's never visited by the media who'll never be told. It will all be buried – Musters, too, if he doesn't co-operate.

'OK,' I reply glumly.

'You're doing well,' she says encouragingly.

I'm doing badly. I know it and she must know it. Normally

she would have told me so. I'm at a loss to understand her tactics.

'Enjoy your lunch?' she asks, suddenly chatty.

'No,' I tell her, 'and I'm not enjoying this solo job either.'

'Stop moaning,' she says, finally provoked into a minor rebuke. 'You complain when you're office-bound. I give you a day out at a luxury hotel and you still complain.'

'Yes, but . . .'

No stopping her now. 'Just do the business and enjoy the ambience while you're at it.' She prattles on, rather like Wigmore, about the hotel where she's dined several times and its history. 'Fascinating. My second-best subject at school,' she says, brightening.

Her best was manipulation, I wager secretly and cynically.

Finally she gets back to business. 'What about Larry Wigmore?'

'Minding a very worried Allen and the money.'

'Keep up the good work then,' she says.

What good work? I ask myself, replacing the phone.

The peace of the lobby ends when the double doors of the conference room open and the delegates escape in babbling groups from fifty-five minutes of the lives and times of Byron and Booth. Smokers amongst them light up.

'Ah.' Lord Kenton, freeing himself from a Turkish delegation, hails me. 'Coming to the 3 p.m. do? There might be some questions for you.'

My role has changed since eleven o'clock. I'm here to ask questions not answer them. 'What is it?' I ask, not having read that far into the timetable.

'Film show on the police security op for the Euro footer.'

I'm not sitting through that, not with all this work to do and no one to help me. 'Sorry. Can't.' I tap the pocket that holds my pager. 'Recalled.'

'Pity.' He winks broadly. Enough said, he's telling me. He strolls away.

Rosalinda Falke steers her chair towards me, looking up at me intently, as if she vaguely recognises me and is half expecting a greeting.

It's the sort of reaction Em still receives out shopping after ten months off screen from viewers who know her face but can't quite place it. For such encounters, she has perfected a standard smile which I try to copy.

Behind the make-up are fine-boned cheeks. Her eyes are a much more restful blue than the shadow that surrounds them. I don't dwell on her face too long. People don't when they see someone in a wheelchair.

Their eyes are automatically drawn, like mine now, to their legs, in the way everyone inspected mine when I was chairbound. They don't mean to do it (it's insensitive) but they do, can't help it. One glance at a thick plaster was enough to tell people my problem, but her ailment isn't so easy to diagnose. In their thick brown trousers they look healthy enough, not withered or anything.

The tyres sizzle slightly on the carpet as she passes by, ignoring me. My smile feels foolish now and I switch it off.

My eyes drift on to other legs on other women and settle on the shapely pair of Irene Kinsley from Interpreting Services. Her shiny black shoes have heels that are unfashionably high, but they do wonders for her calf muscles. They are heading towards the Ladies.

When she comes out, I go straight up and straight in. 'Miss Kinsley, I'd like a word with you.'

She doesn't exactly take it in her stride. She looks furtively at my badge. 'What about?'

'Your suitcase.'

A relieved smile. 'Got it back, thank you.'

'Er.' I'm wrong-footed. 'I still have to see it.'

'Why?'

'There's been a spate. There may be prints.'

Her eyes narrow. 'I have to work.'

'Now, I'm afraid.'

'Come up, say, just after five. Ring first.'

'Sorry. I must insist.'

A petulant look. 'I have to translate again in a minute.'

'We can do it in your room now.' My face sets firm, official. 'Or up at Central nick. My car's outside.' I shrug, couldn't care less. 'It's up to you.'

15.00 hours

I am proceeding heavenwards. Going up in the lift, Irene wears anything but an angelic smile. Her face, not her best feature anyway, has set as hard as concrete.

Two-thirds of the way down the second-floor corridor she unlocks the door of 299 with a key she collected from reception.

The room is the double of Beamish's; same furnishings and green and yellow décor, similar bedspread, but a prettier picture, at least, not so gruesome as the death mask. I can't read the caption from here.

'There.' From the opened door, she points to a fawn fabric suitcase on the floor by the writing table. Beside it stands another, a black leather one.

I soft pedal. 'When was it returned?'

'Left outside the door,' she says, not answering the question.

'Who returned it?'

An impatient little gesture. 'It was there when I nipped up around two. The porter, I presume.'

'Anything missing?'

'No.' Too quick.

'Sure?'

'Certain.'

'Let's check.' I walk in, dropping my folder on the table with the lamp in the tiny lobby.

To make a scientific show of things, I take out my handkerchief, hoping she won't notice it's been used to give my nose a good blow. Holding it in the palm of my hand, I lift the black case by its handle on to the bed.

'The other one,' she says behind me, closing the door.

'You said black at reception this morning.' I tuck a thumb into a corner of the handkerchief. 'Is it locked?'

She appears at my shoulder. 'Yes.'

I nudge the right-hand lock. It clicks open. 'Then someone's been in.'

'Oh.' She bites her bottom lip, concerned.

I repeat the process with the other catch, then with both index fingers lift the lid. The inside looks ransacked.

She walks with a flounce behind me round the bottom of the bed and sits in the wing chair by the window.

In no particular order, I take out and drop on the bedspread two brightly coloured basques and four or five pairs of briefs, a pair of handcuffs, white silk scarfs and a black cat o' nine tails, made out of a velvety material.

'Tut tut.' I give her my sad expression. 'Interpreting isn't the only service you provide, it appears.'

She crosses her long legs with deliberate care; a touch of the Sharon Stones. 'They're for private purposes. No law against it, is there?'

'We've had information.' I pat my chest over my notebook and heart. 'Got a statement from someone who attends lots of these do's.'

She smirks. 'Not from a dissatisfied customer, I'll bet.'

'There's a law against travelling brothels.'

'Really?' She cocks her head and glares. 'That's not the impression a certain chief constable gave me after a Whitehall conference only last week.'

Deserves a wan smile that, so I grant it. 'Provided he's not this force's he's not my worry.'

'No? What is, then?'

'To get information about a delegate here.'

'Who?'

'Mr Musters or Mr Maurer, call him what you like.'

'Oh.' A long, thoughtful pause. 'So this has nothing to do with that, then?' She gestures to the bed.

Not knowing if she means her vice activities or the suitcase, I play safe. 'If you want it that way.'

A longer pause, making up her mind.

I'm going to give her some help. 'Unless it's love . . .'

A stony face. 'Don't make me laugh.'

'Then ask yourself where your loyalty lies.'

'With me,' she replies promptly, then goes silent for a second or two. 'And if you get your information, can we forget what's in there?' She nods at where the notebook is stowed.

I pat it. 'On my heart.'

'Where shall I begin?' she asks, uncrossing her legs, standing and moving gracefully to the drinks cabinet beneath the TV.

She pours herself a glass of whisky from one of those airline-size bottles and puts it on the windowsill within reach of her chair. She hands me the chilled Perrier I request.

She goes back to the cabinet. From the top of it she takes a cigarette from a packet of Silk Cut, uses a match from a hotel book of them to light up, picks up a bottle green ashtray which she places by her glass.

As she moves around, she gives me a quick dip into her background – Daddy an army major, retired now, privately educated, then university for languages. She's thirty-five, looks older in the improving daylight coming through the adjacent window. Another five years, she says, and she'll be out of it – living in the country raising a kid.

They all say that at thirty-five, of course, but she's got a better chance of making it than a street girl from the Meadows or the Green, catering for kerb-crawlers at a tenner a time. Working luxury hotels, Irene will be on ten times that, plus dinner.

She sits, crossing her legs again. I lower myself on to the stool in front of the dresser.

She was introduced to Musters at a conference in London in the mid-eighties where she was translating, she begins, talking through smoke that she's not taking fully into her lungs.

I have to ask an immediate question. 'Who by?'

'Gordon Allen, the magazine man,' she replies. 'Musters invited me out to dinner.'

I aim for an amused smile, but it must have come out off key because she takes it the wrong way.

'Why not?' she snaps. 'It sounds romantic, all this travelling, but it can be very lonely. And the pay's not great – eighty a day. There's lots of days, weeks even, between jobs.'

I respond with a solemn nod, trying to pacify her, wanting no more misunderstandings.

'My French was OK but I needed better German,' she continues, calm again. 'He arranged for me to go on a mature student exchange, six months, all expenses paid.'

'What was his reward?'

She raises a leg, a breathtaking view, and toes the side of the bed.

'Anything else?'

'Such as?'

'Pillow talk.'

'No.'

'Come on.'

'No.' Her voice and face are aggressive and she takes a real drag on her cigarette.

'You're bound to have entertained government employees, military types, quite apart from the occasional chief constable.'

A little laugh, her first. 'Not then. I wasn't into this then.'

'When did this . . .' I cast a hand towards the items on the bedspread. '. . . start?'

'Four, five years ago.'

After the Wall came down, I remind myself, sipping my water silently.

'I was always being propositioned. Why give it away?'

Lots of questions are begging to be asked. Was Musters paying her in the late eighties? If so, for what? Is she having to make up any financial shortfall since German reunification with this sideline? I'm not going to ask them; not yet. This is a new murder inquiry, I repeat to myself, not an old spy probe.

'Pays better than translating. And it can be more fun.'

'Did he ask you to pass on any confidential info?'

'He did, but I didn't.' She gives me a defiant look 'What do you take me for? My father would disown me.'

'Did you know he's on the run?'

'Knew he was in trouble and couldn't go home.' A vague expression as she switches cigarette for glass. 'Something to do with some GDR contingency funds, granted himself a golden handshake or something when his job disappeared.'

'So you've kept in touch these last five years?'

'Now and then.'

I ask the usual when, where and how.

The occasional phone call from him, meetings twice a year on average at various conferences abroad, adding, 'Bruges last December was the last time.'

'Were you with him in Dublin a year ago?'

'Never been there.' He phoned her London flat, she continues, early last month. '"Going to Nottingham? See you there, then. Bring the usual selection," he said.'

For the preliminaries, she explains without a trace of embarrassment, he likes her to wear bras and pants in pastel shades – soft green and pale yellow especially. He likes her in a red wig, too – 'because of some great lost love of his from his Dublin days, I think.' She shrugs, not really bothered.

I point to the whip.

'He likes a bit of baby oil and S&M before the main event.' A giggle. 'He's quite submissive, for a German.' Suddenly she's defensive. 'It's only simulated.'

'So all this gear is for him this weekend?'

A curt nod.

'No other clients?'

'Not on this leg of the trip.'

I put my empty glass on the dresser. 'Tell me, is Gordon Allen a client?'

A sneer. 'You've got to be joking. He's gay.' She keeps on the right side of him because he can put work – 'commercial work' she emphasises – her way, but that's the extent of their relationship.

A dicey question now, but there's no fudging it. 'How about Lord Kenton?'

She sips, works her lips and retrieves her cigarette from the tray. 'He puts it about a bit, they say, but not in my direction.'

At his age and size, there's got to be hope for us all, I think. I back-track. 'But Musters is?'

'Not a client, no. Not paying. He treats me well, buys me things. Goodwill. For old times' sake. Hearts of gold and all that.' A brassy smile.

Mine is intentionally salacious. 'So he was here last night?'

A coy expression, oddly engaging. 'Dinner first, naturally.' She spreads her hands. 'Here in the room.'

Hard-hearted bastard, I think, no longer smiling. He kills Beamish and then orders room service and a whore. Is she Musters' partner in crime as well as bed? Why not? She was with him in Bruges when that woman also died in her bath. I can't ask her outright without revealing why I want to know. 'Did you see him before that yesterday – in the afternoon, say?'

A headshake. 'Dinner at eight in here was the date.'

'Did he arrive on time?'

'Yes. A bit pissed, as usual. Needs to be, he says, to get rid of his inhibitions. He has all the vices, apart from this.' She holds up what's left of her cigarette and leans sideways to stub it out in the tray. She picks up her glass again. 'This is his tipple, Irish, if he can get it.'

'And he stayed all night in here?'

'He has no wife to rush back to, does he? Not like most. We're both unattached. We had breakfast, and then he slipped out to do some shopping for some new knick-knicks before the first session.' A short laugh. 'For us both.'

'And he got back to the hotel, oh, about ten,' I say, more or less thinking out loud.

'If you say so.'

I can say so because I saw him returning with his M&S bag when I was registering; a bag he needed for the switch with Allen at 2 p.m. in the castle grounds, an appointment he didn't keep.

I look at the suitcase. 'When did this go missing?'

She checked in at two-ish yesterday, linked up immediately with her German party and straight to work, she answers. She's two suitcases, because it's Edinburgh tomorrow night for a religious rally.

We both laugh.

She left them at the porter's lodge, she adds. Only the fawn one was in her room when she got to it, about six. She went to reception to make inquiries. The day-shift porter had gone off duty. They phoned him at home. He insisted he'd delivered it to the room.

'Any of the contents missing?' I ask.

'Such as?'

'A white nightie, size 12.'

'Why?'

'Just have a look, will you? It's about your size, isn't it?'

She rises languidly, hunts through the items, saying nothing.

'Did you pack one?' I ask, to keep the conversation going. 'In case of fire?'

She doesn't smile at what's admittedly an old line. 'I may have done. I certainly didn't wear it last night.' She resumes chatting as she rummages. 'It was very annoying because the missing one contained what he likes.'

'Spoilt his night, did it?'

'Not really. The other bag has body stockings. A change is as good as a rest, I would have thought.'

She puts the other bag on the bed and searches that, too. 'But he did rather miss the pastel-coloured panties. He doesn't like white. So he nipped out this morning to buy some for tonight.' She shakes her head, smiling. 'He's a case.'

Tonight, I think, with a professional charge that's got to be greater than Musters' disappointing sexual one last night. Don't rush your fences, an inner voice commands.

She ends her search, looking down vacantly on the mess. 'Can't find it. If I brought it. Why? Have you an underwear bandit loose?'

'Something like that,' I mutter. I wait until she's sitting again. 'Do you know John Beamish, of the Central . . .'

She laughs harshly; an unattractive snort, really. 'MI5, you mean.'

I can only hope my face is unreadable, doubt it. 'What makes you think that?'

'Don't give me that innocent look. Everyone knows. Him and his partner.'

'Larry Wigmore?'

A nod.

'Ever . . . er . . .' I'm talking about colleagues of a sort here and I'm going to phrase this carefully. '. . . have you ever escorted either of them?'

A firm headshake, lips tightly shut.

'How do you know them, then?'

She gives this some thought. 'Musters pointed them out, told me who they were.'

I want the usual where and when. 'Bruges,' she replies. 'They were posing as consulate officials. Half the delegates who came to these things in the eighties were secret service. It's not so bad now, but you still get them. Posing as businessmen, trying to steal each other's secrets.' A grimace. 'Pathetic lot.'

I'm inclined to agree. In training they told the tale of MI5 and the KGB spooks following each other in London, crashing into each other's cars and exchanging names and addresses both drivers knew were false to square the insurance claims.

What did Rebecca West say in that classic book *The Meaning of Treason* which, unsurprisingly, was not required reading on our course? Something about espionage not being recommended as the bricks to build a civilised society. I can't remember word for word, but I'll never forget the next line. 'It's a lout's game.' Too bloody true.

'Did you see either Wigmore or Beamish yesterday?' I ask.

'Wigmore, no. Beamish yes, at one of the lectures, sat quite close to Musters, as a matter of fact.'

I may have asked this before, but I'm going to ask it again. 'Seen either today?'

'No.' A positive headshake.

I inch round a question that's been on hold for some while, one of a whole backlog that's going to keep us here for some time yet. 'You knew Musters was using a false name?'

'Nothing wrong with that. Beamish and his mates do it, too. They all do. It's a standing joke. They're all jokes.'

I feel I must defend them. 'But here, at least, they're booked in under their proper names.'

'Who knows?' she shrugs.

Who indeed? I have to concede.

I've reached a big question. 'So where is Mr Musters or Mr Maurer or whatever we want to call him now?'

'Gone.'

I sit bolt upright on the stool. 'Gone where?'

'God knows. All I know is that he phoned me this lunchtime. "Got to cancel dinner tonight. Business. Sorry." He was going to stay until tomorrow lunchtime, but something unexpected turned up.'

She grumbles on about two other members of her party pulling out unexpectedly, too, but I'm not interested in them. 'Have you seen him since breakfast?'

'He was at your talk.'

I wish people wouldn't keep reminding me. 'And since then?'

'Only to say goodbye.'

The usual when, where.

'In the foyer about an hour ago.'

Shit, I think, close to panic. Between two and two thirty, when we were chasing and grilling Allen.

'Where was he going?'

'To the airport.'

All outstanding questions are forgotten. I can't get up fast enough.

15.25 hours

Breathing laboured and noticeably limping, I am proceeding towards reception. Becky knows me well enough by now to chance a joke when I reach her counter. She waves a slender hand at the wheelchair in its usual berth. 'Looks as if you need that.'

All floors are served by three single-door lifts in a row with a wider service lift opposite. All four buttons were pressed on the second floor but a lift, any lift, was so long coming that I took the stairs faster than my gammy leg wanted to go. It got its own back coming across the foyer.

'Er . . .' I manage a smile while I steady my breath. I'll try the good news first. 'Good news about the missing suitcase.'

Her turn to 'Er'.

I put an elbow on her counter, resting. 'Turned up outside Room 299. Didn't you know?'

'Er,' she repeats, then, 'No,' and then, frowning, 'Good.'

'Left outside her door. Did your porter locate and return it?'

'If he did . . .' She looks puzzled. '. . . he never told me. She goes into her computer. 'It's still listed as missing on here.'

She thinks, shaking her head, disturbing her blonde hair. 'Can't have done. He'd have told me. And he'd use his pass key to put it in the room. He'd never leave it outside.'

We look at each other, both knowing that whoever took the case had returned it. She inquires if anything is missing, a question I haven't really got much of an answer for, so I claim that Miss Kinsley is checking.

'Tell me . . .' We're still looking at each other. '. . . We've had one or two of these jobs in city hotels just lately. Has any delegate left, checked out ahead of time, this afternoon?'

'Only Room . . .' She double checks her memory from her screen. '010. Mr Maurer, Frankfurt.'

My heart misses a beat, and another when, almost simultaneously, the pager sounds in its pocket. I look down to finger
off the bleep but don't slip it out to read who wants me.
'When?'

'Just after two.'

Oh Jesus, I lament, my worst fear confirmed, when I was in
the castle grounds with Allen. Musters had organised a quick
getaway with the money. He must have followed us, seen what
was happening and fled.

I am scratching my brain for something Irene just said, when I
was only half listening, about two of her party also pulling out,
wishing I'd taken more notice, because the delegates I've seen
her with are Germans. 'Any of his fellow countrymen departed
today?'

She looks back at her screen. 'Just him. Else, they'd have all
gone together in the same taxi anyway – or so you'd think, if
they're all German.'

My heart is sinking. 'What taxi?'

'There was a bit of a kerfuffle about it.'

Mr Maurer handed in his key, she recounts, folding her hands
together on the counter. She had receipted the bill, settled with
cash. She hadn't actually seen him going out the automatic
doors. A driver from Yellow Cabs turned up. 'Room 010 for
Birmingham Airport,' he'd said. 'Sorry I'm a bit late.'

Becky looked around the foyer, couldn't see Musters, double
checked his key was in its place, but phoned his room anyway,
got the expected no reply. The driver hung around for a few
minutes. He finally accepted that his fare must have picked up a
taxi outside that had dropped off a guest. He went on his way
moaning about missing a 100-mile round trip and the tip that
would have gone with it.

'The whole thing was a bit strange, if you ask me,' she
continues.

I accept the invitation and ask.

'Well.' One hand vanishes from the counter and she bends
slightly at the knees, talking with her head down. 'He also
handed in this.'

Her head comes up and her hand reappears holding a key
with a leather tag advertising a national car hire firm. 'He asked
me to tell them their car's on the blink and he'd left it outside.

You'd have thought, since he'd paid for it, he'd have got them to send a replacement and he'd have driven himself to the airport; much cheaper.'

I take the key. 'Has the room been cleared?'

She half turns to look at the clock behind her. 'Doubt it. Not yet.'

'Will you instruct the cleaner, the German lady, not to . . .'

'Sorry?'

'Not to touch the room until . . .'

She is shaking her head. 'We've no German staff.'

'French then, perhaps.'

'In the kitchens, yes; but not domestic.'

I describe her, as best I can, tell her where and when I saw her and add, 'She's the bathroom lady.'

'They don't specialise like that. They go right through the room.' A smile is stifled. 'I'd better report this.'

'Leave it with me,' I wink and take the car key. 'Just for a while.'

Six or so parking slots at the foot of the wheelchair ramp have been reserved for disabled drivers with those signs showing a matchstick figure perched on a half-moon.

In one, Musters, the nerveless sod, had left the white M-registered Vauxhall Astra he'd hired. I unlock the passenger door.

Inside is remarkably clean; no tab ends in the ashtray and just the user's manual and the company's paperwork in the glove compartment.

On the passenger seat is a map folded to show a sizeable stretch of the M1 which travellers from north and south use for Nottingham; not much help to me.

The car had been taken out of the firm's Liverpool branch two days earlier with just over 30,000 on the clock. The mileometer shows that only 150 have been added.

The rest I'll leave to Forensics, if and when they finally get round to joining me.

I lock up again and walk several rows back to find the silver-grey Peugeot I spotted from Beamish's bedroom window. I check the number against notes in my book from Malloy's briefing first thing this morning. It's Wigmore's.

Underneath, the asphalt is a pale colour and bone-dry, so it may well not have been moved since he arrived yesterday. On the other hand, the wind has dried out the surface beneath cars parked each side of it.

Proves nothing, one way or the other, I conclude, especially as there's evidence that Beamish's body was moved in a stolen van. Would you transport a corpse in your Volvo and run the risk of a minor bump or being stopped in a traffic check? 'Course not.

I stand there, fingering the branch bunch of keys in my pocket, wondering whether to break in.

'Trouble, old man?' The unmistakable tone of Wigmore behind me.

I turn, trying not to look guilty. 'No. No. Just been for something from my own car.' I flick my head towards my Volvo. 'Spotted yours. Nice job.'

There's a very awkward silence. I don't know whether to explain that Malloy gave me his car number and he doesn't seem to want to query how I knew it. He doesn't volunteer the reason he's here. I've no explanation for what I was supposed to be collecting from my car; a stand-off.

I'm going to have to break it. 'Musters has gone.'

Now he has two queries, both urgent. 'Where? When?'

I tell him what Becky, but not what Irene, had told me, and gesture to the hired car. He takes the motion with my hand as an invitation to walk to it. On the way I tell him what I've found inside.

'Told your office yet?'

I shake my head. 'Just about to. Wanted to check out the car first.'

We inspect it for a few seconds, and then he starts walking up the ramp. He's still not explained what he's doing in the car-park and I'm not going to ask.

He's gone silent and his face wears a hurt look. He knows now, at best, I've not been levelling with him; at worst, I suspect him of some kind of involvement.

I'm going to have to give him something to jolly him along. 'Did you see that cleaner before we ...' a wan smile is turned on. '... met by chance this morning?'

He shakes his head sullenly. 'Why?'

I try to pass it off. 'There's something I want to check with her.' It's not enough. 'My chief's orders.' Still not enough. 'Does Beamish smoke?'

'Told you already. No.' He sighs heavily. 'I'd better inform London.'

I nod and keep my head down to fish out the pager and press up the message: 'Quick call to Malloy.' The number that follows is different to the one she gave earlier.

Crossing the foyer, both of us heading for the phones, Wigmore perks up a bit. 'At least Allen will be relieved that Musters has gone. He's been sticking to me like shit to a blanket.'

He'd finally got rid of him by escorting him back to the press bench for the 3 p.m. film show about the Euro soccer. 'Told him he should be safe enough with two hundred people around him.' He shakes his head. 'Queer cove.'

In more ways than one, I think.

'Had Forensics on.' Malloy goes straight in again, giving me no time to impart my dramatic news. 'From the sewerage farm.'

Suddenly my end of this job doesn't seem so bad after all.

'They isolated drains from the Meadows and put in a sieve. A woman's wig's turned up, been cleaned up and turns out to be red. Too expensive to have been flushed down a loo, they say. Mean anything?'

I brief her on Irene Kinsley and the returned suitcase but explain she can't be a hundred per cent sure about the white nightie. 'She just throws things in for a trip and can't really remember if she packed one or not, but the size is right.'

Malloy starts to try to make some sense of it. 'Musters and his accomplice . . .'

I butt in. 'And I seem to have a hotel half full of suspects for that role.' With a dollop of sarcasm, I add, 'All to myself.'

'. . . drowned Beamish in his bath,' she continues, ignoring the interjection. 'To get rid of him, they put on a stolen red wig, and got him to a ground-floor entrance where the stolen van would be waiting.'

She's missed a line. They might have used a wheelchair to get the body from room to entrance. And I've allowed Wigmore to use the hotel wheelchair, contaminating, if not destroying, any forensic evidence that may have been on it. I'm not going to confess to that – not yet.

'Check that wig with the Kinsley woman, too,' she commands. 'There's nothing on file about her or any translator.'

'Sure,' I say, but first I am going to devastate her with the sensational news that Musters has gone, repeating what Irene and Becky have said.

'Oh, dear.'

Oh, dear? I was expecting to come under a hail of machine-gunned oaths and orders. She must be drowsy from too much Night Nurse or something for her cold.

She undertakes to check taxi firms and to have watches put on all airports, not just Birmingham, and not just for a Mr Maurer since he travels on so many aliases. I update his description, but she asks no questions.

Bearing in mind Musters' Dublin connections and the fact that the car was hired in Liverpool, I suggest a watch on Irish Sea ports, too. 'Good thinking,' she says.

I'm surprised that she didn't think of it herself, but don't say so.

She adds that she expects to have the answer to the loose end on Rosalinda Falke within the hour or so. 'Stick with it.'

She puts down the phone, leaving me thinking: Christ, she's on poor form today. Any international performing like this at the championships in June will find himself dropped for the next game.

What was supposed to be a quick chat has gone on longer than Wigmore's with London because he's not about the lobby when I trail back to Becky on reception.

'Your wheelchair . . .'

'Want to borrow it after all?' she jests.

'Not quite yet. But did anyone borrow it last evening, say, five-ish.'

She goes to her keyboard and screen. 'Room 012. Fraulein Falke. German FA.'

Lots to do, I think, walking back to the lifts, not sure whether to take one.

On the second floor there's Irene to see again about the wig. Here, on the ground floor, there's Fraulein Falke to quiz over why she wanted a wheelchair when hers seems to be working perfectly well. I'll sit on that for a while, until we finally get her bona fides checked. Also on the ground floor is Musters' room to search before that phantom cleaner gets to it.

I make that the top priority and walk beyond the lifts into a corridor with magnolia walls.

The branch bunch of all-purpose keys gets me into Room 010. Almost automatically, I drop my folder, face up, on the lamp table as I walk through the short hallway into the warm main room.

The bed is made, its spread with white roses on a green background smoothed out, but then it would be if Musters was with Irene upstairs all last night.

The tops of bedside cabinet and dresser are clear, apart from a pad of hotel paper. I look down at it, seeking indentations from any notes he may have made, too much to hope for with a slick operator like him.

Could be a longish job, I decide, so I take off my jacket and lay it neatly on the bed.

The wardrobe doors are opened. Empty. Bedside and dresser drawers are pulled out. Empty.

On the wall is a painting of a smallish man in a mauve robe with white knee breeches. He is studying a scroll. 'Edward IV reads the first royal proclamation to come off a printing press in 1476,' says the caption.

There's no suitcase anywhere. The ashtray is empty, the drinks cabinet full. I'm not picking up a single scent of anything.

In the bathroom there's no toilet bag. Only one hand towel seems to have been used. Honeysuckle flavoured foam and shampoo are in their small bottles, unopened. Makes sense, I think. He must have showered with Irene this morning.

Then I see a pink, square, rather large sponge sitting on the bath ledge.

Can't be hotel issue. You don't use other people's sponges. At home, certainly, but not in hotels. You never know where they've been. Has the cleaner left it behind? But it hasn't been cleaned yet, or that hand towel would have gone.

Something at last. I bend forward to feel it. Synthetic, not genuine, soft on the outside; stiff inside. A stiff sponge?

I pick it up. Dry. I put it to my nose. No scent.

It seems to explode. Have I picked up a ...? Your hand. Still there, intact, holding the sponge. A booby-trap. I've picked up a ... Confusion, no, more, panic blasts through me, can't think or focus.

Flames in my head now. Black and reds. I can't see. Oh, God. I'm blinded. On fire.

Water. Running water. Cooling, putting out some of the flames in my head.

My ears are blocked and bursting. I want to scream for help, burble something that I don't hear. Fill your lungs, I order myself. A deep breath. Water fills them.

Someone is behind me. Helping me? No, drowning me.

I stretch my neck with all the strength that's left in me. Air rushes through my lungs.

A soft whirring sound now. Wigmore? In a wheelchair. Must be. Thank God. He'll help. Or ... a sudden thought, terrifying ... will he finish me off?

I'm on my knees now, head on its side, on something soft and dry. I seem to be looking at legs, legs I have seen before.

I can see. Sweet mercy. I can still see. Safe now to close my eyes.

??.?? hours

Cheep. Cheep. Can't be seven, surely? I've only just climbed into bed. I'm not the egg scrambler this morning. I was duty kitchen hand yesterday. Or was it today?

Cheep. Cheep. I am proceeding to lose all sense of time, track of the days.

No, bugger it, I'm right. I'm not getting up. Let her. It's her turn.

No one is next to me on a sheet that seems strangely stiff. She has gone back to work, without even telling me.

Oh, come on. Em won't have taken a job without consulting you. You talk over everything. Go back to sleep. Stay in bed. Take a day off. Ask her to tell Malloy you've got flu.

Think nice, calming thoughts. You know you can never sleep with anger in your heart. Your head goes off into a spin. Like now.

No, I must work this out, work out what I'm going to say, and then we'll have it out.

Who will take care of little Laura? She's virtually the only topic of mutual interest.

And that is starting to trouble Em. Am I vegetating; missing out? she's beginning to ask herself. Twelve years, I worked full-time, she said the other day. Am I throwing all that experience away?

Draw on it, I urged her. Write books like Jacko. If he can, anyone can. We'll get a computer and you can work at home.

It's not just that, though, is it?

Before we became parents, we'd each come home from work and yarn about our jobs and workmates; interesting stuff, loads of gossip, exchanging ideas and thoughts.

Now I've few stories to tell, not in this balls-aching branch, and Em has no job and is getting bored and feeling isolated.

But – and this is the point – Laura needs her mother around, all the time. The same reassuring voice, same smell, the constant presence. I don't want Laura to have a minder.

I mean, it's not as though we need the money. My pay's good enough and, if I do the job on this current inquiry, will get better. If grandad's pay – and he was a constable for most of his service – was enough for a family of three, then so's a super's, soon to be a chief superintendent.

'Look,' I'll say, 'I'm not a woman's place is in the home man, but a mother's is, for the first few years.' And after that? When Laura is of school age, then back to work; a proper, paying job. I won't, I promise, insist on a bit of do-gooding, like outings for a handicapped charity, or giving adult literacy lessons. Might even attend one or the other myself. Good that. I'll tell her that, too. It will make her laugh. I can feel myself smile, then consciously turn it off.

I'm going to get up and go to the kitchen where she'll be whisking the eggs. She'll be there, bound to be. It is her turn, I'm certain of it. She won't have gone back to work; not without consulting me. I know that.

I'm just going to start the debate, a civilised debate, point out some of the difficulties.

I open my eyes.

The ceiling is magnolia anaglypta and isn't ours.

I move my head, just slightly. It's so heavy it pains me and makes me shut my eyes again. I rest a while and reopen them on to a fuzzy face; a woman's face, with gingery hair; not Em's face.

Oh, Christ. A strange woman in a strange bedroom. Where was I last night? What did I do? Sweat envelops me.

I try to speak. Nothing comes. I raise a hand. It falls, with a slap, open palm first, on to my chest. My bare chest.

What did I get up to? A bender? Feels like it, worse than that never-to-be repeated thrash on whisky in my schooldays. God, do I feel ill.

My hand slips down my naked stomach and catches my belt. I haven't even taken my trousers off.

I work my mouth. The effort is so great that I have to close my eyes. 'Where am I?'

'Lie quietly.' A female voice, firm, like a nurse.

'Please. Where?' My voice sounds weak and far away.

119

'You have had a bad blow to the head.' Each word is spaced out, thought through.

'Where am I?'

'In my room.'

'Why?'

'I found you on the floor next door.' The words are precise and accented.

With concentrated effort I open my eyes again and keep them open. The blur firms up as Rosalinda Falke. She is sitting in her wheelchair at my bedside. No, not my bedside. Her bedside. 'What happened?'

'Do you want a doctor, yes?'

'Just tell me how I got here, please.'

'You were next door . . .'

Searching Musters' room, I recall, and nod; wish I hadn't.

'I was coming down the corridor and heard shouting and the splashing of water. I thought someone had slipped in the bath. The door to the room was open a little way. I went in and found you on the bathroom floor. You have a bump to the back of your head.' She cups her own.

I raise my throbbing head to put my hand behind it. My hair, back, side and top, is wet.

'Your shirt is also wet,' she adds.

'What happened?'

A sorrowful smile. 'I think you may have neglected your own advice.'

I shake my head, not understanding.

'Your crime prevention advice at your talk this morning.'

I manage a painful nod.

'I think you were attacked.'

'I didn't see anybody.'

'From behind.'

'How did I get wet?'

'You went head first into the bathwater.'

Bits of it are coming back now, like those mornings after stag do's when you know you've behaved badly but aren't sure how badly. The bath was empty when I went in. Someone hit me from behind. Running water. I remember running water. Who-ever hit me must have started to fill the bath. You know why – to push you under unconscious.

'The outside window to the room is open,' she continues. 'Whoever did it escaped into the car-park, I am afraid. Have you lost anything?'

She picks up my jacket from the dresser behind her.

As she hands it to me, I ask, 'How did this get here?'

'I brought it with us.'

A more important question occurs. 'How did I get here?'

She bends forward slightly. 'I managed to drag you up. You walked some of the way. Don't you remember?'

I keep my head still. 'What room am I in?'

'Mine. Zero one two.' She gives it military style, like Wigmore.

That's right, I think. Next to Musters' – just as Malloy pointed out.

'What time is it, please?'

She looks at a gold wrist-watch: 'Sixteen-ten.' Again, military style.

'If you have memory loss,' she continues in a troubled tone, 'you should see a medical officer. Do you wish me to call one?' Her accent is distinctly Germanic now.

'Have you sent for one?'

'I thought it best to wait a few minutes and for you to decide.' She fingers my name tag. In view of my job, she's telling me. To save me the embarrassment of the gossip sweeping through the hotel that a so-called expert of crime prevention has been mugged; great PR for the force that.

'I remember now,' I lie.

'You do not wish to see a doctor?'

'I'll be fine. How long was I out?'

'Only a few minutes. You have just lain down on the bed.'

'Did you see him – my attacker?'

'No. He must have heard me coming and gone.' She grips the armrests of her chair. 'These are inclined to let people know when you are in reverse. Have you lost anything?' She offers me the coat.

Elbows on the bedspread I slide up my backside and put my head against the bed-head, sigh, stop moving for a few seconds. My eyes find the obligatory portrait on the wall, Richard III, the only one I've recognised all day without reading the caption, because of his humped back.

I reach for and take the jacket, going through all pockets with fumbling fingers.

121

With her freed hand, she feels at her side and finds a packet of cigarettes and a yellow lighter. 'Perhaps not, if you've a headache.' She tucks them away again.

I inspect all pockets. Notebook, pen, chequebook, credit card wallet are all there.

As I feel for the pager, she adds, 'That went off while you were resting.'

So it wasn't an alarm clock, I think, my rambling dream about Em flashing back. I thumb up the message, blink to focus. 'In foyer. Please contact. Larry.'

I feel through all the pockets again. 'No,' I finally answer.

'Good. It was lucky I decided to miss the next lecture. You could have been there for some time. No one else seems to be about.'

'Thanks,' I say sincerely.

She relaxes back in her wheelchair, smiling. 'Do you get much of this sort of crime in England?'

'Increasingly so, I'm afraid.'

A light laugh. 'That is not the impression you gave in your talk this morning.'

I am in no mood for sardonic asides and it must be showing in my expression. Hers becomes serious again. 'In Germany, too, we have these hooligans. Such lawlessness.'

Soccer hooligans, maybe, and I am tempted to ask her the question Em's father first planted in my mind this morning: what is a representative of the German FA doing in a place their team will not visit?

I'd dearly like to know, too, why a wheelchair was delivered to this room when her own is in such good working order.

I decide to wait until Malloy has checked her out. Besides, it seems ungrateful right now, having just thanked her for coming to my aid.

I swing my legs off the bed. 'Is my shirt in a bad state?'

'Too wet for you to wear.'

I know I can't wander about the hotel like this. 'Mind if I use the phone?'

She gestures to it to tell me to help myself, then backs with that jarring noise with her chair in reverse to make room for me.

A few even more jarring bounces on my bottom on the edge of the bed and my knees are against the cabinet. I pick up the phone and realise I don't know the internal numbers. 'What's reception?'

She puts the chair in forward and purrs almost silently close to me, puts out a hand and presses 9. I ask the woman who answers if Mr Wigmore is around. She says she'll put him on a house line.

'Phillip,' he says, gratingly cheerful.

'Got a spare shirt?'

'Say again?' A posh, puzzled tone.

'A shirt. I need one. Mine's damaged.'

'Sure. White, fifteen and a half top collar. Shall I bring it round to you?' A sudden pause, as if he's realising I'm not booked in. 'Where are you?'

Bring it round to me? I repeat to myself. If he doesn't know what room I'm in, why didn't he say, 'Shall I bring it up to you?' Most rooms are upstairs in any hotel. Does 'round' mean he knows I'm on the ground floor? If so, how?

No time to think it through as Rosalinda gestures rather frantically at me. With her heavy facial make-up, she looks for all the world like someone out of opera – overacting, too.

'Just a minute.' I lower the phone.

She points to two suitcases by the drinks cabinet. I take in the room; a ringer for next door, lots of whites and cream. 'My colleague is your build.'

What colleague? I ask myself. What's a bloke doing doubling up with her in a single room?

I am so distracted that I can only think of saying, 'Sorry?'

She speaks more slowly. 'My colleague. He has left his case here temporarily. He has shirts.'

I look at her, unable to work anything out.

She gives me a reassuring smile. 'He will not mind.'

I resume speaking into the mouthpiece. 'It's OK. I can borrow one here.'

Rosalinda manoeuvres in a three point turn, the reverse part noisy, across the room towards the suitcases.

'Where are you?' asks Wigmore, alarmed. 'What's happened? What's that noise?'

I don't quite know how to answer with (to my mind anyway) yet another suspect sitting with her back to me, able to hear every word, so I tell the truth. 'I'm not quite sure. I was visiting a room in connection with that missing suitcase. Now I lie. 'I passed out. Must be this chill.'

Straight away Wigmore gets the message, whispering, 'Musters?'

'Could be.'

'You all right?'

'I am now.'

'Sure?'

'Perfectly.'

'Need any help?'

'No. I'm fine. Just a shirt and I'm getting one.'

Wigmore groans. 'Oh, lord. Allen. I've let him go.'

'Where to?'

'Back into the conference. Thought with Musters gone any danger to him was over. Shall I babysit him again?'

To have Allen turn up dead in a drain would complete a perfect day, I think. 'Perhaps you'd better take close order, to be on the safe side.'

'OK,' he agrees, then goes silent.

'What do you want?' I ask.

'Pardon?' He seems surprised – at my bluntness, I guess, after showing me such concern.

'You bleeped me.'

'Oh, sorry, yes. I briefed London, went off to the loo, came back to the phones and you'd gone.'

'What did they say?'

'Couldn't raise Major Merryweather again. The duty man said he'd check out the Heritage Foundation withdrawal, but reckons it could take time with it being a bank holiday.'

'Everyone's using that excuse today,' I commiserate.

'Just wondered what you wanted me to do now, that's all. It's a query that's been somewhat overtaken by events, what?'

He asks again if I need anything else. I say no thanks, tell him I have other calls to make, arrange to see him in the bar later and hang up.

Rosalinda noisily about-turns her chair and then soothingly purrs towards me. Across her knees is a neatly folded white shirt in a plastic bag which she hands to me. It's been freshly laundered at the hotel.

Sitting on the bed, among white climbing roses, I take it out,

124

slip it on and begin to button up. It feels good, cotton, a nice fit. I fiddle when I reach the top button.

'Your tie is wet,' she says. 'Do you also wish to borrow one?'

I shake my head, not hurting so much now, stand with heavy legs and put on my coat. 'Thanks.' I pinch the shirt. 'Whose is it?'

'A colleague's.'

One of two Germans who, according to Irene, have left? I need more of them. 'I'll nip to Marks & . . .'

'Do not worry. Please. He has plenty.' Her reply is almost flustered.

'Can't I return or replace it?'

She shakes her head resolutely and repeats, 'He has plenty.'

I'm not going to get more without alerting her to the fact that I'm on to her. One more question is added to a growing list to be asked when Malloy finally gets round to checking her credentials.

I reach the door and turn.

She points to the pot lamp on the hallway table. 'You were hit with that.'

I feel my head and summon up a weak smile. 'You've been terrific, thank you.'

She is looking at me very intently. 'We will meet again before I leave, I hope.'

I nod, sure we will.

16.25 hours

No stairs on the return trip to see Irene. It took lots of effort just to walk to and catch the lift up.

More out of habit than politeness I tap on the door, not anticipating a reply, intending to use the branch bunch of keys to get in.

Unexpectedly, a woman's voice calls, 'It's open.'

I go in. The main room is unoccupied and untidy, black two-piece suit thrown on to the bed, black pantyhose, white blouse and bra, black briefs on the green carpet.

'With you in a tick.' The same voice, Irene's, comes from behind the bathroom door.

Carefully, I pull the wing chair from under the close-curtained window and sit, back to the wall, facing the door to the corridor, the safest place, and close my eyes, bushed.

'Hi.' I haven't heard, much less seen, her coming.

Wondering if I'd passed out again, my eyes open on a view that no married man in a bedroom not his own could regard as safe.

She's approaching in a white towelling robe so short there's thigh muscle as well as calf to admire. Her hair is turbanned in a white towel. The robe is tied tight to her waist by a thin cord.

She is surprised, certainly not delighted, to see me. 'You look awful.'

'I feel awful.'

'What happened?'

I stroke the back of my head. 'I've been mugged.'

'You poor thing.' She unwinds the towel from her short hair, its blondeness darkened by dampness. She places it tenderly over my head, patting me even more tenderly. The movements of her arms make her robe open slightly at the front to give a peek at not very deep cleavage, glistening. Even with two or three thirds of my senses impaired, she's sensational, smelling of oils, not powder. 'Where?'

The wet towel is taking some of the sting out of the pain. 'There.'

'No, silly. Where did it happen?'

'I went to have a look at your lover's room and . . .'

'He's not my lover.' She rubs harder and the sting returns. I say, 'Ouch.' She stops, looks down at me. 'Like that?'

'No.' Our eyes meet. 'Someone clobbered me.'

'Can't be him. He's gone.'

'He could have come back.'

Her eyes drift away. She is patting my hair again, gently. 'And you've come to ask me to kiss it better?'

A thought occurs to me. 'You're not . . .' I stop and begin again. 'I'm not interrupting anything, am I?'

'Always time for you, my wounded little hero.' She has a professional woman's way of making you think you are the most important man in her life. Then she ruins it immediately. 'Till five. And then . . .' A carefree shrug. '. . . who knows?'

'I came', I resume, 'to ask you to look in your suitcase . . .'

She sighs heavily. 'We've done that. I can't be certain.'

'. . . for a red wig.'

No protest this time; no questions, either. She just leaves the towel piled on my head, walks with swaying hips to the two suitcases, bends with bottom well out to pick up first the black one, then the fabric one.

She puts both on the bedspread. She rummages through, throwing some things out. Holding a black G-string against her stomach for me to view, she smiles saucily. 'Like it, eh?'

'I prefer virginal white.' I drop the towel on to the carpet, adding to the debris of the room.

'That can be arranged,' she says flatly, returning to her rummaging. 'No,' she says finally. 'It's not here.'

'You do remember packing it?'

'Oh, yes.'

'Which case?'

'This one.' Her puzzled gaze is on the black case.

'What for?'

'What for?' Her hands disappear to feel inside it. 'To wear, of course. Out to dinner. He likes me in it.'

Her hands reappear holding about half a dozen pairs of briefs, assorted pastels. Her face is still puzzled. 'But I didn't bring these.'

'A parting gift, perhaps?'

'Who from?'

'Guess.'

Confusion still fills her face. 'Why would he take the wig?'

If she's involved in Beamish's death, she would have given it to him. Maybe she did. Maybe she hasn't had time to buy a replacement to cover their tracks. Maybe this is just play-acting – what did she call it, simulated?

I remind myself I am dealing with a woman with a university degree, higher than the one I achieved; not very difficult, but she's mixed in high-powered company, too.

'How did you know it was missing?' she asks; an understandable question.

'It's turned up on a related inquiry,' I reply guardedly.

Whether he stole it or she gave it to him, he needed it to dress up Beamish. Then he ordered a wheelchair from reception to be delivered to Rosalinda's room next to his, brought it up in the lift. He put Beamish in it, maybe tucked a blanket round him to hold him in, and took him down to the waiting van; a well-planned getaway.

Anyone seeing them would think Fräulein Falke was being pushed out of the hotel for a pre-dinner breath of fresh air. He's some operator, a formidable adversary.

'Can I have it back? It cost a packet.'

I'd like to reply, 'You won't want it when you know where it's been,' but that would only provoke more questions. 'Soon,' I lie.

She sways back towards me. I stop her a yard away, close enough, nodding at the bed. 'Sit down.'

'Oh, masterful.' She does as she's told on what little space is free, folding her hands demurely on her almost completely visible lap, a told-off schoolgirl.

I open the offensive. 'Where were you earlier last evening, say, about six?'

'Why?'

'Just answer the question, please,' I tell her, injecting a touch of tetchiness into my voice.

'In here.'

'Who with?'

'You don't really expect me to answer that, do you?' she says, even more tetchy. Before I can say, 'Yes – or else,' she goes on, 'Because I'm not.'

'You've told me about Musters, why not about your six o'clock caller?'

She goes silent, lips sealed, face set and sullen.

I could take her in, I suppose, sweat her. But those are not Malloy's orders. We'll return to this topic later when I've got authority to conduct a no-holds-barred interrogation.

Meanwhile, another topic. 'Did I hear you right? Did you say earlier that two delegates have left your party?' She nods. 'And both are German?'

Another nod. 'Why do you ask?'

'Because, according to reception, Musters is the only German, the only delegate, in fact, to have checked out this afternoon.'

'Well,' she replies huffily, 'they said they were leaving. They said goodbye at lunchtime.'

'Who were they?'

'From the German FA. They weren't in my official party. They're all arty-farts, culture tour operators. They just tagged on.'

Shit, I think. I've lost my folder. I feel naked without it. Where did I leave it? Reception? Falke's room? Musters'? 'Names?'

She flares. 'You bloody well know, don't you?'

No is the answer to that, not a clue what's upset her.

'All these questions and you know the answer,' she grumbles on.

'I have to check,' I respond evasively. 'Got your list?'

She gets up and strides erect, no vamping, to the drinks cabinet. She picks up her pink folder from beside the TV, studies the delegates list and puts it down again. 'Fancy a pick-me-up? You look as though you need one.'

I need something, feel faint, and nod.

She crouches, rather inelegantly, opens the door, making the bottles tinkle, and talks to the inside of the cabinet. 'A Speyside special, eh? Twelve years old. Fancy sharing that?'

I fancy anything that will give me a jump start. 'OK.'

She stands to pour one small bottle of pale golden liquid into two glasses. No water is added.

129

She brings mine, then collects hers and comes back again with the folder in one hand and her cigarettes and lighter in the other. 'Rooms 298 and 159,' she reads from the folder.

I park the glass on the windowsill beside me, take out my book and pen and note the numbers. Then the pen is swapped for the glass, which I hold to my nose. It takes in a rich peaty aroma. I sip and taste a sharp cleanliness warming my tongue and tingling the inside of my upper lip. 'Names?'

'Letts and Altmann.' She drops the delegates list on my lap, reaches across me, her chest so close that the peaty smell is overwhelmed by the more seductive scent of her body oils. She takes the ashtray from the sill, backs away and sits on the bed on top of her legs. She lights up as I read the list.

Both Letts and Altmann are listed as being from the German Football Association. Strange that they should have departed before the film show on the Euro games. Strange that they should be here at all. They're in with Fraulein Falke. A three-handed operation. Not for the first time I feel lonely and exposed.

I look up at Irene. 'Ever been to their rooms?'

'No. The . . .' She thinks. '. . . the chap from the floor below.'

I look down to cross check. 'Altmann?'

She nods. 'He came up here.'

'When?'

'You know.'

I know nothing. 'When?'

'Last evening.'

I complete a hat-trick of whens.

'Six o'clock.'

Her alibi, I think. A second ago she wouldn't give me his name and now he's conveniently vanished. Some alibi. How many more guests are going to disappear from this hotel? I fret. Worse than an Agatha Christie, this case.

I take another sip which goes down much more smoothly.

'Like that?' She tips her glass towards me.

I work my tongue around the after-glow. 'What sort of whisky did you say it is?'

'Good lord.' She looks surprised. 'Don't you know?'

'All I know is that it's making me feel better.'

A friendly laugh. 'A single malt.'

130

I peer into the glass, cursing what I've been missing all those years from schooldays. 'Ever been to Musters' room this trip?'

The palm of her hand holding the cigarette upright between the first two fingers runs along the bedspread. 'He came here.'

I put on an impatient expression. 'Ever been to Room 010 at any time for whatever reason?'

'No.' The irritation on her face soon gives way to curiosity. 'What were you looking for in there anyway?'

'I don't really . . .' I feel myself frowning. 'A sponge.' I don't know whether it's come out as a question or an involuntary answer.

'Oh, that.' There's total comprehension on her face. 'Find it?'

It's coming back and I talk more or less to myself. 'I had it in my hand and then I was whacked.'

'Bad luck.' She sighs sympathetically through cigarette smoke. 'Sounds like you're right.'

My expression is lost.

'He could be back.'

There's no way out of this maze, but silence.

'He'd never leave without it.'

I can no longer string her along. 'What are you talking about?'

'Don't you know what's in it?'

I shake my head, clearing all the time.

'Passports, traveller's cheques. He's obsessed about their security.'

My head goes cloudy again, I take a long gulp at my drink, but the medicine is no longer working.

She takes a shorter sip. 'Musters has lots of aliases but no fixed abode, right? Because he's always on the move, on the run from his own ex-colleagues as well as Western intelligence.'

'Why his own side?'

'Because of the money he pocketed in Dublin.' She looks unsure. 'I don't know.' She pauses. 'Ever met any spies?' She doesn't wait for an answer. 'Met loads, on my travels, over the years. He entertained them, introduced me to some.'

She stops, thinks. 'They're not like they're depicted on TV, black leather jackets and "We have ways of making you talk."'

'Smoothies, you mean, like your mate Musters?'

'Not all of them, no. They're . . .' A thoughtful second, getting it right. 'Lots of them, not all, are more like, oh . . .'

131

She thinks again. '. . . like, say, our old British colonial service taking civilisation and Christianity to far-flung places. They never asked themselves if the natives really wanted or needed it.

'They saw spreading their country's philosophy as their national duty. They never questioned whether it was right or wrong any more than their fathers questioned Hitler. Orders is orders. A bit like you, I suppose.'

I smile, unoffended, because she's not altogether wrong.

'Musters is different. He regards them as puppets. He was in it for a good time. Made no secret of it, not to me anyway. He likes the West, our ways. If the Wall had stayed up, he'd have defected by now and, with all that he'd have been able to tell, got a nice British pension for life.'

A pensive expression. 'But, of course, when it did come down, he was out of work with no prospects. So he took off.'

'And you approve of him, do you?' I ask sourly.

She straightens. 'I don't approve or disapprove of anything or anybody, you included. I owe him, that's all, for my German.'

I'm going to have to firm my questions up. 'You know what he's been doing, don't you?' I don't expect a reply, so I go on. 'He's spent up his Dublin dough, so he's been going around, calling in loans, advances he made to his old sources. He's demanding pay-backs. Were you with him when he called in any loans?'

'No.' She says it sharply.

'In Dublin?'

'Told you. How many times? Never been there.'

'But Bruges?'

'Saw him, yes, and yes, he had money.'

'Know how he came by it?'

She shakes her head.

'It was in *Talking Points*.'

'I only read the ads.'

'The woman PR who died . . .'

'Denise?'

'Know her, then?'

'Met her there. Nice girl.'

'She paid him back and finished up broke and dead in a bath.'

'Eh?' She appears horror-stricken. 'That was accidental, surely? Slipped and banged her head.'

'Who told you that?'

132

'It went right round the hotel like wildfire at the dinner soon after they found her.'

I shake my head solemnly, hoping she's getting the message: Murder.

What little colour she has fades from her face. 'I didn't know that. Honestly.' She got the message. There's nothing, nothing in this world, that gets ladies of the night, as my grandad used to call 'em, on the police side more than the murder of a woman.

She extinguishes her cigarette in the ashtray beside her, reaches forward and touches my knee, just briefly. 'Does that make me an accomplice?'

'What did you do?'

'I don't want trouble, publicity.'

I touch my chest. 'On my heart.'

'He pulled out of town, very suddenly. Like today. So suddenly he didn't have time to pack his bag and settle his bill. He phoned. "Go to my room and collect my sponge. Forget everything else. Just collect my sponge." He hides all his docos there. "Just post it," he said, "to . . ."' She shrugs. '. . . and he gave me a PO box number in, oh, I forget, Zurich, I think.'

I put on my incredulous face. 'A top spy handler, and he confided all of this to you?'

'He had to. He sleeps with the bloody thing under his pillow.' She yanks her head towards the top of the bed. 'Had it here last night, took it with him when he left. Never uses it to shower. When I first saw it, I thought: Hallo. Is this a gag or something? A girl in my position needs to know. I badgered him. It became a joke between us.'

I groan inwardly, feeling all the stress flooding back. And I had it in my hand. All his passports and bank details that would have led us to all his accounts, all his contacts, his paperwork. The day just goes from bad to worse. 'He asked you to post it just that once from Bruges?'

She nods. 'Normally, I presume, he has time to do it himself.'

I'm not following and say so.

'He never travels with the sponge in his luggage, can't. If he's stopped by Customs, in a drugs search, say, and they find what's inside, he's blown it. So he always posts it ahead of him, registered or courier service, to a different box number each time.'

133

I think about it, believe it, but I'm not sure that I believe her. 'He didn't, when you said goodbye in the foyer, add, by any chance, "Forgotten my sponge again. Don't want to keep the taxi waiting. Nip up and post it on," did he?'

'No.'

'And you didn't by any chance get to his room just behind me . . .' I feel my sore head. '. . . and give me this, did you?'

'No.' Gasped.

Slipping my notebook back in its pocket, I struggle up out of my chair. 'Mind if I look around?'

'Help yourself.' She throws out her hands, then seems to change her mind. 'Make it fast.'

I make it slow and thorough, bathroom first, shelves filled with toiletries that aren't all supplied by the hotel; no sponge.

I sort through the contents of her cases on the bed, the pockets of outer garments which hang behind the sliding door, and shoes on the carpet. Nothing is concealed in them.

I disturb King John signing the Magna Carta at Runnymede by lifting a painting of the scene away from the wall. Nothing hides behind it.

All the time, she talks, non-stop, friendly mostly, questions mainly, wanting to know if I'm married, where we holiday, how long I've been a policeman.

I answer in monosyllables, if at all. The almost empty drawers yield nothing. I am patting my way through the dresses and coats that hang in the wardrobe again, double checking, when there's a timid tap on the door.

'Go away,' calls Irene in an unusually shrill voice.

I reach the door in three or four long and jarring strides and start to open it, wondering if I'm about to come face to face with the third man.

17.00 hours

'Ah.' Standing in the corridor is Larry Wigmore. Seeing me his face crumbles into that hapless, helpless, hopeless expression of a man caught in public with his pin-striped pants down.

'I, er . . .' He coughs to clear his throat and tries to collect himself. He has another stab. 'Hoped I might find you here.' All he's done is add to the utter farce.

Grim-faced, I sigh at such an obvious and pathetic lie. I'm not even going to dignify it with a reply, just wave with a hand to tell him to come in.

He enters the hallway slowly, shoulders hunched, eyes glued on me to avoid looking at Irene who is now kneeling on the bed, hands clasped at her lap. She is wearing an impish grin.

Wigmore grins, too, a glaze-eyed grin, shocked and embarrassed. By the table lamp, he tilts his head in no particular direction. 'Just escorted Gordon Allen to his room down the corridor.'

I nod, unsmiling, thinking: And to think the defence of the realm is in the hands of a tripe hound like this.

'You . . . I mean . . .' He rids himself of a near stammer by gabbling the rest. 'That's all right, isn't it? Wants to write up. He's locked in. That's all right? I mean, that's secure enough, isn't it?'

At last he gives Irene the briefest of glances. 'You're early, my little Jimmy Bond,' she says maliciously, not helping him at all. 'I told you to come after five.'

He reddens around his fine cheek-bones.

Looking round, I vent my mounting anger on her. 'I thought you told me you only knew him by sight.'

'Ah.' An amused smile. 'I also told you I'm discreet.'

Treacherous, more like, catching in the spying business, I silently fume, turning back to Wigmore. 'And now you're free you've come to babysit her, have you?'

135

'Hang on.' There's dissent in his face and voice. 'No ... Well, to chat to her, yes. But if you've already...' The sentence dribbles away.

I stare at him. 'Get on with it then.' I feel for and find the handle and yank the door open.

He follows me out, almost dancing round me, a tough task for a man with a leg that appears to be stiffer than mine. 'Look, Phil...'

I close the door and lean against it. 'You look. Don't come knocking on her door and telling me that you hoped to find me here.'

'No.' He hangs his head slightly for a second. His eyes come up, mournful, a scolded dog's. 'You all right?' He nods at my shirt. 'Not hurt or anything? You look pretty rough.'

It's a diversion and I'll not take it. 'You been following me?'

'No.' Blurted.

'Then you could have no idea where I'd be.'

'No.' He surrenders, shame-faced. 'I was taken unawares. Sorry.'

'And why didn't you tell me she's been bedding Musters?'

'Should have.' No more than a mumble.

My face is set as stern as I can make it. 'What's the bloody game, Larry?'

He is looking thoroughly miserable, a schoolboy on the headmaster's mat. 'I did as you suggested, and got back to Allen. He told me he wanted to draft some stuff.' He flicks his head down the corridor. 'Ask him, if you like.'

Oh, I will, sunshine, I will. All in good time.

'So, I thought, while I was up here, I'd find out if, er...' He nods at the door. '... she's seen or heard anything. Why not?'

I am shaking my head sadly. 'You're expected. You're not just dropping in. You made an appointment.'

'Well, yes, I phoned ...'

Our voices must be raised, mine anyway, or Irene is listening behind the door, because it half opens. Through the gap she says, 'He did.'

'When?' I snap.

Simultaneously he says, 'While I was waiting for you,' and she says, 'About an hour ago.'

Four-ish, well, they've got that story more or less together, I have to concede.

'Just for a quiet chat,' adds Larry lamely.

'Then why's she dressed like that?' I'm conscious that I'm speaking about Irene as if she isn't present, rather like well-meaning people in my wheelchair days.

She elects to answer for herself with a giggle. 'A girl never knows her luck.'

I bring up the palm of a hand, to push her back inside, think better of making physical contact and running the risk of the indecent assault charge that could go with it. I halt the hand in mid-air. 'Do you mind? We need to talk privately.'

'Then keep it down,' she says reprimandingly. 'Think of the neighbours.'

My hand drops to the door knob. Her hand appears in the gap. My pen, Em's gift, is in it. 'No need to be rude,' she says in a hurt tone. 'You forgot this.'

I take it, mumbling an embarrassed 'Thanks'. She shuts the door quietly.

'Why', I ask Wigmore, speaking more softly, 'didn't you tell me about her when you briefed me in Beamish's room first thing this morning?'

'I, er . . .' He has no immediate answer.

'Why wait for Allen to tell me?'

'Difficult,' he mutters.

'What's difficult about it?' I demand.

His head comes up. 'Well, yes, we did work out, John and me, the relationship between them. Not from Allen. He told us nothing about them or anybody until this trip.'

'Then how?'

'Witnesses, delegates who had seen them eating together at previous conferences. I got some good descriptions.'

'Why didn't you tell me? Why leave it for me to find out from Allen?'

'No one's briefed me on how much background I'm supposed to give out.'

I put on a threatening face. 'Look. You've frightened the life out of me with a gun. Now I've been hit over the head. All of it while I'm trying to find your missing mate.' I pause, softening

137

my tone. 'I'd like the whole story now, please, or it's back to HQ for me. I don't need this shit.'

He looks defeated. 'Well, John suggested he fix a little assignation with her.' He nods beyond me at the door. 'In Bruges.'

'And did he?'

A mournful nod. 'On the last night. She might help us get a line on Musters' whereabouts, we thought.'

I double check. 'On the night of the dinner and the PR girl's death?'

Another nod.

'But he missed out on dinner.' I tilt my head back. 'She didn't. She was there. At least she claims she was.'

'She was,' he confirms. 'Definitely. Saw her myself. Sat close by, as a matter of fact. John asked me to keep observations on her.'

'What time was their assignation?'

'Late. He missed the meal to see a contact. When he got back it was all round the hotel that Denise Albert had been found dead in her bath. Knowing what had happened with that woman researcher in the river in Dublin, we suspected the hand of Musters immediately. So it became vital to find him before he vanished again.'

'And did she?'

'Sorry?' A puzzled frown.

Like a teacher patiently explaining something to a confused small boy, I slowly spell out what, to me, had been a natural follow-up question. 'Did Irene put John on to Musters?'

'Obviously not – or we wouldn't be here now, would we?' he replies. I've overdone it, because there's an irked 'Don't patronise me' tone to the answer. 'She confirmed he'd gone, John said afterwards, but that's about all.'

'Did she tell John anything about posting a package on after him?'

'No.' A deeper frown. 'Why?'

I tell him about the package she'd dispatched to Switzerland from Belgium for Musters, but not what was in it. Naturally, he asks. If he's going to hold back on me, I am on him and reply vaguely, 'Paperwork.'

While I talked I've been inching away from the door, a half-circle in shuffling steps. Now I'm going to back him against the wall, mentally, if not physically. 'How close did you personally get to her in Bruges?'

'John introduced us, that's all, in the bar. We all had a drink together.'

'You mentioned Kenton and Allen to me immediately, volunteered info about them. Why not her?'

He seems to see a way out of the corner into which he's heading. 'You asked me specifically about Musters' sources, his ex-Joes. Remember? She's not a source. We've checked her out. I had no idea anyone was even suggesting it until Allen named her on the way back from the castle. We didn't know he had introduced her to Musters. He wouldn't talk.'

I have no way of discovering for myself if Irene was an eighties source of secrets to Musters. A nineties screw, I can prove, but not a source. Nor am I interested. All I want to know is who helped Musters kill Beamish and dump the body, and where Musters is now. 'But you knew Musters was sleeping with her?'

'Suspected, yes, and established as a fact in Bruges.'

'Did John sleep with her?'

His head drops.

'Tell me.'

'Oh, God, well, er, yes. I suppose so.'

'Why didn't you tell me that, too? She would have been my first port of call after meeting up with you this morning.'

He gathers himself. 'I don't know what your orders are, what you'll report at the end of all this or to whom. I don't want John compromised, that's all. I don't want Merryweather to know. I'm not going to drop him in it via you or anybody. He looked after me, retrained me after the army binned me.'

'So when you got back to London it wasn't reported to Merryweather then?'

'Of course not.' There's understandable horror on his face at a question that was ambiguous.

I shake my head sternly. 'I don't mean that John screwed Irene and probably charged for it on his out-of-town exes. I mean, Irene's proven relationship with Musters.'

Enlightenment has replaced the horror. 'Oh, of course. Yes. Sorry. John drafted a full report on Bruges for Merryweather. He handed it to me to check before submission. He listed her among Musters' known associates. Absolutely. No doubt about it.'

I move closer to him. 'Have you slept with her?'

'Good grief.' The horror is back; sheer horror. 'No. Honestly.'

I don't know whether to believe him. I do know I'm not going to give him a lecture about sleeping on the job. I'm not going to point out the dangers of following a spy into a woman's bed. He and his boss Beamish should have been taught about poor old Profumo in training.

'And you fixed her up again?'

'Nothing like that. Not to do anything like that. I'm well catered for in that respect, thanks very much.'

'To do what then?'

'When I saw her crossing the foyer, I thought, well, John'd want her questioned. And since I'm on speaking terms with her from Bruges, well, I sort of marked her down exclusively to me.' His eyes meet mine, squaring up for the first time. 'Just a discreet inquiry to see if she's seen John or Musters while she's been here. That's all.'

I say nothing.

'If she came up with anything, then I'd tell you, I decided.' He pauses. 'And the source. If she knew nothing, then I wouldn't have said anything to anybody and John's night with her would have remained a secret.'

He laughs awkwardly. 'I knew Allen was planning to knock off work. I thought I'd just pop along.'

He's walked right into it. 'When did Allen tell you that?'

'After I last spoke to you on the phone. After I got back to him when we . . .' He stops, snared.

'But by then you had already phoned her to make this appointment.' For good measure, piling on the agony, I add, 'Behind my back.'

'Yes. Sorry.'

'You're still holding back on me.' A bit rich, that reprimand, admittedly, in view of what I'm holding back on him, but a much more important notion is growing on me. 'The truth now, Larry.'

He goes through it all again, at some length – how he spotted Irene while staking out the foyer at lunchtime and decided to make unilateral inquiries of her to establish if she'd seen or heard from Beamish in the last twenty-four hours. The reason he hadn't confided in me was because I'd ask questions and he didn't want

140

me – or anyone – to know that his partner had been poking Irene for fear that it would all get back to Merryweather and cost Beamish his job.

I don't interrupt – just let that thought flower, and it blossoms into this: Wigmore has no alibi for the time I was hit over the head. He was floating about between the phones in the foyer while Allen was at the lecture. Just as he was floating around the hotels at six o'clock last night – or so he says – when Beamish's body was dumped.

Allen has an alibi for this afternoon, if not last night. Kenton, subject to him chairing the 4 p.m. session – and that's easily checked – is in exactly the same position.

Go back a bit. Forget Dublin for the time being. You don't have the details. He's claiming an alibi for Bruges and giving Irene one. But, if they are in it together, he, Irene and Musters, he would, wouldn't he?

Maybe Beamish went to the dinner and Wigmore didn't. Maybe *Talking Points* have photos of other diners. They took Kenton. Why not the rest of the guests?

The game plan is working. Elimination. That trusted, old-fashioned technique is working a treat. Just a few more questions to ask and I could have this wrapped up in time for baked halibut for dinner.

A charge of excitement – that thrilling feeling of being on the brink – shoots through me as I look at him in his pin-stripes, but it's blunted when I remember what's at the left armpit under his well-cut jacket.

I'll take no chances, been down that road once and it's crippling. Next time it could be fatal.

He plays it dim, but nice, but he's smart and hard and armed. A few more answers and I'll whistle for Malloy's back-up.

'Now that you know, will you report it?' he asks.

It would have been the easiest thing in the world to say 'No', but, playing the hard man, too, I don't. Instead, I just flick my head sideways. 'Best get on with your unilateral inquiries, then.'

I don't know if he is flannelling me with all this loyalty to my mentor bit, not yet.

Meantime, if he wants to run the risk of compromising himself, that's up to him. It's madness. Irene's trouble.

When the story breaks of Beamish's murder – and with an

inquest coming up I can't see a way for Merryweather or the Home Secretary himself to keep it quiet – this hotel will be full of more journalists than it has delegates at present.

One of the tabloids will find Irene and offer her more than she'd earn in ten years in both her jobs. She'll sell and tell her story without a qualm of conscience. All the VIPs she's bedded, her involvement with a spymaster and MI5 agents will make a rattling good read. Sex and spying. The perfect scandal.

She's not going to stitch me up, though. Never sleep with a client, I was taught.

'What are you going to do?' he asks plaintively.

I am holding his gaze. 'See Allen.'

For the first time in any of our chats, there's fight in his eyes. 'Checking up on me, are you?'

'You invited me.' An easy smile. 'You held back on me, so what do you fucking well expect?'

He smiles nervously. 'See you in the bar, then.'

I don't answer, walk away from him, as fast as I can, towards the lift. He stands at the door, watching as I press the button and wait.

Stepping inside, I'm quietly confident that I'll be back up here soon, probably with Malloy's back-up, to make an arrest.

17.10 hours

I am proceeding up and down in the lift, not so much like a yo-yo, more a passenger on a slow suburban stopper; so slow that I have time to work out most of the colour codes on the square buttons for each floor.

White is for ground and the House of York, red for first floor and Lancaster, green for second and the Plantagenets. The button for the top floor, which I haven't visited, has a child-like drawing of a dwarf bowman in green, so maybe the interior designer did succumb to the legend of Robin Hood after all.

First stop is white and my bunch of keys is used to gain a nervy re-entry into Musters' room.

For a second or two, I stand perfectly still, listening, hearing nothing but noises from the car-park and street beyond coming through the opened window, white net curtains billowing.

Like a schoolboy observing his road safety drill, I look right. My pink folder is on the lampless table in the little lobby, the scribblings from Em's briefing topside up.

Then, a glance left and right again before walking slowly into the bathroom, treading carefully on the tiles and wet mat to avoid stepping on the shattered pieces from the pot lamp-holder that KO'd me.

The plug is in its hole and a thread of blood worms just below the surface in about a foot of water. My blood. Feeling the matted hairs on the back of my head, the full horror of it begins to dawn. Someone was going to drown me in here, like Beamish upstairs last evening.

If Fräulein Falke next door hadn't arrived, I'd be dead by now, tucked up in a wheelchair, wearing a wig and heading for the river in a stolen vehicle.

My gut tightens with a tremor. Em would be a widow and Laura fatherless. I would not have seen her first steps and heard

143

her say 'Dada' for the first time. Some bastard wanted to rob me of that.

And for what? Private papers inside a sodding sponge. More than that. The secrets of a secret life. Well, you bastard, I'm going to expose you and those secrets. You've made it personal now.

Becky has kept her word. The cleaner has not been in. Edward IV, after more than five hundred years, has still not reached the end of his printed scroll.

There's no sponge on the ledge, but that's no surprise. I scout around for some time, deep in thought. Apart from the window, the shattered lamp and the water in the bath, the rest is as I left it an hour ago; a long hour in which my life could have ended.

The folder tucked underneath my arm, I move next door and tap, rehearsing my intro. On second thoughts, I'm going to say, fingering my undone collar, I will borrow that tie because I feel a bit conspicuous wandering around this posh place with an open neck.

Anything will do to get in and get her talking again. Just a gentle probe, about those fellow Germans, using the suitcase inquiry as cover. An hour ago I was too dazed to seize the opportunity.

Even as I stand here, glancing like a fugitive up and down the deserted corridor, a fresh question bubbles up.

This room is closer to the lifts and the lobby than next door; a forward drive, virtually soundless, all the way from the conference room for Fräulein Falke in her motorised wheelchair, no need to go into reverse. How come, then, that her buggy made so much din backing that my assailant was halted in mid-attack and fled?

No reply after a second tap, and I toy with the branch bunch. She has the habit of disturbing intruders, I decide. I pocket them again.

Seated behind her counter, Becky's mouth drops open when I stand before her, no quip this visit. 'Are you poorly?'

'Just a slip.' I don't want the management to think it's about to be hit with an insurance claim and for her to push complicated forms across the counter for me to fill in, so I flick my head to the front doors. 'On a pavement outside the castle.'

The fact that I must look ill makes me feel it. Wearily, I sit down in the wheelchair parked beneath Charles and his standard; may as well. Between us, Wigmore and I have buggered all the forensic clues it might hold.

'Herr Letts and Herr Altmann.' I give their room numbers after pulling out the delegates list from the folder resting on my knees. 'Have they checked out?'

Her eyes follow her fingers to her keyboard, then go up to look up at her screen. 'Tomorrow.' She swivels on her chair to face the pigeon-hole of keys. 'They're not in their rooms, but they should be about somewhere. Why?'

'This suitcase business. They may have seen . . .' Not yet thinking straight, I was about to say Musters, stop myself, but can't recall in this very second the alias he's using. ' . . . the man we want to interview.'

She reminds me. 'Mr Maurer?'

I glance at the 'Special Needs' notice above her. 'Tell me, what was his special need?'

Her fingers clack away again. She waits for the answer to come up. 'Vertigo.'

You've really got to give it to him, haven't you? He'll be ill with anything for a ground-floor room and a quick getaway.

'Can we put a cleaner in now?' asks Becky.

I've destroyed enough forensics and am going to dodge it. 'When did he reserve the room?'

A ringing phone interrupts her tapping. 'Sorry,' she says, picking it up.

Normally, I'd be annoyed. This afternoon I'm glad of the break. I fill in time thumbing through my complimentary copy of *Talking Points* to the Bruges pages. There's no group photos from the last night dinner. Now I am annoyed.

'Back again,' Becky says, coming off the phone. She looks at the screen. 'Monday, March 11.'

'And the lady in the wheelchair next door, Ms Falke . . .'

The introduction of a name that's already cropped up in questions about the borrowed wheelchair provokes a suspicious look from Becky.

I nip the shirt. 'She fixed me up with this. Mine's torn. In the fall. I just want to send her some flowers.' I yank my head towards the row of boutiques across the foyer, hoping one sells flowers. 'When's she leaving?'

More clacking. 'Tomorrow.'

'And when did she reserve the room?'

'Monday, April 1. By phone against a credit card. Special needs, too, obviously.'

Less than a week ago and three weeks after Musters, I calculate. She'd asked for a ground-floor room by phone, avoiding paperwork with German FA on it. Surely, in what, five hours, Malloy should have cracked that simple query with them by now?

'How about Herr Letts and Herr Altmann?'

More fingerwork. 'Same day. Same order.'

So they are on Fräulein Falke's team and they've not come here for the football.

I get up, ask her to leave Mr Maurer's room as it is for a while, and 'Thanks'.

'Take care,' she calls after me.

Next stop is red, various tones of which are used in the carpet and on the walls of the corridor on the first floor.

The branch bunch gets me into 159 where the colour theme is continued and Henry V is defeating the French, single-handed by the looks of it, at Agincourt.

The room is immaculate, carpet swept, bed made, surfaces dusted, clean towels in the sparkling bathroom, but you'd expect that mid-afternoon in a first-class hotel.

What you'd also expect to find in a room that's reserved until tomorrow are clothes in the wardrobe, personal effects on the dresser or tables, spare shoes on the carpet, a razor and toothbrush on the shelf below the bathroom mirror.

There's nothing, not a single item, to indicate Herr Altmann is staying or ever stayed here.

Passing Room 150, on the opposite side of the corridor, I resist an urge to break into Wigmore's room. Judging from this morning's encounter, he doesn't take too kindly to uninvited visitors. I'll wait until Malloy's heavies have relieved him of his gun.

Green now, and walking down the second-floor corridor I wonder what Wigmore and Irene are getting up to at the far end.

Not much, I would have thought, after the strength-sapping shock of seeing me on the doorstep, but enough, I hope, to keep him busy while I'm talking myself into Gordon Allen's room.

'Who's there?' he calls in answer to my tap.

I tell him.

'Captain Wigmore with you?'

'Engaged up the corridor.'

'He told me not to answer the door to anyone.'

Odd that, because I can hear in the background another voice with a tinny tone. 'He didn't mean me.'

The tinny voice stops in mid-sentence and Allen speaks solo. 'Got the pass name?'

Oh, Christ. They're playing silly boys' game. 'No, but I've got a pass key. Now open up or I'll use it.'

The door is unlocked and pulled back a couple of inches. The fear in the one eye that's visible doesn't seem to subside when he sees me.

Allen pulls the door open. I walk in. He's changed into scruffy casuals – to feel at home, I presume, because the room is in as big a mess as Irene's, with papers as well as clothes. Heaven knows what Richard I, in a Persil white smock with a red cross on it, is making of it.

As he shuts and locks the door, he repeats, 'He told me not to answer without it.'

'Well, he didn't tell me.' I am worrying about who's hiding in the bathroom. 'What is it in case I need to call again?'

'Henry Caxton,' he says.

Henry Caxton? I think, unable to make sense of it. 'Why?'

'Don't really know,' he says with an uncertain shrug.

He moves from behind and beyond me, heading towards the writing table. A small, portable word processor, lid up, screen alive, sits on it, next to a mini-printer and a much smaller, silver tape recorder.

His folder has been emptied out and spread, not only across the writing table, but over parts of the bed-cover.

'Any news of Musters?' he asks. 'I gather from Captain Wigmore he's gone.'

'We'll get him,' I say easily. 'Don't worry.'

He pulls the stool from the leg space at the centre of the dresser, sits on it, picks up a cigarette that's burning in a bottle green ashtray, turns away from the mirror to face me. He looks very worried indeed.

Still standing, I jerk my thumb at the closed bathroom. 'Someone in there?'

'No. Why?'

'Thought I heard a voice.'

'Must be this.' He picks up the silver recorder, which makes a whizzing noise under his thumb. When the sound stops, he lifts his thumb up and down again in quick succession. 'Welcome to our four o'clock seminar . . .' It's Kenton, booming. '. . . in which our subject is D.H. Lawrence country.'

'I'm trying to drag a couple of hundred words out of it.' He is speaking over Kenton's recorded voice, making it sound as though it's a tough job, so tough that the ends of two cigarettes are already in the ashtray.

He turns Kenton off and stubs out. 'Pain in the neck, isn't he?'

I'm not, as a public servant, going to knock a powerful peer, so I'm not going to answer that. Instead, 'You're skipping the 5 p.m. session, then?'

He waves a hand towards the papers on his bedspread. 'Catching up.'

I take that as an invitation to sit but there's no room on the bed among items that include a stack of padded envelopes with high denomination stamps, plus his Nikon with flash attachment.

I head for the wing chair and sit, wearily, lounging a little. I toss my folder on about the only spare space that's left on the bed. 'Were you with Lord Kenton in Bruges three months back?'

'Eh?' He's distracted, miles away.

I repeat the question.

A surprised expression now. 'Took his picture, didn't I? Seen it?'

I answer that I'd seen it in *Talking Points*, but didn't realise it was his work.

'That's what all the fuss is about.'

'What fuss?'

He nods at the bedside phone. 'He's been on, complaining that it makes him look smug. Well, the camera can't lie, can it?'

He laughs grimly at a joke I bet he never told Kenton, so dependent on his patronage is he.

'He's demanding I take another,' he continues. '"More artistic," he says.' He sighs, put upon. 'As if I haven't enough to do.'

He looks directly at me. 'What do you make of him?'

This time I can't think of a get-out, forcing him to go on. 'Any more oily and he'd be self-basting. Hypocritical bastard.'

I'll chance a simple question. 'Why?'

'Making a speech warning against honeypots, sleeping around, when he's at it himself.'

A more difficult question. 'We're not talking about our old friend Irene Kinsley, are we?'

He pulls a dismissive face to tell me: 'No.'

'Who then?'

'Well . . .' A short pause before the plunge. '. . . that PR woman who died.'

I start coming out of my lounge. 'In Bruges?'

A nod.

'Denise Albert?' I am sitting up and taking more notice all the time.

Another nod, then a sigh. 'So they say.'

'Who says?'

'Some of the delegates there. Saw him going into her room.'

'The night she died?'

He shakes his head. 'The night before.'

Not sure what I've got, not wanting to display too much interest until I am sure, I need a distraction. 'Tell me . . .' I lean forward to recover my folder. He watches me intently.

Sorting through it, I'm trying to think of a safe question. 'Do you get all this bumf in advance?'

Some hand-outs from draft speeches, yes, he replies, plus a preliminary timetable and a list of delegates who had made early bookings. 'A waste of time. It's all changed or updated by the time we get to the conference.'

I have found the updated delegates list. 'How about Messrs Wigmore and Beamish – see them in Bruges?'

'Yes, but I didn't speak to them. I've tended to avoid them since our confrontation.'

That interrogation, he means, some years back when he would tell them nothing about his eighties dealings with Musters, though he turned to Beamish for help quickly enough yesterday when his ex-paymaster put the bite on him.

'And Irene Kinsley?'

'She was there. I didn't speak to her, either, but yes, I saw her. She comes to most of them.'

'Do you?'

'Always. My job.'

'Dublin?'

A nod.

'Was she there?'

He pulls on his beard. 'Difficult. They all merge into one. Don't really recall, one way or the other.'

'Messrs Beamish and Wigmore?'

He shakes his head. 'Can't remember.'

'Musters?

'Until today, I haven't seen him since . . .' His voice tails away.

Since he was taking the East German schillings to set up his magazine in return for introductions to potential traitors, but he doesn't want to talk about that. Like hot war criminals, cold war traitors have to block out their shameful memories.

I reach the question I really came to ask, pleased I didn't put it at the outset, because I've learned so much more. 'As well as taking Kenton's photo at the Bruges dinner, did you take any others – group photos of other guests that you haven't published?'

Even before I'd finished an admittedly long question he is shaking his head, but I am not too disappointed.

We chat a while, me listening in the main to grumbles about the hours he works, jack of all trades, and the miles he travels.

He throws a hand around the room. 'This is why I'm keen for new tech. I have to post everything to the printers. It would be much easier if I'd direct input. Save all this transcribing into hard copy and postage.'

I tell him my wife was a journalist (I'm not sure if the use of past tense is deliberate) and he wants to know where she went to university.

She didn't, I reply. He went to some place I've never heard of for the sociology of communications, he goes on.

I frown.

'Media studies, they call it these days,' he explains.

Media studies? I muse. Wigmore told me communications. Has he been misleading me? Or is it a misunderstanding?

Either way, it gives Allen no experience in secret communications of the sort East Germany would have been happy to buy. He could be telling the truth, I conjecture, when he claimed he gave Musters only names of sympathisers, agents of influence.

I am anxious to get away, but he asks about her career. A weekly, then local radio and finally regional TV. I smile maliciously. 'I gather you cut your journalistic teeth on the old *Daily Worker*.'

'Yes,' he says, and then he shuts up.

I repeat a question I asked him in the castle grounds. 'Where were you at six o'clock last night?'

'In here. Working.' He goes silent, not too chatty since he was reminded of his radical youth.

No change there and no alibi still, I think. Then again, he was busy reporting Kenton at four this afternoon, when I was being whacked over the head, so that clears him. It clears Kenton, too, come to think of it, despite his rumoured connection with yet another victim. Unless, of course, I've missed something.

I'm wasting valuable time here. I tell him I'll not waste any more of his.

The branch bunch of keys is busy again in the lock of 298, the mysterious Herr Letts' room, directly opposite Irene who has hung a 'Do Not Disturb' sign on the knob.

Obligingly, I go very, very quietly about the task.

Silently, I push the door open and step inside.

My eyes fall on the backs of legs, legs I've seen before, and travel over a woman's broad rear, on and up to red hair, hair I have seen before.

17.35 hours

Right now it's her hands I want to view, must see. Not her legs, her backside, her hair. Beamish's gun is missing somewhere so I must see her hands.

They're out of sight. She is bent forward over the bed, back to me. In front of her, on the yellow flowered cover, is a brown leather suitcase, lid thrown back.

What's she feeling for inside? I don't know, can't be sure, but I can be safe. Her hands. I must see her hands. Quickly. Now.

From the opened door, I call, rather than shout, 'Armed police.' It's coming out astonishingly calmly. 'Arms out. Straight out. Now.'

Her head turns, just an inch or two.

'Keep facing front,' I say, quite quietly now.

Her head is stilled. Slowly her back straightens. Her arms rise gracefully to horizontal, the scarecrow position. Her hands, limp at the wrists, hold nothing.

As quickly as I can, I walk up behind her and look over her shoulder into the case. Men's clothes have been hastily packed.

Her head turns towards me. 'You have made a good recovery, Mr Todd,' says Fräulein Falke with a tight smile.

Not as miraculous as you, I think starchily. 'Move away from the bed.'

She shuffles, more nimble than me, towards the end of it. Her arms are beginning to sag.

'Arms up.' I order her to go to the standard wing chair beside the window, not her wheelchair which is parked between bed and wall.

She walks, arms still out, like an ageing ballerina making a curtain call in shoes of heavy brogue. She turns towards me and sits. Small hands grip the ends of both armrests.

I drop the folder on the bed and ransack the suitcase, looking

152

across at her every few seconds. All I can detect in her heavily made-up blue eyes is curiosity, not a trace of fear.

All I can find are men's clothes, some dirty in a white plastic bin liner; no weapon and no sponge in the toilet bag.

I sit on the end of the bed, eyes fixed on her. 'You've got some explaining to do.'

'Well done.' She smiles faintly. 'You have no gun.'

I flick my head at the door. 'A colleague does across the corridor, so no fast foot work.'

Whether she caught the gag or not, her smile is more relaxed. 'Obviously, you will have questions.'

Lots, the first of which is not so blindingly obvious but it's been nagging at me since 11 a.m. 'What's a representative of the German FA doing in a city where her national team isn't going to play and which their supporters aren't going to visit?'

'Ah.' A mournful sigh. 'I can see that is not one of the more successful parts of this operation.'

Try this one, lady. 'Who are you and what operation are you on?'

One hand goes to her lap. With the other elbow, she lifts her backside off the cushion and sits further back in the chair, making herself comfortable. 'My name is Hilda Braund.'

I was right. The old con trick ploy. When you are acting a role, use an unforgettable name. 'Not another character from *Die Fledermaus*, then?'

'Ah.' A warmer smile. 'A man of music. I was forewarned not to underestimate you.'

'Who by?'

She doesn't answer.

'Who are you?'

Her eyes drop to my name tag. 'You are not who you claim to be either.'

I speak very slowly. 'W-h-o a-r-e y-o-u?'

'Nobody, really.' She braces herself. 'Stasi until 1990, currently unemployed as most of us are, regrettably.'

'What are you doing here?'

'Looking for Mr Musters.'

'Have you found him?'

She glances at a silver wrist-watch. 'That will be answered soon.'

153

'You'll answer it now.'

'Truthfully,' she replies with great emphasis, 'I will not know his precise whereabouts for an hour or so and the information will be shared then. You have my word.'

'For what it's worth,' I reply sarcastically.

A hurt expression fills her face. Her lips purse.

'A friend of yours, is he?' I ask.

'Not at all.' Her lips hardly move.

'Listen, lady.' I bounce myself into a more relaxed position on the bed, stretching out my legs, crossing them at the ankles, trying to tell her that I've got all night. 'I've got you for entering this country illegally and for breaking and entering this room.'

'I am here with permission,' she answers, unconcerned.

'In this room or in this country?'

'Here.' She throws out a hand languidly.

It's only half an answer, but I'll let her think she's got away with it – for now. 'Where is the occupant of this room, your colleague Mr Letts?'

'He did not have time to pack.' With the same hand, she gestures to the case on the bed. 'I am doing it for him, at his request.'

I nod at the green carpet. 'And Mr Altmann one floor down?'

She smiles broadly. 'His shirt fits you well.'

'Where are they?'

'Gone. Both of them.'

'Where to?'

She thinks. 'Home.'

'Without checking out?' I cock my head. 'Aiding and abetting decamping from a hotel without paying the bill is another charge.'

'I shall be signing theirs and my own when I depart tomorrow.'

'Friends of yours, too, are they?'

A stiff nod. 'Former colleagues.'

'Ex-Stasi?'

Another nod.

Now for that other half of an answer. 'And are you in this country on a false passport with permission?'

She gives this some thought. 'By arrangement.'

'What's the arrangement?'

'To locate Musters.'

154

'Why?'

'I'll tell you what I can,' she replies, making it sound like a big favour.

'You'll answer any questions that I care to put to you, lady, or I'm wheeling you into the nearest nick.'

I'm not sure if she caught that one either.

She was an analyst, not a field operator, based in East Berlin, she begins. She'd been recruited straight from university where she'd studied English. She'd hoped to travel. 'This is my first journey overseas,' she adds with a sad little smile.

She'd handled Musters' dispatches from London. He didn't use his own name. His code was Danny Boy.

Ties in with his connections with Ireland, I think. 'Good, was he?'

'Oh, yes,' she answers immediately. 'His information was top grade, particularly towards the end, at a time when our leaders were placing a great priority on high technology, with the declared aim of making the state world leaders in communications inside five years.'

She pulls a face. 'Ludicrous, of course. We were way behind the West. One of the reasons for our fall . . .'

She is becoming discursive, like Wigmore first thing, and I wonder if it's a trait of their profession; gabbling about inconsequentials, because they dare not speak of their jobs.

I lie further back, very casual, propped up by an elbow, and take in the room as she talks.

On the wall Thomas à Becket is about to be martyred for putting two fingers up to Henry II. His dying posture is not dissimilar to mine and I sit up again.

'We threw everything into information technology,' she goes on. 'Traditional heavy industries which had been doing quite well were starved of funds. Thus . . .' A matter-of-fact shrug. '. . . the economy collapsed.'

I don't really want any more of this lecture on why the Wall came down. 'Musters' sources were delivering the goods, you say?'

'At a high price.'

'In the late eighties?'

155

A nod.

New to me this, totally contradicting everything Wigmore's been telling me all day. 'Like what?'

'Covert monitoring equipment, for instance. Transmitters, pressure pad to trigger cameras and recorders and so on.'

Old hat, I think dismissively. 'You'd already have those, surely?'

'It was the miniaturisation of them that was so much more advanced. We knew of it, of course, but didn't have the technical expertise to replicate it. We bought the designs. They were ...' She can't think of the English word to express her admiration.

'*Wunderbar*,' I offer.

She laughs lightly.

Can't have come from Kenton. OK, he was a bigwig in his élite union for communication boffins then, but the stuff he gave to Musters was vetted by Beamish and was mostly duff.

Can't have been Allen because he's not, and never was, into these sort of communications. There must be a third man after all and I think I know who. 'Who was his source?'

'The code name is all I know. He had one of our biggest budgets from funds held in Dublin.'

'What was it?'

'Flora.'

Margarine? I think. Flowers? The second sticks longer than the first. Flowers? Wigmore and his botany. He's spent his adult lifetime in communications.

Kenton let MI5 see everything that passed over his union desk. Beamish selected bits and pieces to be handed on to Musters, misinformation mainly, the occasional useful titbit to make the dross look good. He packaged them. But it was Wigmore who delivered to Kenton to make the drop. Could Wigmore have switched items in the package, substituting hot info for duff? An inside job?

His hair was wet at seven last night. He misled me about Allen's degree, held back on Irene Kinsley. His room number was engaged at about the time that registration was getting that phone message from the already dead Beamish. Now Flora.

The case is building nicely, I compliment myself.

When the Wall disappeared, she continues, so did Musters, his files and the Dublin funds.

'As for the rest of us, nothing. No work. The smallest of pensions, barely enough to live on.'

That's what comes from being on the losing side, I think without sympathy.

'A year ago,' she goes on, 'we got together to campaign for a better pension, a more fair deal. Bonn said there could be no arrangements for alternative employment or better compensation while amongst our number was a renegade, acting against the interest of the newly unified country.'

She shakes her head disgustedly. 'He was harming us all, bringing disrepute down upon us, raising questions as to our trustworthiness. They were not prepared to consider our request with that matter unresolved.'

'The matter of Musters?' I prompt.

A curt nod. 'We were informed that he had committed blackmail and murder in Ireland, causing maximum diplomatic embarrassment.'

'How were the three of you going to resolve the matter?'

'Use our expertise and contacts to locate Musters and the missing funds and Bonn would then negotiate on pensions.'

'Did you go to Dublin?'

'No, but we were told what happened there.'

'Who told you?'

'We were briefed in Bonn.'

'Bruges, three months ago?'

'Yes, but far too late. We started, a small group of us, to monitor arrangements for other similar conferences and we worked out he may well come here. A calculated guess, you would call it.'

Her face brightens. 'When we checked the credentials of enrolled delegates, we discovered Mr Maurer's were false.'

I'm going to have to take her back through this, because something is wrong and I can't quite work out what. 'When, precisely, did you do this research on delegates?'

'We started about two weeks ago.'

After Musters enrolled as Maurer and booked his room, according to records in reception, I recall. 'From a list you obtained from the conference organisers?'

'Obtained for us, yes.'

She's confirming what Allen said about receiving timetables

157

and names of delegates in advance. 'When did you discover that Maurer was a phoney?'

'It took most of the week to work through all the names.'

'When did the breakthrough come?'

'Saturday.'

A week ago tomorrow. It confirms everything Becky told me, but there's still something wrong. I throw my head back in the direction of the redundant wheelchair. 'So, by Monday of this week, you'd enrolled and booked in next door to him on the ground floor, posing as a disabled delegate?'

'And my two colleagues took rooms on the two other floors,' she adds, looking pleased with herself.

They had the whole building covered, I think admiringly. 'And you positively identified Maurer as Musters?'

'Last night.'

Before or after Beamish was bumped off? I ask myself. Have I got a witness here? Or the killer? 'And you watched him?'

A satisfied smile. 'We know in which room he spent last night. This morning he was followed to Marks & Spencer. We know what he bought and how much it cost.'

She lists women's briefs and a man's maroon pyjamas and gives their prices, showing off for me.

'Upon his return,' she continues, 'I saw him at the same time as you were in the foyer and I saw him speak to you after your small speech.'

When he was pointing me in the direction of Gordon Allen on the press bench to divert attention from his getaway, I lament, anything but pleased with myself.

Did he decide to flee after I'd made an appeal for information about the missing Beamish? Or maybe Fräulein Falke's team are not as good as she thinks they are and he rumbled his time was about up.

'We know about his liaison with the lady on the second floor,' she continues, preening now.

'How?'

'As a result of much hard work in follow-up inquiries from our visit to Bruges, confirmed here yesterday.' She smiles to herself. 'Mr Altmann checked her out personally last night.'

'What time?'

'Six o'clock.'

Confirms Irene's alibi, I think; definitely clears her on Beamish.

'As a result of information he gleaned, we became satisfied that we had indeed identified the right man. We started observations when he called on her for dinner.'

At eight, I recall, which means, if I'm to believe all or any of this, that their surveillance on Musters started two hours after he had bumped off Beamish.

Still grandstanding, she's telling me what they ordered from room service, but I'm not overly impressed. With a man in the room directly opposite, it wasn't a difficult stake-out. 'What were you, yourself, personally, doing at six o'clock?'

'In my room downstairs.'

No alibi then, and she was on hand when I was whacked. My saviour or my assailant? Let's get some other names out of the way first. 'Do you know of Gordon Allen, the magazine writer?'

'I have seen him here sitting behind his name plate at the press table.'

'Do you know him?'

'Of his writing, yes. We have been studying past issues of his publication. Not personally, no.'

'Lord Kenton?'

'One could hardly miss him,' she replies mischievously, 'but again he is of no concern to us.'

I'm tempted to ask if she knows both were sources of Musters' spying, both of questionable value, but hold fire, not sure how much I should be telling an ex-enemy.

'Have you met Beamish and Wigmore?'

A headshake.

I tap my name tag. 'In the way you worked out that I'm not Community Relations, have you worked out their real role?'

She answers after careful thought. 'We are aware, if this is what you mean, that British security are also taking an understandable interest in Musters.'

In other words, she knows – or certainly believes – they are MI5.

'Who made you aware of that?'

'Bonn.'

'What did they tell you?'

'That two of your colleagues had got close to Musters in Bruges, but that he escaped their net.'

A cloud appears on the horizon of my mind.

'Our analysis of the delegates enrolled for that conference disclosed that they were not employed in the government departments shown on the list but they were immediately ruled out as being Musters.'

That cloud is fully formed now and is very black indeed. Is this a joint operation from which I've been excluded, deliberately cut out? 'Are you co-operating with any of our security services?'

She totally avoids a straight answer. 'Our instructions are merely to locate Musters and to recover the monies of the state. It is essential to any settlement of our monetary grievances.'

'Are you working with us?'

'We only report to Bonn.'

They are. They must be ... and yet. 'What were you doing, disguised as a cleaner, in Mr Beamish's room, the room of someone you believed to be MI5, at 10 a.m?'

She has no answer at all.

'What were you looking for?'

No reply still.

I smile. 'Your legs, or rather your ankles, gave you away.'

'Yes.' She looks down at them. 'They have enlarged with all this inactivity.' She pauses, recognises she's trapped. 'Documents. We thought he might have beaten us to Musters' documents.'

'Why do you want them so badly?'

'Because they will lead to the misappropriated funds and, as I have said, their recovery is part of any future financial arrangement with Bonn.'

She's good, very good. Now get out of this. 'Why did you order a spare wheelchair to be delivered to your room when your own works so well?'

No hesitation this time. 'I did not.' She sits up, startled.

'According to reception, someone asked for the hotel wheelchair to be delivered to your room around six last evening.'

'It was not me.'

'Mr Letts or Mr Altmann, perhaps?'

'Why should we? What is the purpose?'

If she doesn't know it was used to transport the late John Beamish out of the hotel, maybe she doesn't know he's dead. I'm going to have to take her in, take advice from Malloy on how

160

much I can tell her. 'Why did you steal a suitcase belonging to the lady on the second floor?'

Her face is indignant. 'I know of no stolen suitcase.'

'Did your colleagues intercept it *en route* to Room 299? Looking for Musters' documents, perhaps? Or was it the red wig?'

That hurt look again, her honour questioned. 'Most certainly not.'

'Were you still looking for those documents around 4 p.m. when you hit me over the head?' I feel it and yank it in the direction of Musters' room next door.

'I did not hit you.' An aggrieved tone. 'I heard you being hit. I arrived too late to see who did it. I helped you back to my room. You don't remember, do you?'

'Only your ankles.' I look at them, then her. 'What I can't work out is why my attacker heard you.'

Nowhere along her route from the conference room to her room on the ground floor, I tell her, is it necessary for her to put her wheelchair in reverse. 'So why should he have heard that noise it makes?'

She has no answer and I sit and smile through a long silence. Then: 'Did you find what you were looking for?'

'No.' She looks distinctly downcast.

'So there's a race on for these documents. Who beat you to it? Where is your precious prize now?'

'That, too, will be answered later this evening.'

Before that, lady, I'm vowing, but first answer this. 'You say you will settle the bills for all three of you when you depart tomorrow. Two nights, full board, in a hotel like this, plus your fares to get here and the conference fees and the hire of an expensive wheelchair. They don't come cheap. Tell me, if your pensions are so paltry, where's the money coming from?'

'It is arranged.'

'By whom?'

'Bonn.' She sort of sinks into her chair, appears to be getting smaller, body language to say she is going into her shell.

I look at my watch. Nearly six. I have a drinks date with Wigmore, my No. 1 suspect, in the bar. Should I cancel it and take her in?

Not wanting to quote the advice on not to underestimate me, I ask, 'Who told you about me?'

'They were right,' she smiles, coming round a bit. 'You have a retentive memory.'

'Who was right?'

'Bonn.'

'What did they tell you?'

'That one of the British team was out of the operation . . .'

'Why?'

A headshake. 'I was not told. Illness, I presume.'

A fatal one, I think macabrely.

She finishes her sentence. '. . . and they had replaced him with the best investigator they could find at short notice.'

Flattery will get you nowhere, lady. 'What time was this?'

'Nine thirty this morning.'

Half-nine? I wasn't even here then, only *en route* after Malloy's briefing. There is collusion between Bonn and London, no doubt about it; no other explanation. 'I'm going to have to take you in and sort this out.'

A deeply worried look. 'I am supposed to sit by the phone in my room.'

'Sorry.' I am shaking my head. 'Your two friends have gone, as well as Musters. I can't afford to lose you, too.'

'Well.' She fiddles in a jacket pocket. 'You have that right, for I am but a guest in your country.' She takes out a paper handkerchief. 'But I have a telephone number here for such eventualities.'

She hands it over, explaining that Bonn had passed it on less than an hour ago. A number that is vaguely familiar is written in pencil down one edge. I fish out my pager and scroll back the day's messages.

It is the same as the one Malloy gave me; the number for Bingham, where, I suspect, Merryweather and the half of White-hall that isn't on holiday will be pulling all the strings.

On second thoughts, maybe flattery will work on this one occasion. I stand, pick up the folder and nod at the wheelchair. 'Hop in and I'll push you.'

162

18.00 hours

The cunning, conniving bitch, the manipulative witch, I rage, walking behind the gently purring wheelchair along the second-floor corridor, carrying the repacked suitcase.

With Rosalinda completely withdrawn into her shell now, not a word is being exchanged and I am free to fume.

Fancy Malloy setting me up like this, pitting me against an armed and trained killer with a bleep my only weapon; a bloody bleep, not even a portable phone to use in emergencies.

A lift is waiting, door open. A woman passenger greets Rosalinda with a sympathetic smile.

I jab, rather than finger, the white button. As we descend in silence, I begin to visualise the scene.

Half-eight this morning Merryweather phones Malloy, acting chief constable for the holiday weekend. 'Spot of bother, old girl. One of our operatives, our top surveillance bod, is missing, feared dead, murdered.'

A précis follows on Musters' background and crimes in Dublin and Bruges. 'Bonn tipped us he's likely to be on our patch. Didn't tell you, of course, because normally we don't work with a load of provincial plods. We assigned Beamish and Wigmore. Trouble is, Beamish has vanished and, embarrassingly, we're pretty damn sure Wigmore did it.'

So swiftly do I step into the lobby, still deep into the mental scene, that I cannon into a waiting delegate. A half-hearted apology is mumbled.

I follow Rosalinda in the wheelchair down the ground-floor corridor, open and hold her door for her to pass through, and lower the case on to the carpet just inside the room.

'You'll be able to manage that now, won't you?' I say facetiously. 'Don't move from here without my say-so or our next trip together will be to the station.' Whether the bigwigs in Bonn and Bingham like it or not, I add to myself.

She replies with a dumb, defeated nod.

I close her bedroom door. So . . . Where was I? What next? So . . . The spell is broken, the vision gone and I think in words, not pictures – 'Radio, rather than TV terms,' my Em would call it.

The tip that Musters might be here didn't come from contacts. Either Beamish was bullshitting Wigmore, or Wigmore is bullshitting me, yet again.

It came from Bonn as a result of painstaking research by the ex-Stasi trio. And, if Bonn is co-operating that closely, they were bound to have told London all that Fräulein Falke has just told me.

Emerging into the foyer, heading for the phones, the vision reappears.

Merryweather (and I see and hear him in my mind's eye, Savile Row-suited and talking like a Queen's Counsel) would say something like, 'Had our eye on Wiggers for some time, ever since Bonn got hold of old Stasi records which disclosed that info we thought was tame was, whoops, very spicy indeed.

'He's had his hand in our packages, it seems, after we doctored Kenton's documents. He reinstated the secrets, as it were. A good ploy. Impossible to detect. Only the code name Bonn came up with gave him away. Beamish was hoping to catch him out this weekend. Instead he appears to have bought it.'

All four phones are engaged. A couple wait close by. I start to circle the busy foyer, thinking on the move.

'How can I help?' Malloy would ask obligingly.

'Need a man to stand in for Beamish – dead man's shoes, what? – and get close to Wigmore. Don't want him fully briefed or armed, just blundering about, like you do up there. Certainly don't want him to know that we have three ex-Stasi members in the hotel independently seeking Musters. A sort of bull-in-the-china-shop type. Can do?'

'I've got just the man, sitting downstairs, twiddling his thumbs, going through the overnight log and reading a day-old *Morning Star*, as a matter of fact, name of Todd.'

'What's he like?'

And Malloy would have told him what she told me after I was

164

turned down for chief super in charge of CID. 'You're at your hottest working on your own, a solitary cat among the pigeons' – a typecasting that's based entirely on the only two decent jobs I've done for her in two years in the branch. 'What are our objectives?'

'To find Beamish's body and prove it was Wigmore who killed him. This Toddy chappie can Rambo around . . .'

Passing the row of boutiques, my feet start to drag and I'm feeling drained.

'He doesn't Rambo. He limps,' I hear Malloy saying in that mischievous tone of hers.

'Ha, ha . . . looking for Musters as a cover for his inquiries, if he likes, but he won't find him. Bonn's bods have had tabs on him since dinner last night and they are taking care of him.'

Becky, behind reception, is looking rather anxiously across in my direction, wondering, no doubt, if I'm concussed. I haven't had a cigarette for ten years, but I'm pining for one now, can almost taste one soothing the stress away. I retrace my steps towards the phones. The TV switch in my mind flicks back on.

'Smashing,' says Merryweather. 'On my way up there, chauffeured, of course. Find us a nice quiet little ops room where we won't be disturbed by press pests. No publicity is an absolute must. Hush-hush. The whole thing's got to be totally deniable. Can't have this leaking, can we?'

The phones are still engaged, but the queue has gone. I come out of my reverie.

Makes sense. Why else would Malloy stall all afternoon on a simple query to check Rosalinda Falke with the German FA? Because she knew all along, but didn't want me to know, that's bloody why.

And, if these Stasi bods had Musters located by eight, they'd tell Bonn and Bonn would tell London, yet no one's told Wigmore. Why? It's obvious. Because he's Suspect No. 1.

Malloy located Beamish fast enough. How else could she have made the link between a body in drag in a sewer? Because she was checking all corpses this morning, easily identifiable by a missing finger. And that old-time cop's entry in the log confirmed that the stolen van at the scene was taken a few streets from here. And still she's kept me in the dark. Used me.

Well, bugger it. I'm not having it. I've had a gun pointed at me, been whacked on the head, almost drowned, and this shift's not over yet.

Well, it is for me. It's all over. I've got a wife and kid and I'm not running bloody risks like this any more.

When a phone comes free I'm going to call that Bingham number and tell Malloy to stick the job where Edward of whatever Roman numerals had that red hot poker lodged.

I don't need the money, this job, this shit. Em can go back to work and I'll be house husband. And when the kid's old enough I'll go private, set up my own inquiry bureau.

So gripped am I in the turmoil of this inner rant, this perfect paddy, that I don't move fast enough when a phone comes free and am beaten to it by a far nimbler Frenchwoman.

Yes, but will you be happy house-bound? Why not? Won't you miss the challenge, the battles of wits and for promotion, the gossip, the fun? Won't you feel out of it, no stories to tell Em?

My fighting spirit is ebbing. A new vision occurs, no dialogue, just me, alone for hours on end, dusting, ironing, cleaning the inside windows, mopping the kitchen floor, spoon-feeding Laura.

Now it flows back. Sod it. Bugger it. I've faced a gun and been hit with a pot lamp. I'm not handing this over. This is my case. She found the body. I'll bring in the killer.

No cunning, conniving bitch is going to rob me of my pinch, the supreme moment when you've taken the knocks and knocked off the villain, job done; no feeling like it.

A phone comes free. A polite Portuguese gestures 'After you' towards it.

I motion him to it, smile, mumble 'Change of mind' and walk away towards the bar.

Suspect No. 1 is standing at a long bar lined with people, several on stools. In his hand is a glass of water in which ice cubes tinkle. 'What'll ya have?'

If he's going to keep his head clear, I'm going to clear mine. 'Whisky and Lemsip.'

He hee-haws. 'Doubt they do that. Have a look-see.' Sounding like the Merryweather of my mind, he hands me a stiff red card headed 'Popular Drinks made with Scotch Whisky'.

Judging by the number of delegates clamouring to be served by two tartan-waistcoated waiters, there'll be plenty of time to make a selection.

A banner – 'The World of Whisky' in white capitals on dark blue plastic – stretches out behind the mirrored bar above a wide cream ledge stacked from end to end with differently labelled bottles.

My eyes run through lethal-sounding concoctions like Horse's Neck, Whisper, Earthquake, stop at Bannockburn which lists scotch (for Scottish spirit) and tomato juice (for English blood) with a slice of this and a dash of that.

Wigmore points further down and laughs again. 'That's appropriate.'

'Hot Toddy,' I read. 'Fine,' I say, smiling faintly.

What with language difficulties and bulk orders going on room bills and subsequently expenses, there's ample time to survey the scene.

Having sat down all day, nearly all of the delegates have opted to stand around the bar. Only a few sit on sofas and single seats in a cosy lounge with tartan curtains and matching fabric in panels on darkly stained wooden walls. All up to standard, I'd say.

I try to calm myself, lest I start thinking out loud, fatal with Wigmore beside me; attempt to slow down my churning mind, but fail. For safety's sake I allow one rant to be replaced by another.

What a doddle of a job, eh? Corner shops may be putting up their shutters because of out-of-town malls. High Street chains are being downsized – chilling word, that – putting up 'Sale' signs and then 'For Sale' signs.

One shop that will never close is the talking shop. They're springing up all over, the great growth industry, consultants who couldn't hack it in their chosen professions on speaking tours, charging the earth; talks about talks subsidised by us taxpayers forking out for hotel and drinks bills.

When the Wall came down, you'd have thought civil defence planners who spent forty-five years talking among themselves

167

about nuclear attacks that never came would be stood down. Not a bit of it. Overnight, they became emergency planners talking among themselves about civil disasters like air and rail crashes, as if they'd just discovered them. Stop meeting your mates on a freebie? Perish the thought. Dale, whose place I've taken, spends half his life at junkets like this.

The only two people actually working for their living, earning their corn, in this entire room are the two hard-pressed waiters.

Perish these thoughts, too, and get back to business, I urge myself.

Kenton has made his customary appearance, sitting on a stool, laughing heartily through cigar smoke at the centre of a large, mainly female, group. Allen must still be hiding and Irene resting, because they aren't around.

Before I can even take a bored guess at the royals who adorn the wall, one of the real workers is heading towards us, ignoring customers leaning across the bar, calling, 'Thank you' and 'Please.'

Wigmore has a ten-pound note in his hand, holding it in the air, like a referee with a red card. He passes it over a shoulder in front of him. 'Hot Toddy and another Perrier, please. And keep the change.'

The waiter takes the note and turns to the shelf to switch on a kettle of water. Out the corner of his mouth, Wigmore explains, 'A trick I learned in crowded clubs.'

With so many people around us, I'm still sticking to safe subjects. 'You married?' It comes out bluntly.

'No, no.' He's slightly flustered. 'I have a . . . I . . .' He stretches out the consonant and I am expecting 'lady', but 'lover' comes out.

I tell him of my domestic set-up until the water is boiled and poured over sugar, with a large Grants added, half a lemon squeezed in and then the whole lot stirred with a silver spoon.

Warm glass in hand, I lead the way from the bar, but the few delegates that are seated are widely scattered and there's no table free that's completely out of earshot.

I walk into the lobby, on to the almost empty Tudor Room next door, and take one of three seats round a low table near the opened door with a view of the comings and goings in the foyer.

'Good health,' says Wigmore, raising his glass towards me as he sits. We both sip.

Warm air wafts up my nose. A sting hits the back of my throat; strong and sharp. My throat is soothed and soon my stomach gently warmed.

'I've been poking around.' I smile salaciously, close to sadistically. 'You too?'

He colours slightly. 'Look. I am sorry about that. I was watching John's back, that's all.'

'Any joy?' I ask, hoping he'll misunderstand.

True to form, he does. 'She holds no interest for me. Not like that.' He looks at me, almost affectionately, telling me – well, what?

Is he gay? Why did he say lover instead of lady? Does it matter? Yes, it does. Homosexuality and spying go back a long way. Musters and Wigmore may not trip off the tongue like Burgess and Maclean, but you have to think about it.

There's time enough as Wigmore recounts in detail what Irene told him. It's far less than she told me. No surprise. MI5 may be great watchers and analysers, but they're so inept at interrogation for evidential proof that, in my jaundiced view, they couldn't grill bacon.

I open a new front. 'Have you checked with your office lately?'

He nods. 'To tell them about Musters.'

'Caused a panic, I'll bet.'

A disappointed expression. 'They didn't seem that fussed.'

Well, they wouldn't be. They know his whereabouts from Bonn. 'Speak to Merryweather?'

'Out still.'

Up here, I'm sure, and they're still cutting him out. At least I've been told Beamish is dead. He's not even privy to that.

'How about the Central Office of Information?'

'Eh?'

'Well, Beamish's cover is CoI and yours is Heritage.'

'Oh.' He sees what I'm driving at. 'Our visiting cards give their addresses but the phone numbers on them come straight into our office. No messages from him on either.'

Short of new ideas, I go silent.

Short of a new subject, he returns to an old one. 'I'm sorry I didn't tell you about John and Irene.'

I wave away his apology. 'It doesn't matter.'

'How did you find Allen?' he asks.

I try a lazy smile, not difficult, beginning to feel exhausted. 'Only by talking the password out of him.'

He laughs, a trifle shyly. 'Sorry about that, too. Amazing, aren't they, these turned Joes? They become converts to security.'

Like health freaks who've given up cigarettes, I suppose, and can smell their stale smoke a mile off.

He is looking at me attentively. 'Hope you don't think that was my idea.'

'Why Henry Caxton?' I ask.

He shrugs a Don't know. 'He just blurted it. I was humouring him. Got to nursemaid your informants, haven't you?'

'He calls you captain.'

'Ah.' He's distinctly embarrassed now. 'John mentioned my old rank when we were putting him through the hoop.'

I wonder about his army service – communications, Ulster – and wonder, too, knowing what's at his left armpit under his pin-striped jacket, if he was SAS. It's just the way that he says a lot, but none of it means much, never criticises or questions orders, accepts everything with unflappable resignation.

I give him a summary of what Allen said, concluding, 'All a waste of time.'

We review our inquiries so far, he beginning with his supposed tour round other hotels last evening. Worryingly, he knows all their names and whereabouts, but then again he covered the same ground this morning.

I go further back. 'When did you first realise that Musters might be coming here?'

'John was called in and tasked by the major on Sunday . . .'

The day after Fräulein Falke's team homed in on the name of Maurer in the preliminary list of delegates, so Bonn must have tipped off London.

'. . . and he came straight round to my place to brief me.'

He's going into great detail about how he and Beamish enrolled for the conference, booked their hotel rooms and laid on their transport and plans, but I am hardly listening.

I look around at the paintings on the wall and remember others I have seen in rooms I've visited, not always by invitation; whose rooms they were and what I learned in them.

A bubble is developing inside me, like gripe, as if I'd drunk something ice cold and sweetly fizzy instead of warm and soothing, and it's uncomfortable.

Through the opened doors I see Lord Kenton waddling unhurriedly across the lobby, stopping to talk to Simon from registration, heads close together.

Finally the bubble bursts and I feel light-headed with relief.

'What now?' Wigmore asks.

'More calls for me, I'm afraid.' I empty my glass.

He picks it up. 'Another?'

I shake my head.

It is an inside job and I need to stay sober to prove it.

18.30 hours

A deliberate dawdle across the quiet foyer pretending to be hunting for something in the pink folder allows time for Kenton to free himself with his usual hearty parting. He overtakes me. 'Can I have a quick word, please?' I ask across my shoulder.

'Had better be.' With a chummy smile he slows but doesn't stop; his routine for his retinue, of which he clearly regards me as a part.

'Bruges,' I say, falling into steady step. 'The lady in the bath.'

'Denise Albert, the PR girl,' he replies immediately.

I'm not sure if he has an old politician's knack of remembering names, or only those of women he's supposedly slept with. 'Did you know her well?'

He stares fixedly ahead of him, his chummy smile gone. He lengthens his stride into a march. 'Follow me, please.'

A small gathering of guests waits for the lifts. 'Off to say your prayers,' says a smiling Englishman with a name tag that identifies him as a Sir and a tourist board chief.

'Ha, ha,' Kenton responds with an insincere smile, not at all amused.

The lift arrives. The door opens. We crowd in. 'Top, please,' says Kenton to the passenger who has elected himself button pusher.

'Nearer my God to thee,' pipes the tourist chief, who clearly knows Kenton well enough to make mock of his picture at prayer in *Talking Points*.

'Dreadful, wasn't it?' Kenton agrees over several heads. 'I'm having a new one taken, a more scenic snap, I hope.'

There's a bit more banter till the lift half empties at red, a few complaints about *Talking Points* which doesn't appear to be highly rated in the trade, until everyone else gets out at green.

'Prat,' growls Kenton as the doors slide shut on his titled

172

tormentor. The two of us continue the trip in silence, Kenton's simmering, not having enjoyed being a figure of fun. The button with the dwarf green bowman pings and lights up. The doors open.

The décor of the corridor is a surprise, no Robin and his merry men in Lincoln green. The walls are shades of sand and green, no more than tints, and the colours are separated with a foot-high border that runs the whole length of the corridor. On the edges, top and bottom, are strangely shaped animals. In between are little bowmen and swordsmen, and bigger horsemen who look like circus acts in dotted costume.

A reproduction in miniature of the Bayeux Tapestry, I realise, so this is the Norman floor. Must be. Normans, then Planta-genets, Lancaster and York with rooms for the Tudors and Stuarts below. All the royal houses from the time the castle was built until it was destroyed after the Civil War. Wigmore was right. It is clever.

A surge of pleasure swells through me. All at once everything seems to be panning out.

Half-way down the corridor, Kenton stops. He unlocks the door and ushers me into what looks to be, as Jacko speculated at lunchtime, the honeymoon suite. The separate sitting-room is spacious with a dark three-piece, a much bigger writing table than normal, a coffee table with a white phone and a cut-glass vase filled with spring flowers, a TV in one corner, a small, well-stocked bar in another and a door half open on to a room with a four-poster bed. The management have done him proud, a thank-you, I conjecture, for bringing in so much trade.

He locks the door behind me. 'What do you mean by that?' It's almost a snarl.

I turn. 'Sorry?'

His face is decidedly unfriendly. 'Downstairs. What do you mean? Did I know the Albert girl well?'

A wrong chord has been struck, but I'm stuck with it. 'Exactly that.'

'What have you heard?' Kenton, expression thunderous now, doesn't wait for a reply. 'I know damn fine what you've heard. Just because I enjoy young company, certain people have me sleeping with them all.'

There's no invitation to sit down. He stands there, facing me, broad shoulders braced, almost toe to toe, close enough to see grey bristles in amongst a five o'clock shadow that has taken the shine off his face. There's no longer a trace of aftershave, just cigar smoke on his breath. He is looking his age.

Lapsing into traces of his native accent, he launches into a rant more paranoid than my private one in the lift and foyer. 'Enemies out to destroy me rob me of my position . . .'

The attack becomes personal. 'Wish I'd never helped you. Should have only dealt with Merryweather or Beamish. What are you playing at?'

Again, there's no time for an answer; just as well because I can't think of one.

'I know your game. Vetting me, aren't you? Looking for scandal.'

He pauses to permit time for a baffled headshake. 'Not at all.'

'If it comes out that I helped you lot in my union days, it will finish me. There's lots of leftie hot-heads, you know, still waiting in the wings. Think what the press will make of it. Think of the damage it will do. There aren't many of us with experience in government, you know.'

He grumbles on about maybe Harold Wilson getting it right after all; maybe the security services always have been opposed to democratically elected governments of the left.

The self-opinionated old fart, I think, quite staggered by his onslaught. Sixty-five and he believes he will form part of the next Labour government. Not in the cabinet, of course. Even New Labour won't have an unelected peer as a cabinet minister, but as under-secretary of this or minor minister of that, perhaps, answering questions in a reformed Lords.

He's so far up his own backside that he can't see what a daydreaming egotist he has become. He just can't give up the spotlight, the issuing of orders, the chauffeured car. There's nothing more pathetic, I reflect, than a man of the people who's fallen in love with the trappings of power.

'Now,' he says, 'if you want to know something, don't keep sidling up to me with trick questions in public. Make an appointment and ask me openly but privately. That's the standard procedure, isn't it?'

I've worked him out now. He thinks my presence here today

is a sort of on-the-spot vetting of his fitness to return to the corridors of Whitehall.

Not finished yet, he recaps on his proven record of patriotism stretching from the sixties to yesterday. 'Pleased enough for my help then, Beamish was.' His soft hands are waving in front of his chest. 'Oh, yes.

'And you . . .' He jabs out a podgy finger. '. . . helped you, didn't I, at lunchtime, answered all your questions?'

How do I play this when I do get a word in? I begin to fret. The bell from the white telephone on the coffee table puts the decision on hold.

He turns away, walks rather heavily, drained by his anger, to it, snatches it up and puts it to his mouth with a gruff, rude, 'Yes.'

There's a short pause, then another 'Yes' and longer pause while he listens.

Not wanting to be accused of eavesdropping, on top of everything else, I seek sanctuary by gazing round the room, spot yet another painting on the wall furthest away and stroll to it without much enthusiasm.

'Not there, no,' grunts Kenton. 'Out of the question.'

The picture shows one posse of sword-waving horsemen chasing another armed with lances up a slope towards a castle on a hilltop, too gentle a slope to be Nottingham.

'Better,' Kenton pronounces. 'On the gun emplacement, perhaps, overlooking the city. First thing tomorrow?' Something said draws an 'Oh' from him. He goes quiet again.

In the short silence I read the framed caption: 'Battle of Lincoln – 1141. Royal troops desert King Stephen as rebels advance with swords drawn intent on close quarter combat rather than a joust with lowered lances.'

'Simon should have,' says Kenton doubtfully, then, firmer: 'Must have by now.' A short pause. 'In the foyer then.' Another pause. 'Outside the castle gates then, if you like. In half an hour; say three-quarters.' He hangs up and returns to me. 'Well?'

Well? I ask myself. Drawn swords for close combat, or a playful joust? Go for it, I decide. You've nothing to lose. If you're wrong, it can't get worse. 'Did you ever sleep with Denise Albert?'

He gathers in so much air that his chest puffs out. 'No.' The air comes out in a strong sound-wave. 'Now . . .'

I shake my head vigorously to tell him: It's still my turn. 'The night before she died?'

He has the open-mouthed, stunned, disbelieving look of a world heavyweight champion who's been hit on the nose by a no-hoper. 'Most certainly not.'

'Did you see her socially?'

'For a drink, yes.' He is shaking his head, trying to get his senses back. 'But I don't see . . .'

'And escorted her to her room afterwards?'

'Cert . . .' He stops in mid-word. 'Well.' His guard crumbles. 'Well, we went up together in the lift. A few of us did. We were on the same floor. But I didn't go in, most certainly not. She was tired.' He hurriedly adds, 'We were both tired.' He collects himself for a counter-attack. 'Who's been telling . . .?'

'Thank you, sir,' I butt in.

'But . . .'

Now I have him in disarray, I'm not going to stop. 'You obviously knew Denise Albert well enough to tell me if she was present at the last night dinner in Bruges.'

His face twists. 'Of course she wasn't.'

'Why so sure?'

'Haven't you read up on it?'

Time to back pedal. 'I was only assigned to this case today.'

He tuts. 'She was due at the dinner. She didn't take her place. A friend became worried because she'd been off colour all day.'

She would be, I acknowledge, having just emptied her bank accounts to pay back Musters the money he gave her for eighties secrets, rooked for every rotten franc she'd got.

'The friend went to her room, knocked, got no reply, but heard a noise. Help was summoned. A porter opened the door. He went in and found Denise. It should be well documented.'

'What time was that?'

'Eight, give or take a minute or two either side.'

'While you were having your photo taken by Allen?' I prompt. Witnessed by Wigmore, I remind myself privately.

Kenton nods at the phone. 'Let's hope he makes a better job of it tonight.'

He doesn't explain further, just gets back to where he left off.

176

'But, of course, the news was held back for some while, till after the dinner, and it was only the following day as we were leaving that we heard it was an accidental fall.'

'I see.' I lapse into thought.

'If that's it . . .' Kenton turns away from me stroppily. '. . . I have to spruce myself up.'

I don't move. 'Tell me, in your early union days and when you were an MP, did you read the old *Daily Worker*?'

He swings back, squaring up. 'What are you driving at now?' He's wagging his finger, back in charge. 'Now, see here. I was carefully vetted; dozens of times, formally and officially. If for one moment . . .'

'Did you see any contributions in it from Allen?'

'No.' A puzzled face, confused by the different directions from which the questions are coming. 'I knew, of course, that Allen used to be far left, but then so were many graduates in those days.'

'Me, too,' I break in, giving him an encouraging smile. 'In my youth.'

He shrugs, weakening. 'And me, I suppose, before being in government and seeing the state of the economy, the damage inflation was doing.'

So, yes, he agrees, relaxing slightly, he did read the *Worker* regularly to see what red-dominated unions were getting up to, and yes, he did use it for press releases in his days as a full-time union official in the Post Office. 'Had to. The Tory press always ganged up on us.'

I bide my time through another little rant with the twin targets of the Tory press and trade unionists who never grew up in the seventies and brought down his government.

He gets back to Allen. 'Sound enough now, I would have thought, unless you know better.'

I work my chin into a 'No'. 'How long have you known him?'

'Ten years, a bit longer. Came to me with his magazine idea when the conference circuit was beginning to build up.'

Talking Points, he explains at some length, was originally established as a workers' co-operative. 'Allen wanted me to put up some money. Didn't, of course, but I've helped him all I can since in other ways.'

I let him harp on (no choice really) about the shortcomings of

177

management by co-op committee, while I think on. So, when Allen couldn't raise the money to set up a workers' co-op, Musters staked him with Stasi cash and Kenton pushed lots of adverts his way.

'What was the *Worker*'s address?' I ask.

A frown. 'Farringdon something. Street or Road.'

I introduce a final loose end. 'This 10 a.m. message that Beamish . . .'

'No sign of him yet then?'

I shake my head.

'Aren't you concerned?'

'That's the sole reason I'm here. Nothing to do with vetting, official or unofficial.' I pause, watching some of the anxiety and anger slip from his face, then resume, 'The message Beamish left for you. According to your clerk on registration, Beamish didn't phone it in personally. Someone else did, on his behalf. Not an English accent. Faintly German, perhaps. Did you see him talking to any Germans yesterday?'

'Why?'

'Because there was a possibility Beamish may have gone off chasing some lead on Musters and we're worried about him.'

He thinks before he speaks. 'The only German I saw him talking to yesterday afternoon was from their Football Association. Chap about your size.'

Altmann, I think, whose shirt I'm wearing. I nod. 'You've been very helpful.'

He gives me a long, serious look. 'You have a very strange way of going about your business, Mr Todd.'

'It's a strange business we're in, sir,' I reply truthfully.

'I'll second that.' He smiles, declaring a truce. 'All right if I have my bath now?'

I'd like to smile back and say, 'Lock your door – we've already lost two that way' and to report here 'collapse of stout party', but I've upset him enough.

Waiting for the lift, I pull *Talking Points* out of its, by now, rather dog-eared folder. A flick through finds the piece on the castle.

Descending, I read up on Mortimer's Hole and how the

Roundheads broke through the rock half-way down to create a platform for a cannon in the Civil War.

All the phones beneath the stairs are free. I call Bingham, burying my head deep into the soundproof hood above the box to drown the laughter floating across the foyer from the 'World of Whisky' where happy hour is well warmed up.

When Malloy comes on, I go straight in, in the mood. 'Tell me, when did Major Merryweather first hear that Musters might be coming here?'

There's an intake of breath and a longish pause. 'I don't really know.'

'Well, ask him,' I say perkily. 'He's sitting next door, isn't he?'

Mumbled conversation before Malloy clears her throat. 'A week ago tomorrow – late. Why?'

I tell her why and where I'm going and what my plan is. 'Fix that for me, will you, with whoever is in charge?'

'Right away,' she agrees enthusiastically. 'Want that back-up now?'

'I've got back-up of my own. Can I tell him now?'

'Even so,' she says slowly, deliberately ignoring my question, 'there's still a gun missing.'

Leave it to her, I decide. She knows what I'm doing and where I'll be. 'Remind me, what Queen of England had a deformity – a toe missing or something?'

'Oh, Sweeney.' She uses my nickname, with an exasperated sigh, for the first time all day. 'Not at a time like this, please. Not now.'

I tell her I've assured Wigmore that she, whose second-best subject was history, would have the answer and a double malt is riding on it.

She sighs again. 'None, as far as I know. Anne Boleyn reportedly had a sixth finger on her left hand.'

'That'll do. Thanks.'

'Anything else you need?' she asks, sounding deeply worried.

I repeat my question. 'Can I tell him now?'

'One second,' she says.

I wait around thirty seconds through a distant consultation I can't hear. 'Yes,' she finally agrees. 'Anything else I can do?'

179

'Well . . .' I'm going to assign Malloy to the worst job of the day. 'Give Em a ring, will you, and tell her to start the baked halibut without me.'

'Christ, Sweeney. Anything else?' she asks.

'Got to dash,' I reply, hanging up, allowing no time for more questions, giving her something to worry about for a change, the manipulative bitch.

Back in the deserted Tudor Room, I sit down and quietly break the news to Wigmore that his partner and mentor is dead, murdered.

To paper over an almost seven-hour delay, I jerk my thumb at the phones and say, 'Just confirmed,' but he's not really listening. He's so stunned his questions are few and my answers short.

Now he seems to be smiling, but it's one of those faint, uncomprehending smiles, blue eyes glistening, at a fond memory of him, perhaps, the beginnings of grief, and I'll not add to it by making this briefing too detailed.

19.00 hours

Wigmore slides his room key across the polished counter towards the approaching Becky, who seems somewhat careworn at the end of a nine-hour shift.

Know the feeling, I think sympathetically.

He turns to me, face grave and pale. 'Is this going to be a long stake-out?'

I shrug uncertainly.

'In that case . . .' Becky has reached us and he addresses her. '. . . can we borrow that again?' He gestures to the hotel wheelchair.

She looks nonplussed; no surprise. We've been in and out of the bloody thing all day. The wonder is that she doesn't ask: 'Ever thought of buying one yourself?'

From somewhere deep inside himself he dredges up that lovable labrador face, making his request almost impossible to refuse. 'Just for a short spin.'

Becky smiles wearily, doesn't ask for his room number again and, still standing, taps her keyboard to log it out.

I push my folder across the counter. 'And take care of this for me, will you?' It was a bit like parting with a favourite woolly jumper to a Christian Aid collector.

Wigmore climbs into the chair, tucks the blanket round his legs, and, leaning forward, speeds down a tiled gangway across the foyer. There's nothing of the gleeful overgrown schoolboy about him this evening, just grim determination.

Elbows pumping like pistons, he's well ahead of me through the automatic doors and down the outside ramp. Beneath it, Musters' hired Astra is still parked.

Going down Standard Hill, he rides on the brakes. On the curved uphill path to the gatehouse I catch up and push.

The sun has gone. A nip in the air preludes an overnight frost.

A man in a black uniform on the lighted gatehouse greets us with, 'Been expecting you,' and gives directions up a path neither of us took at lunchtime; straight ahead and steep.

Wigmore swivels round in the chair. 'What's the major's plan?'

Actually, it's mine, but I'll let it go. 'To get close and listen for as long as possible. Move only when we have to.'

The path turns sharp left at three circular flower beds set in a grass bank. No tourists wander. 'Can't we bug it?' he asks.

'No time,' I reply.

At the bottom of two flights of steps, with stone bird-baths on retaining walls, Wigmore gets out and walks up, but leaves me to lift and carry the chair. All he carries is the blanket.

At the top of the stairs, he resumes his seat with a preoccupied 'Thank you' and tucks himself up again.

An asphalt path flanked by heavily pruned sycamore trees runs the length of the eastern side of the floodlit ducal palace, giving a close-up view of the fussy, Flemish-style stonework and a statue beneath the flat terraced roof of a man on a horse, both, disturbingly, headless.

Wigmore doesn't look up, just talks ahead of himself. 'Why doesn't Merryweather let us take him in and give him to the analysers?'

Because, I think sourly, those desk jockeys have had the answer staring up from the paperwork all week and missed it, but to say so gives too much away. 'It's very thin, conjecture mainly, and, unless he's offered a deal, he might not co-operate.'

'Do you think the major will make him an offer?' asks Wigmore.

I don't really want to answer this, so concentrate on the building. The main door is small, wooden and mushroom-coloured, anything but a grand entrance. That apart, the palace is as good as anything in my native Derbyshire, the shire of stately homes.

'Do you?' Wigmore does want an answer.

'Not if I can help it,' I finally reply. 'I want the bastard in court.'

'Doubt you'll get that,' says Wigmore sorrowfully. 'Not with all this dirty washing.'

You don't know the half yet, matey, of what's going to be laundered in public, I think, if I have my way.

At the southern end, the path opens out in a wide slabbed terrace with the white flag-pole we saw from below – taller than the palace itself.

The view from here is panoramic, but hardly spectacular – a mishmash of roofs and chimneys and pylons, the soccer stadium's floodlights among them, from industries that sprang up on the once green fields of the Meadows. It's too heavily built up to permit a sight of the river and get a bearing on Farringdon Street where it ended yesterday for Beamish.

Another attendant in a black uniform waits at a black gate tipped with spikes in the stone wall that surrounds the terrace. He reads our badges, concentrating on mine.

'It's open,' he says, pulling back the gate to prove it. 'So's all the other doors. All lights are on. That's what your boss requested, right?'

'What other doors?' I ask, disturbed.

'There's two or three on the way down, plus the bottom entrance, but . . .'

Wigmore breaks in, rather rudely. 'Where's that?'

'Street level, of course,' he replies testily. He looks at Wigmore, but addresses me. 'He won't be able to manage it in that.'

Both of us grin knowingly at each other, close to smirks. 'Thank you, sir,' says Wigmore condescendingly.

'You won't be able to get out the bottom till the other key comes back when the rest arrive.' The attendant is understandably irked at our self-satisfied smiles. 'Leave you to it, then.' He turns away in a huff.

I look at Wigmore. Both our smiles have gone. I walk as fast as I can to catch up with the attendant. 'I don't quite follow what you just said.'

He doesn't slow down or look round. 'You've got a big party coming, haven't you? From your conference?'

I reply with two quick nods.

'They're coming up that way for the lecture in here.' He motions with his left hand towards the palace. 'Your clerk's got the key – collected this afternoon – to let them in and guide them up.'

I ask him to describe the clerk.

Young, tall, fair-haired, he answers. Simon, I think. Shit. It explains Kenton's reference to him, of course, in that overheard phone call, but again I think: Shit. A flaw has been exposed in the planning. 'What's down there?'

He rattles it off, the product of numerous guided tours each day. Loads of steps, steep tunnels and half-way down an open platform, the roof knocked away during the Civil War for a gun emplacement. 'He'll never make it in a wheelchair, you know.' Now he looks at me with a hurt expression. 'I was only trying to help.'

I tell him I'm sure he was, politely thank him and turn back some distance short of the mushroom-coloured door.

Reaching the southern terrace, I slow from stroll to dawdle to full stop as Wigmore steps, stiff leg first, out of the chair and, raising his good leg to hip height, rests it on the stone wall beside the opened gate. With a mighty heave, all of him rises in slow motion into the air, squats on top of the wall, then drops with his bad leg on a narrow grassy bank on the other side.

'Here,' he calls, not looking behind him. 'Have a shufty at this.'

Stupid bastard, I chafe, breaking into a trot. Fancy going in search of Plantagenet broom for his mum on a stake-out.

I don't try to copy his climb. Instead, I put my back to the wall, hutch myself up into a sitting position and swing my stiff leg over first.

I follow him into a thicket of young sycamores, ash and maple trees that falls away, sharply and alarmingly, into . . . what? . . . impossible to tell from here, thin air, by the looks of it.

When I struggle up alongside him, almost out of breath, he is standing in a straggly bed of wild ivy, pointing down through the last line of saplings.

All I can see is that we are on the very edge of a very long drop. My lord. I try to catch my breath, can't.

He grips my upper arm, not too tightly. Dear lord. Panic charges through me.

I've misread it, him – yet again. Fucked it up. Totally. He's going to push me, push me over the top. Make it look like an accident. Because I got too close to a truth I failed to fully work out.

Christ. It's him. It is him. Since lunchtime I've sensed it. Those two whiskies addled your brain, put you off the scent.

You've no proof, no evidence. You admitted as much yourself; just a hunch, a wrong hunch, and you've walked into a traitor's trap, face to face with a man you're convinced is SAS trained. Get your strike in first, an inner voice orders.

I flex my knees, setting feet firmly and wide apart in the undergrowth, lowering my centre of gravity, as ready as I ever will be for the life or death struggle that's bound to come.

As casually as I can, I move my right arm slowly across my midriff. My hand just touches the back of his, ready to grip his wrist, step a pace back and try to throw him over my good leg; unconcerned where or how far he falls; his problem.

That pace back now, slowly, every sense on full alert, every sinew tensed.

A false step, I realise immediately. Disaster. My heel is caught up in something as strong as wire. All of me is pitched backwards. Lost it. I've lost it. Done for.

A grip like a vice now on my bicep, hurting me. 'Steady, old man.'

Our eyes meet across our shoulders. His are wary, but concerned. He relaxes his hold.

My eyes disengage downwards and on to Allen and Kenton walking side by side from the direction of the well-lit, white-walled corner of the Trip to Jerusalem.

'They're using the bottom entrance,' says Wigmore quietly but urgently into my left ear. 'And we're uncovered at ground level.'

Much more than a flaw, a gaping hole, appears in the plan now. Panic of a different sort now, for an operation going wrong.

Kenton stops to talk to a group with guidebooks – delegates, I presume, returning to the hotel, but I can't be sure from this distance with this obstructed view.

Allen walks on ahead, camera hanging from a cord round his neck, something silver swinging in his left hand.

'Where will the entrance be?' I wonder out loud.

'Directly below or thereabouts,' Wigmore ventures. 'Let's take a bearing.' He looks out from the thicket across the road to a long red-brick Victorian building with identical spires in a grey slate roof. Then, urgently, 'Come on.'

He lets go of my arm and leaves my side. I about-turn slowly, head down, careful where I put my feet.

185

At last, it's safe to look up. He is threading his way, sure-footed as a mountain guide, back through the thicket. 'I'll cover that end,' he calls, climbing the wall. 'It's downhill all the way.'

By the time I'm off the bank, over the wall and back on the terrace, he's reached the end of the path beside the eastern front of the palace. He straightens his hunched shoulders, steps forward out of the chair before it stops. Carrying it high and in front of him, he sinks rapidly from sight down the stone steps.

A steep flight of stone stairs leads down from the black gate, fenced on either side, the last few steps overhung by thick green ivy.

A barred arched door is pushed open. Lamps on the dark brown ceiling and walls bathe another flight of stairs in yellow. They're steeper still, like going down into a ship's hold, depths all different, hard going.

A subterranean tunnel now, feet crunching on grit which has flaked off walls six feet apart. There's plenty of headroom, two feet to spare, and the rock is firm enough to hold up the roof without supports.

A seaside smell from the damp sand fills my nostrils. It's comfortably warm, but that could be me in a sweat.

A hairpin bend and then the tunnel seems to corkscrew dizzily into the bowels of the earth, following the face of the cliff, it seems, only a few yards inside it.

All of a sudden, natural but fast-fading light and I step out into fresh air.

The Roundheads' gun emplacement is a platform twelve yards long cut out of rock. At the far end the path burrows back into the massive face of sandstone.

On the high back wall are semicircular indentations made, I guess, by Cavalier cannon-balls.

Just two steps from that is a wall of irregular height, face high at the far end, chest high this end, directly in front of me.

On top of it is not so much a ledge as a narrow bank overgrown with rough grass, moss and creeping plants. Beyond that, a sheer drop of sixty feet or so.

I look over the wall and down on the view I had seen from above. The Victorian building with double spires is much closer.

186

I worry about Beamish's missing gun, comfort myself with the thought that Malloy's back-up will be just across the road and Wigmore will soon be here.

Voices echo from the tunnel at the far end of the platform, distantly at first, getting closer all the time, Kenton grumbling. Heavy breathing and heavy footsteps are all I can hear now above the noise of the traffic from the street below.

I step back into the yellowy shadows.

Nothing is said until they regain their breath. Then Kenton begins to grumble again, this time about the view. 'No real landmarks,' he complains. 'Dreadful backdrop.'

Allen complains about the light.

Shuffling footsteps. 'Try here,' Allen says. 'Fold your arms.' Click. Flash. Whirr. 'Look away.' Click. Flash. Whirr. 'Now at me.'

Kenton again. 'What about that distant skyline – those wooded hills and the church tower? That's rather nice.'

'Too far away.' A tinny scraping. 'Perch yourself up here.'

'Arghhhhh.' Hollow steps, just two or three, and a grunting sound.

'At me.' Click. Flash. Whirr. 'Head to your right.' Click. 'Further.' He sounds disconsolate. 'Too near.'

Kenton, brightly: 'Isn't that white building that lovely head-quarters at the university? Can you get that in?'

'Let's see,' says Allen above more tinny scraping.

A long silence is broken only by Kenton's cautious 'Careful'.

Click. Flash. Whirr. 'Fine. Better.' Then: 'Lean out a bit more.'

It's not what I hoped for, none of it.

But it's dangerous ground this, for everybody. I dare lie in wait no longer.

I step out on to the platform. From the tunnel at the other end Wigmore silently emerges. His face is tense but unreddened by his long uphill climb, his breathing normal.

Kenton is seated on the grass bank. On the stone floor below him a set of three aluminium steps are folded out.

He's leaning out at five to the hour, close to overbalancing; a heart-stopping sight. Wigmore moves soundlessly with his back

187

to the rear rock wall and takes him by an elbow. 'Don't move,' he says very softly.

Allen sits, legs crossed, higher up the grassy ledge. He lowers his camera from eye level with both hands, holds it to his chest and stares at me vacantly.

'Don't move either,' I say.

No one moves while I choose between a sword drawn for verbal combat, straight in and at him, frightening the truth out of him, or tactical fencing with words, hoping his guard slips.

19.30 hours

'Gordon Allen.' My steely tone. 'I am arresting you for complicity in the murder of John Beamish yester . . .'

'No, no, no,' groans Allen, clutching his camera tightly.

'Imposs . . .' Kenton tries to say.

'Honestly.' Allen, his face in agony, has that Merseyside whine to his voice, higher pitched than normal.

Kenton manages, '. . . ible.'

'Quiet,' snaps Wigmore, gripping Kenton's elbow tighter, pulling him upright.

A pause, a silence so deafening that, for me, it blocks out all street sounds.

'Already dead when I got there, he was,' Allen gasps. He signals surrender, a complete and immediate cave-in, by lowering his chin-strap beard. 'Honestly.'

'What? Dead?' Kenton, incredulous. 'When? How?'

Wigmore tilts his upper body towards him, alarming in view of Kenton's still precarious position. 'I said shut up.'

Not bad questions, though, simple and direct, I have to concede. The new caution I've used so infrequently is recited parrot-fashion, along with the usual rights to a solicitor. Then, relaxing, already half-way home, I add, 'Start with yesterday.'

Musters came to his room, Allen begins, at barely above a whisper. He reports his greeting, 'Good to see you again.'

Allen, huddled, cowered, on his knees, wears a tortured expression to indicate it was anything but good for him.

He starts to tell his story in quotes. 'I find myself out of money,' Musters said. 'Can you help, say, with twenty-five thousand pounds?'

'Out of the question,' replied Allen. 'All I've got is an overdraft.'

'Well, think about it,' said Musters. 'If you want to retain your reputation and stay in business. You know what I mean.' He went away.

Allen knew what he meant: exposure of his own eighties dealings with Musters, the names he'd given him, the Stasi money he had taken. He thought about it and went to see John Beamish in the hotel and told him everything from yesterday back to the eighties.

'Good,' enthused Beamish. 'Leave it with me. I'll arrange the money. You make the delivery. We'll pounce.'

He signed the indemnity absolving Allen from any financial loss, prosecution or publicity for helping the security service to nail Musters.

At five, Allen came out of the final session of the first day of the conference. A message was waiting for him behind the registration desk. 'Please come to Room 224 – John.'

It was Musters who opened the door to Beamish's room. He ushered Allen into the bathroom. Beamish lay under the water, dead.

'I couldn't speak, hardly move apart from trembling,' he says, trembling now.

'Scandalous,' Kenton interjects. 'Appalling.'

Allen ignores him and returns to the verbatim.

'Now you're going to help me get rid of him,' Musters told him.

'Madness,' Allen protested. 'You're mad. A member of the security service? You'll never get away with it.'

'A turncoat,' said Musters dully. 'A renegade, you mean.'

Wigmore works his chin and swallows.

They walked into the bedroom, Allen continues. On the green bedspread was a black pistol.

Hand on his lapel, covering his name tag, Wigmore opens the left side of his pin-striped jacket. 'Like this?'

Allen nods.

'Go on,' I say quietly.

'May I have a cigarette?' Allen asks me.

'Keep your hands where I can see them all the time,' Wigmore replies on my behalf. Left to me, I would have let him.

Allen cups the camera with both hands and goes on, unable to look at either of us, such a shameful secret about to be revealed.

190

'Musters told me that Beamish had been his best source for years,' he says with a deep sigh.

Wigmore grits his teeth. 'Lies,' snaps Kenton, his whole flabby frame appearing to wobble.

Allen looks at him rather pityingly. 'They'd worked out a foolproof system, he said. You gave MI5 reports from your scientists. Instead of weeding them, Beamish copied them, and made up the packages for him . . .' He nods down at Wigmore. '. . . to return to you to drop off at dead letter boxes. Correct?'

'I don't believe it,' blusters Kenton.

Allen ignores him, wanting it all off his chest. 'In case MI6 had a spy operating inside Stasi, Musters gave Bonn a code name that would point away from his source and to the courier – him.' Another nod at Wigmore.

'What was it?' Wigmore asks, barely able to talk.

'Flora.'

Wigmore doesn't even blanch.

Musters, Allen resumes, described how he fled with his files when the Wall came down and cleaned out a Stasi account in Dublin which funded a good life in Co. Cork for four years.

A year ago, running short of money, he returned to Dublin and, by telephoned arrangement, met up with Beamish, struggling financially on basic pay now that his cold war perk had ended. They hatched a plot to blackmail an academic, a woman, who'd been a paid contact in the geological field.

'They cleaned her out, then killed her, he said.'

'They?' queries Wigmore. 'Who?'

'He didn't say.'

It's obvious, I would have thought – Musters and Beamish.

'He just pointed to a picture on the wall' – the royal death mask, I recall – 'and said that was how she ended up. And he asked: "Do you want to finish up like that, too?"'

I nod him on, thinking: That, happily, would increase his cigarette consumption in Beamish's room.

Allen recounts how Musters described getting the body out of the hotel in Dublin in a wheelchair and throwing her in the river.

'And what about poor Denise in Bruges?' asks Kenton, unusually quietly for him.

'Same thing, but she struggled in the bath and shouted.

191

Beamish', he says, 'finished her off by dropping her hair-drier into the water.'

'So it wasn't an accidental fall after all.' Kenton closes his eyes, groans, sways slightly, and Wigmore, face impassive, grips him harder at the elbow, making him wince.

Nothing compared to the pain that Wigmore must be feeling inside, I acknowledge, the poor, loyal, betrayed sod.

I wonder momentarily whether to order both down and on to the stone floor, at the point of Wigmore's gun, if necessary, but don't want to interrupt the flow, break the spell. 'What happened then?'

Allen looks at me blankly. 'He didn't say. I don't know.'

I do. Then came the knock on the door by the worried dinner guest. They fled when the caller went away to get the porter, leaving the body behind. I ask if he originally introduced Denise Albert to Musters as a potential source.

'You mean,' says Kenton, face disbelieving, 'she was an enemy agent?' The enormity of it sinks in. 'My God.'

Allen ignores him, and claims not to have met her until three months ago in Bruges, repeating that he didn't know how she'd died until Musters told him.

'Then', I say slowly, 'why, in reporting her death in your current issue, did you used the word "shocking"?'

'Eh?'

'Shocking.' I cock my head. 'Electrocution.'

He's too wound up to see what I'm driving at. 'It's a usual word to describe a sudden death. Stunned, devastated, shocked. Means the same thing.' He looks at me pleadingly. 'Believe me.'

I'm not sure I do believe him. Some informers, either by auto-suggestion or deliberately to display their secret knowledge, too clever by half, reveal glimpses of their hidden lives now and then. Most pay dearly. Another task for Merryweather and his analysers, I decide, and I move him back to Nottingham.

On his arrival, Musters, Allen reports second-hand, told Beamish the target was Kenton. 'Out of the question,' replied Beamish. 'He was following MI5 orders. He's in the clear. We can't blackmail him. He'll go straight to the authorities.'

Kenton is nodding solemn agreement.

'They had a huge row about it, he said. Musters was desperate for money, so he asked if there was another target.'

192

'And Beamish suggested you?' I butt in.

Allen nods mournfully. 'Beamish knew I had no cash but he told Musters he'd get him . . .' He nods towards Kenton. '. . . to release twenty-five thousand from some special fund.'

'Outrageous,' chimes Kenton.

I can work out where his story is heading from here. Musters went to see Allen to activate the plot. Allen went running to Beamish, thinking he was doing the right thing. Beamish, posing as a good guy, made the arrangements.

He also arranged for Wigmore to go on a pointless trail around other hotels to make sure he didn't accidentally come across Musters at the Standard Hill.

'What happened last evening?' I ask.

Allen goes back a bit with more hearsay evidence. 'All day Musters was getting suspicious, felt Beamish was about to spring a double cross, shift all the blame on to him for Dublin and Bruges, refute all and any allegations Musters would make when he was caught. He feared capture, dreaded it. They had another row, worse, he said.'

'What about?' asks Wigmore.

'The fact that Beamish hadn't told him earlier that Lord Kenton wasn't a suitable target, the risk he'd run coming here and the money he'd spent. He thought Beamish was about to wash his hands of him.'

So Musters, I reflect, sneaked into Room 224 and drowned him. Just like that.

Allen looks at me with eyes that are more than defeated now – dead.

'And Musters told you all of this?' I ask. 'Why?'

'To frighten me, I suppose. Let me know how clever and ruthless he is. And he succeeded. He was boozed-up, boasting. He kept toying with the gun.'

Fingering his camera absent-mindedly, Allen returns to direct speech. 'Now, help me get rid of the body and earn yourself ten thousand or . . .'

He shrugs, and I make a stab at the rest. '"Or you'll go the same way," Musters said?'

Allen begins to talk very rapidly, almost gabbling. 'And he meant it. I could tell. He would have done it. He'd killed three times. Why not me?'

'You should have gone to him,' says Kenton sternly, craning towards Wigmore.

'I know,' Allen admits to his chest. 'But I didn't know who to trust any more.'

Must be hard in this game of double agent and triple cross, I have to concede, but that's the life they've all chosen and it's difficult to feel sorry for them. 'What did Musters tell you to do?'

'Carry out Beamish's briefing to the letter. Collect the money he'd arranged. Go to the castle and Musters would come to me and we'd split it.' A doubtful silence. 'Or so he said.'

He's got ahead of himself, so I haul him back to last evening.

'Well, what could I do?' he sighs. 'I hadn't killed him. Honestly. Took no part in it. Truthfully. I feared for my life. I thought that if I helped him he'd let me go.'

He could have walked into Central nick last night while Musters was with Irene but that would have meant passing up ten grand, I think cynically. 'What did you do?'

Went round to the Playhouse and stole the van, he confesses. When he got back Beamish was dressed in drag and sitting in a wheelchair. 'Musters was highly amused,' he adds. 'You know, we're dealing with a psycho here. He terrifies me.'

They got Beamish off the second floor via the service lift down to Musters' room on the ground, where they waited until the car-park was clear. Then they got him to the van.

Allen drove. 'Musters didn't know the way. He'd had too much to drink anyway.'

Their destination was the River Trent. They couldn't drop him off the bridge in rush-hour traffic. They got lost in side streets trying to find the river and ran into a traffic jam which a policeman was sorting out.

'Musters panicked,' Allen goes on. 'All that tough talk and he panicked. Me, too. It was only a matter of time before the policeman got round to us and realised that the van was stolen. We dumped him down a drain.'

'Remember the name of the street?' I ask casually.

'Will I ever forget?'

'Why?'

'Used to write regular letters to the *Worker* in my, er, student days. Seeing that street name plate, Farringdon Street, that along . . .' He stops to think.

194

I help him out. 'Along with seeing the picture hanging on the wall in Musters' room of that king reading the first printed proclamation from the presses of . . .'

He finishes it. 'Caxton. Oh, God. Is that what gave me away?'

Honest answer? Not really.

All I do know is that it helped me snap out of the tunnel vision I'd developed over Wigmore.

I don't know why Allen gave Wigmore the name of Caxton for the password. He probably doesn't himself. His mind still back in Farringdon Street, subliminally thinking of printing presses? Being clever?

But it made me start to suspect that at some time he had been in Musters' ground-floor room and seen that picture on the wall.

Mooching round the foyer, pining for a smoke, forced me to recall the stale smell of cigarettes on the blinds in Beamish's room.

Who else smoked cigarettes? Not Wigmore. Not Kenton, a cigar man. Irene, true, but she was in the clear for six last night. Fräulein Falke had a packet, but, these days, she's supposed to be on our side.

Maybe it was an inside job after all, but maybe I was homing in on the wrong insider. Since Beamish was dead and beyond questioning, I was forced to question myself. If it wasn't Wigmore, who helped Musters in Bruges?

Can't have been Allen, Wigmore, Irene or Kenton. They were all at the dinner. Only Beamish missed it.

Then I recalled what Fräulein Falke had told me. They only IDed Maurer as Musters a week ago. Merryweather via Malloy confirmed it.

Yet Beamish had drafted a report naming Irene as a known associate three months ago. So why hadn't Merryweather taken the simple, routine step of ordering a tap on Irene's phone? He should have known well before Bonn that Musters had called her to arrange a meeting here.

Why didn't he? Because he never knew. Because Beamish hadn't actually filed that report. He'd done what he'd been doing for years when feeding high-grade info to Musters, shuffled the paperwork, telling Wigmore one thing, doing the other.

So, yes, it was an inside job that explained Bruges, but left a question unresolved over Nottingham: Who helped Musters either kill or, at the very least, dispose of Beamish, and who hit me?

Kenton had an alibi in front of two hundred witnesses for four o'clock when I was whacked, plus Allen's recording of him talking.

But what, I asked myself, was to stop Allen turning on the tape and leaving it running?

So I pondered on Allen, put myself in his position. You've helped a foreign spy for years, taken his money. Now, you've helped him get rid of a murder victim. And that, I'm prepared to accept at this stage, is all he did, plus later trying to drown me.

You see the body in the bath, an armed and whisky-filled killer hovering over it, and the death mask on the wall. Is there any wonder his cigarette consumption went up in Room 224? You get the body downstairs and there, again on the wall, is the first royal scroll to come off Caxton's printing press. You have to abandon the body in Farringdon Street, a macabre reminder of your radical, idealistic youth.

At lunchtime, you go for a quiet snack, and what's on that bloody wall? One of Henry's wives with six fingers while the body in the bath only had four.

Everything is conspiring against you.

Is there any wonder that when Wigmore allowed him to pick a password he blurted, 'Henry Caxton'?

And it made me think, that's all; above all, about the money. I mean, come on, who's ever heard of a blackmail victim turning up at the pay-off with a camera and a tape? That's going to get you killed. It can't have been genuine. It had to be a set-up.

Yet, I'd missed it. I'm going to have to hope that others will, too.

'So what happened in Farringdon Street?' I ask.

They backed away from the traffic jam, Allen resumes, chin-strap beard almost on his chest, but only up a cul-de-sac. They were trapped in a dead end. They got out, saw the road-works barriers, pulled back the drain lid together, dropped Beamish in, then returned on foot to the hotel.

I inch him on. 'And this morning?'

'Well.' A heavy shrug, a heavier sigh. 'You made that appeal for info about Beamish of the CoI and I knew we were in trouble, thought you'd found him. Have you?'

My head stays still.

'Then, without even checking with me, Musters pointed me out to you. When I spoke to him later I was furious . . .'

Not too furious with a psycho with a gun, I'm willing to bet.

'He claimed he was trying to cause confusion.'

And he'd created more by leaving that 10 a.m. message for Kenton to give the impression that Beamish was out and about, still alive, I realise.

'Stick to the plan and story,' Musters instructed Allen. 'Collect the money where Beamish told you, go to the castle. If it's safe, I'll take my share off you there. If I smell trouble, I'll pull out. Keep the money and send me my share.'

Wigmore faces shadows with deep unhappiness. He thinks, I presume, that Musters spotted us there and we've let him go. He doesn't yet know about the ex-Stasi team at the hotel and I'm not going to tell him here.

Allen is explaining that Musters gave him a box number. 'Here somewhere.' Distractedly, he reaches towards a pocket.

With Kenton sitting upright, legs dangling inside the wall, Wigmore judges it safe to finally let go of his arm. His freed hand shoots to his left armpit. 'Leave it there,' Wigmore commands.

Allen gulps so deeply I can see his Adam's apple wobble behind his chin whiskers. He hugs the camera to his chest.

'Er . . .' He clears his throat, looks directly at me and lapses back into verbatim. '"Come back here," he told me.' He's lost the thread. 'The hotel, I mean . . . he meant. "And send my sponge, too, with my share."'

He's confused, drained, and I tell him to slow down.

He doesn't. 'He'd got paperwork hidden in it, you see, which he daren't take through Customs. He told me where I'd find it.'

He can't hold my eyes any longer, just kneels there on the ledge, head hanging, fingering his camera.

He's dried up and I am going to have to help him out. 'Instead, you were detained by us in the castle and relieved of the money.'

A barely noticeable nod, just a tic really.

'Just after four o'clock when he . . .' I gesture at Wigmore. '. . .
went off to the phones, you switched on your tape, left it running,
but left the press bench, bound for Room 010?'

Another tic.

'But I was there first.'

'Sorry,' he mumbles into his chest.

I feel the back of my head. 'And you gave me this.'

He looks at me again. 'I've been in a dream all day; a walking
nightmare. It's been like seeing a horror film, but it's me up there
on the screen.' He is jiffling now, pointing briefly into the air.

'I couldn't send him his money because you had it.'

'What did you do with the sponge?' I ask.

'Popped it into a padded bag, loaded it with stamps and
posted it, just to get rid of it.'

I want to ask 'Where to?' but Kenton prevents me. 'That's
right. When we were on the phone, arranging to meet, he told
me he was going to . . .'

Allen won't let him finish. 'If I failed with his documents, too,
I was a dead man. He's mad. Where is he? Have you found him
yet?' He is extremely agitated, beside himself, ready to crack up.
'Will this help?'

A hand comes away from his camera towards a pocket.

'Don't,' screams Wigmore.

There's a vivid flash, pale yellow, more blinding than the noon
sun, an explosion so loud that a cannon-ball seems to have made
a direct hit on our position, and a scream so horrifying that I
can't hear anything else at all for a moment or two.

I blink my eyes open.

The sky all round is full of birds, black and white, fleeing from
every cranny in the rock face, wheeling, screeching.

Only three of us remain on the gun platform.

A MONTH LATER
10.00 hours

The public gallery is nearly full. All stand respectfully when the coroner walks briskly into a small courtroom on the first floor of the Victorian terraced house across the road from the Playhouse.

A slight, white-haired man with half-moon spectacles, he begins by explaining apologetically that the regular coroner and his deputy are away at an unspecified Home Office conference and he is acting in their place.

He looks across his pine bench at a civilian clerk who reads out the five inquests to be heard, with the usual preamble; phrases like 'touching the death' and 'draw near and give your attendance'.

We sit through a suicide and a fatal domestic fall, the end of which half empties the gallery.

'Next', the clerk announces, 'is John Beamish.'

His widow, fair-haired, dark-suited and maturely attractive, is called forward from the back row. Yes, she confirms identity. Yes, her husband was a civil servant here for a conference. Yes, he did have a keen interest in Victoriana.

And, well, yes, Mrs Beamish continues with a sorrowful face, he might well – 'when off duty, of course' – explore the back streets for second-hand shops and bargains. He'd have to use public transport or walk because he hadn't driven north in his car.

'Did he drink?' asks the coroner, his first blunt question.

'He liked to relax with a whisky after a hard day.' She smiles sadly, 'Provided he wasn't driving, of course.'

The veteran constable, overweight despite his daily cycling, follows her into the witness box next to the coroner's raised bench.

Yes, he agrees, he located a stolen van during a traffic incident

199

in Farringdon Street, but there were no fingerprints to link it to the deceased. Yes, he goes on, there was a second-hand furniture shop in the vicinity.

A water board engineer comes next, deposing that work had been taking place on a drainage pipe. The iron cover, he insists, had been replaced at the end of the shift on that Thursday, but it was not unknown for vandals to remove them. He'd found the body next morning and called the police.

A Home Office pathologist is told by the coroner that he need not take the oath, because he'd been sworn in at the formal opening of the inquest last month.

Not true, as it happens. He wasn't even here. He'd merely submitted via the constable a half-completed written report so the body could be released for a funeral service. He doesn't correct the coroner.

He testifies that Beamish had died from drowning but he isn't asked about the state of his lungs. He gets round the fact that Beamish had been dressed in drag by not mentioning his clothing at all.

He had drunk the equivalent of two double whiskies, which would have made him unfit to drive. 'Since he wasn't in a vehicle,' the coroner decrees, 'that's not an issue in this case.'

He blasts mindless vandalism at some length. He decides that drink might be an issue after all, in that it could have impaired his vision and account for his failure to see the manhole cover was missing. He records a verdict of accidental death.

Mrs Beamish departs with the condolences of the court and, I'd imagine, a hefty pension for as long as she keeps quiet.

A fatal fire now on a drunk who had fallen asleep in his bedsit with a cigarette in his hand.

'Finally,' intones the clerk, 'Gordon Allen.'

A forensic scientist goes first, producing maps and measurements of the scene, and two sets of photos – the first of the body, the second he'd managed to develop from a semi-exposed roll found in Allen's smashed camera.

The pathologist is recalled to testify that cause of death was multiple head injuries, but doesn't add the usual 'consistent with a long fall'. He submits a written report from Allen's doctor stating he was suffering from work-related stress which might result in dizzy spells.

Lord Kenton, in a sombre suit with a face to match, goes into the box. He'd known the deceased for many years as a photo journalist from *Talking Points* and, he says very gravely, in the absence of any immediate family, he'd formally identified the broken body at the foot of the rock.

He tells of an appointment they had made at the Standard Hill Hotel to go together to Mortimer's Hole. 'It was his idea. He wanted some scenic shots.'

The coroner studies the first batch of photos. 'He sat on the ledge to take these pictures?'

'Some of them, yes.'

'Did you regard that as dangerous?'

A lazy smile. 'I sat on it myself, as I think the photos, subsequently recovered and developed, will show.'

The coroner studies the second set, looks up. 'And it's true to say that an interview of considerable length took place there?'

'Yes,' said Kenton, not expanding.

'And, as this progressed, he was fingering his camera.'

'All the time.'

'Then, quite suddenly, out of the blue as it were, a flash went off and he disappeared from the ledge where he'd been sitting.'

'Yes. Sadly.' Kenton wears a funereal face.

I replace him in the box and give my new rank and department: chief superintendent, transferred to Complaints and Discipline last week.

I say on oath that I, with a fellow delegate, joined Lord Kenton and Allen half-way down Mortimer's Hole, witnessed the photo session and confirm an interview took place.

'Towards the end of it, you were totally blinded by an unexpected flash as if a camera bulb went off?'

'Completely blinded.'

'Did you know, as his family doctor states, that he was suffering from stress which might make him liable to sudden dizziness?'

'Not until today,' I reply honestly.

'Let's get this out in the open.' He leans forward. 'Did he at any stage threaten to take his own life?'

'Never.' Well, that was the truth, I comfort myself, but nothing like the whole truth.

The coroner thanks and dismisses me. 'As we've heard, there

was another delegate with the last witness.' He peers at a short typed statement. 'All he can do is corroborate all that's been said. Does anyone wish to hear him?' He leans forward, offering Wigmore to the court, but, since the family and the creditors of *Talking Points* aren't represented, there are no takers.

'Very well then.' He leans back in his seat. A tragedy, he calls it. 'Here we have an experienced professional merely trying to do his job well.' He begins to speculate. 'In a sudden attack of dizziness, he fired off his flash unintentionally and, disorientated, fell to his death. My verdict: Accident.'

He packs his papers together and gets up. So do we. He departs as swiftly as he entered, never to be seen hereabouts again, I'll wager.

Kenton pumps our hands, declines lunch, explaining he's returning immediately to London with Beamish's widow, who is waiting for a lift in the Playhouse bar. He beams and winks.

12.00 hours

I am proceeding at a stroll towards the Standard Hill Hotel, Wigmore at my side, on a lovely May day, blue skies, sunshine, windless.

The Playhouse at our backs, he says, 'That was smooth.'

As malt whisky, I think admiringly.

He smiles across at me. 'Guess who was behind it?'

No need. Without a doubt, Major Merryweather; a small, tubby man, as it turned out, in sports coat and flannels and with a northern accent.

He'd read the joint report we typed into a word processor, thanked me, and pocketed the disc. If Fräulein Falke did get in touch with Bingham via Bonn, he never told us or, Malloy grumbled later, her.

Now she knows how it feels to be kept in the dark, I thought with private glee.

Wigmore flicks his head in the direction from which we've walked. 'Did I hear you right? Have you been promoted and transferred?'

Yes, I say, not adding that probing corrupt or incompetent fellow officers is not the job I'd have chosen myself, but at least I'm out of the louts' game.

'Congratulations,' he smiles. 'I've gone up a grade, too.'

The least Merryweather could do, after falling for that suspicion Musters cleverly planted with his Flora code to divert attention from Beamish.

His face goes sad. 'There was a big turn-out at John's funeral.'

I nod, thinking: More than the watchers reported from Liverpool.

They'd cremated him, of course. They don't want, in years to come, some investigative reporter tracing, say, a pedestrian on Castle Boulevard recalling an explosion that couldn't be accounted for, and putting that together with another statement from someone who'd seen Malloy's marksmen taking up firing positions among the slate spires on the building opposite.

Imagine some bloody-minded paper like the *Morning Star* – long may it survive – running that, with leftie MPs and civil righters clamouring for answers. So Merryweather had arranged for nothing of Allen or his story to be left to be dug up. No one who does need to know will ever find out that a police bullet caused those head injuries.

Sometimes I upbraid myself for not searching Allen's room while I was there to rule out a gun that's still not been found or asking Wigmore to frisk him before he talked.

But then again, I remind myself, I suspect he was going to kill me.

Becky gives us a wave when we cross the foyer, motions jestingly to the wheelchair. Wigmore shakes his head and blows her a kiss. 'Lovely girl,' he says.

'How's your, er, lover?' I ask pointedly.

He smiles rather shyly. 'He's fine.'

At least, I think contentedly, I got something right about him.

'And your wife?' he hurries on.

Back at work, I inform him. A job share three mornings a week, up at four, home at ten after reading regional bulletins on breakfast-time TV.

'Is that OK with you?' he asks.

I tell him a young domestic comes in on those mornings and looks after Laura until her mother gets home, but I know he means: Do you approve?

Well, how can I disapprove now that I accept how badly I would miss this job, would never give it up? If me, why not her?

There's another conference – textiles this time – but the delegates are still ensconced in the Plantagenet Suite and there's plenty of tables in the Tudor Room.

He pays for Lincolnshire sausages for himself and a more expensive smoked salmon salad for me and I get a celebratory bottle of Chablis, the least I can do after my unfounded suspicions about him.

Tucking in, I ask, 'Seen or heard anything of you know who?'

He shakes his head. 'Never mentioned these days.'

'Who won the race to his documents?'

'Don't know.' A puzzled frown. 'Curious, wasn't it, the way the major never acted when we told him they had been posted and gave him the box number from Allen's pocket?' He pauses in thought. 'Still, he'd have his reasons, I suppose.'

Larry the Loyal, I think, to the very end.

Soon delegates pour into the dining-room, taking up all spare tables around us. He talks of the films he and his beloved have seen and I of a trip with Em to the opera at the Theatre Royal.

'*Die Fledermaus*?' he asks, and we laugh.

Outside, at his car, we shake hands, promising to keep in touch and see each other soon, but I know we never will.

14.00 hours

The in-tray has hardly piled up in my absence – just three extra papers.

An inspector has breath-tested positive driving home from a retirement party. I order office duties, not suspension. A vice squad detective is accused of thumping a pimp. I order him back into uniform, pending inquiries which I'll conduct.

And there's a memo from Malloy pinned to a pink print-out from Interpol:

Police in Belgium seek assistance in identifying the body of a man found in their territorial waters, believed to have fallen from a North Sea ferry. Age: about 50. Height: five feet ten. Weight: nine stone ten. Eyes: Brown. Hair: Natural light brown, but dyed a sandy colour. Distinguishing feature: Toothless, no dentures in place.

Autopsy estimates the body had been in sea for about four weeks. Badly mutilated by ship's propellers. Death due to drowning, but an unexplained finding is that fresh water was in his lungs.

Wearing the remains of maroon pyjamas of a Marks & Spencer make.

I sit with head in hands, let my mind wander. So Fräulein Falke's team took care of him, then. They tracked him so closely that they knew he was about to flee by cab, leaving Allen with the cash.

They'd switched taxis on him, whisked him away to Hull or Harwich and a ferry across the North Sea.

I begin to suspect that Falke would have got a call from them *en route* to a port at around 4 p.m. that Friday. 'We can't find his documents. Take a look in his room.'

So maybe she didn't hear noises. Whatever way it happened I'm pleased she came when she did.

They'd get him on board, into a cabin and into the bath. Maybe he gave them his post office box number with his final breath. Then they'd dress him for bed, get him on deck, lob him over, a sleep-walking accident. His gun would go after him. It was one way of ensuring that he never sang in some foreign courtroom or wrote his memoirs.

Bonn would tell Merryweather, which explains why he didn't search the post office for the padded bag Allen mailed. He let Fräulein Falke and her team have it, a reward, the bargaining chip for the better pensions they deserve.

Justice of a kind for all, I suppose, apart from Allen. I search my heart but can find no sorrow in it for Musters, only for Allen whose death will always trouble me, regret I can never express.

I flip up Malloy's memo, read: 'If we can't help on this, please mark for file.'

File is ticked and it goes in my out-tray, job done.